The Colourless

– KITTY LEWIS –

To Louise !!
Kitty Lewis

An environmentally friendly book printed and bound in England by
www.printondemand-worldwide.com

http://www.fast-print.net/bookshop

THE COLOURLESS
Copyright © Kitty Lewis 2016

All rights reserved

No part of this book may be reproduced in any form by photocopying or any electronic or mechanical means, including information storage or retrieval systems, without permission in writing from both the copyright owner and the publisher of the book.

All characters are fictional.
Any similarity to any actual person is purely coincidental.

The right of Kitty Lewis to be identified as the author of this work has been asserted by her in accordance with the Copyright, Designs and Patents Act 1988 and any subsequent amendments thereto.

A catalogue record for this book is available from the British Library

ISBN 978-178456-346-2

First published 2016 by
FAST-PRINT PUBLISHING
Peterborough, England.

Acknowledgements

Firstly, thank you to my mum Carole and dad Ian, who encouraged me to keep going and put up with my distant moods while I thought up new ideas. To my big sisters, Tracey and Sharon, who read my work and convinced me it was actually quite good. Thanks to Debbie and Lauren at The Cover Collection for the amazing artwork, and Theresa at Fast Print for helping me get this in print. Big shout outs to Sarah, for all the red writing; Alex, for the punctuation advice; Ryan, for being brilliant; and Naomi, for the weird tea. Last but not least, to Millie, just for being you.

Characters

Kandrina: Young scholar

Enkarini: Kandrina's little sister

Harndak: blacksmith, Kandrina's father

Remlik: Kandrina's mentor

Remlika: Sorceress and Remlik's twin sister

Braklarn: Powerful sorcerer

Wordarla: Alchemist and Braklarn's half-sister

Jindar: Chief of the People

Gondrun: Assistant and scribe to the chief

Jindara: Chief's eldest daughter

Semark: Son of the

Mala: Elf woman

Krin: Elf man

Falp: Elf boy

Dranjari: Aspect of the Goddess of time

Yantrola: Priestess of Dranj-Aria

Crenkari: Acolyte of Talri-Pekra

Dranj-Aria: Goddess of time

Talri-Pekra: Goddess of magic and knowledge

Ralor-Kanj: God of balance

Vrenid-Malchor: Creator God of the People

Fakro-Umdar: God of

Chief	death
Lerdran: Exiled for heresy	Somri-Galin: God of suffering
Nerlarina: Face of the Colourless	Aikra-Lora: Goddess of children

THE COLOURLESS

Chapter One:
Blasphemous Thoughts

Kandrina stirred, woken gently by the early morning sunlight filtering through the curtains. Her little sister, Enkarini, snored softly in the other bed. Kandrina threw back her covers and tiptoed across to the wardrobe. She could hear her father speaking to someone downstairs – probably scolding her older brother Perlak for staying out all night again. Kandrina smiled faintly to herself. Much as she adored her big brother, it was always nice to hear other people being shouted at; usually she was the one being told off. Most of the time, it was because she had said or done something that her obsessively religious father disagreed with. He had become highly devout after her mother's death seven years ago, and had forced it onto all three of his children ever since.

At first, Kandrina didn't mind, because there were wonderful stories of a glorious afterlife; she had often imagined her mother looking down on her from a beautiful green meadow, keeping her safe. As she got older, however, she had begun to wonder why the gods had taken her mother away. Looking for an answer, and finding none, she began to question the faith. Her father had already been blinded by that point, and refused to listen to anything that contradicted the temples. Perlak had been more willing to talk about it with her; the two of them had often rebelled against their father by refusing to dress properly when they attended sermons, or by sneaking out of the house so that he couldn't find them. She smiled at the memory of one incident last year, when they had run off and spent a day out on the plains with the hunter Perlak had been apprenticed to. The master hunter had even given her a chance to shoot a few arrows at a target tree. She hadn't been very accurate, but she'd enjoyed it a lot. She made her way down to the kitchen to begin the breakfast preparations, still smiling to herself.

She found a few slices of bread and some cheese in the pantry; that would do for her and Enkarini. Her father and brother preferred meat for breakfast though, so she lit a fire, dug out a pan and a largish ibikona wing, and began cooking it. As the pan heated up, she went to listen by the door. Her father's voice was quiet – that was odd. Maybe he was just keeping his voice down because he thought she and Enkarini were still sleeping. She shrugged and went back to the meat. It was starting to sizzle, so she took the tongs from the side and turned it over. More sizzling as the uncooked side hit the hot pan. It smelt good; she decided to put another wing in for Perlak. Though if he had been out all night, it was more than likely he had already had breakfast before coming home. Quite often he would go to visit one of his lady friends instead of coming home after a late night hunt. She heard a few words drift through from the other room; judging by the tone of voice, it sounded as though her father was upset rather than angry. Wondering what Perlak could possibly have done, she took the pan off the fire and poked her head round the door to see what had been going on.

Automatically, she raised a hand to wave at Perlak over her father's shoulder, like she always did when he came home in trouble. He always grinned at her when she was being told off, too. Sometimes he pulled silly faces as well, making her laugh and frustrating their father even further. Looking into the room, she couldn't see much beyond her father's broad back. He stood in the centre of the room, leaning heavily against the high-backed chair he usually sat in. She couldn't see Perlak anywhere, but another man was speaking, an unfamiliar voice. Wondering who it could be, Kandrina pushed the door open a little wider and peered around her father. A sandy-haired, bearded man stood just inside the open front door, a sympathetic expression on his face. She vaguely recognised him after a few seconds; the Chief's scribe had clearly come to deliver some news. She looked back at her father, who had collapsed onto the arm of his chair with his head in his hands. Something was obviously wrong.

"Father?" she said hesitantly, looking over at the two men. "What is it?"

Harndak looked at his daughter. "Kandrina, I'm sorry..." He ran a calloused hand through his dark hair. "Perlak..." Words seemed to fail him; his lips moved but no sound emerged. He lowered his head again and began to sob quietly.

The scribe looked over at her. "My deepest condolences. Your brother Perlak was taken by the Demons last night. I will have his remains returned to you later today, so that you can begin preparing for the funeral." He inclined his head and left, closing the door behind him.

Kandrina stood frozen in the doorway. Waves of emotion crashed over her, each one obliterating the one that had come before. Disbelief, anger, despair, pain, disbelief again. Her head span, she couldn't take it in. Was this just some awful nightmare? Would she wake up in a moment, safe and warm in her bed, in time to hear Perlak sneaking upstairs to his room? The sharp pain in her heart told her otherwise; no dream could ever hurt so much. First her mother had been taken, years ago; now her beloved older brother. Slowly but surely, the terrible Demons were taking everything she loved away from her. Somehow, she found herself standing by her father's chair, tears running down her face as she looked into his eyes. "Why? Why would they take him?" she cried.

Harndak stood and held his oldest daughter tightly, his own tears running down into her hair. "I don't know, Kandrina. Nobody knows," he said, stroking the girl's hair. "At least Perlak is with your mother now."

Kandrina sobbed into her father's shirt. "It's not fair, they shouldn't keep taking people from us," she said, her voice muffled by tears and shirt. "Why doesn't the Chief do something about it?"

"He prays to the gods to stop them, just like we all do," Harndak reminded his daughter. "There's nothing else we can do. After sending an entire battalion to their deaths a few years ago, Chief Jindar is reluctant to send out any more soldiers. The temples tell us they cannot be destroyed, that the only way to keep them at bay is to pray."

Kandrina pushed away slightly. She did not believe that anything was completely indestructible, and could not understand the attitude most people had towards the Demons. "Father, there has to be something else they can do. We have been praying ever since Mother was taken, and still the Demons came back to us. What of the people who pray every day, and still lose family and friends?"

"Kandrina, why must you harbour such misgivings?" Harndak asked in exasperation. "You know the Demons are called closer to our lands by the words of non-believers, and the priests are always on the lookout for those who doubt. Why do you cause friction?"

Attempting to remain calm, though her temper was beginning to rise, Kandrina tried to explain once again to her narrow minded father. "I don't intend to cause trouble. But I simply can't see why everyone is so hopeless about this. Surely if everyone pulled together, maybe if the Chief sent some mages out..."

"As I just said, Kandrina, the temples say there is no way to vanquish the Demons. If there was a way, don't you think they would have done something by now?" said Harndak, holding his daughter's shoulders at arm's length. "Perhaps the Demons returned to our family because we weren't praying enough," he said, looking into her eyes.

"Oh, blast praying, and blast the damned temples!" Kandrina cried, her temper getting the better of her at what she took to be a subtle accusation. "We pray for everything, and it makes no difference! Every spring we pray for good rains to make the crops grow, and every year it doesn't change anything; the rain comes or not, as it wishes, without a care for our prayers." She pulled herself away from her father and began pacing. "Why are you so afraid, Father? The holy books talk more of acceptance and peace; why do you blindly obey everything the priests say about sin and damnation? What if they're wrong, and the old religions were right?"

"I will not have this argument with you again, Kandrina. Not now, and certainly not while your sister is upstairs sleeping," Harndak said, quietly but firmly. "You know perfectly well that the holy books were written years ago, at the time of the merging, when peace and tolerance were the most important things to preach. The gods speak directly to the priests, and to us through the priests. And the old religions are all false truth, as well you know. The Manak faith is the only true religion."

Kandrina stopped in front of the cold hearth and turned slowly to face her father. "If all the old religions are false truth, Father, then why do the temples acknowledge some of the old gods? Dranj-Aria was first worshipped by the Tewen tribe; Aikra-Lora came from the Astator religion. We only have shamans because of the nature-worshipping Wirba tribe. If the faith of the Manak tribe was the one true path to Paradise, why would they have altered it so to incorporate gods from other faiths?"

Harndak stared at her, and she could see him closing off, shutting his mind and refusing to accept the sense of what she was saying. "How do you know all of that? I expressly forbade your tutor from telling you anything about the old faiths. They are irrelevant heresies, Kandrina," he said.

"I read of my own accord, Father. There is a wealth of information in the library, if you know where to look," she replied sarcastically. Her mother had insisted she be taught privately, away from the temples' influence, and Kandrina was eternally grateful to her for it. "I find the old religions make a lot more sense; they speak of gods who prefer not to interfere much with mortal life. Those are the gods we seem to have, not the prayer answering, 'vengeful yet forgiving' gods preached about in our temples," Kandrina said.

"Kandrina, stop! This is heresy, and I will not hear it spoken in this house," Harndak said sternly. "Now go and wake your sister. We have a funeral to begin preparations for."

Kandrina turned and stormed back up the stairs. Grief at her brother's death now mingled with boiling hatred of her father's blind faith. She loved her father, but hated that he had been so easily frightened into believing fanatically in the temple doctrines. As far as she was concerned, the priests had taken advantage of his grief after her mother's death.

Harndak shook his head. "I knew having that girl educated would create problems," he muttered to himself, watching her go. "I just hope she doesn't speak her mind outside of her mentor's house."

"Enkarini," Kandrina called softly as she entered the room she shared with her younger sister. "Wake up. Father needs to speak to you." She gently shook the younger girl's shoulder.

Enkarini stirred. "What's wrong?" she asked muzzily. Enkarini was the exact image of her departed mother. Long, wavy brown hair, startling green eyes, and flawless alabaster skin. Kandrina looked into her sister's eyes, wondering what Mother might have said, how she might have broken the terrible news to her little girl. Since Meradina had died when Enkarini was still a baby, Kandrina had been more of a mother figure to her than an older sister, yet she still found herself wondering if she was leading the little girl wrongly somehow. Alone of the three children, Kandrina had inherited their mother's independent mind, which was why she had been sent to a private tutor rather than the temple-run schools. As she watched her sister rubbing sleep from the corners of her eyes, Kandrina felt a sudden, overwhelming urge to protect her sister from indoctrination, whatever it took. Discarding the notion of sugar-coating the truth, she blurted it out quickly.

"It's Perlak, Enkarini." She didn't need to say anymore. The sisters held each other for a long time, silently coming to terms with their brother's death.

Fakro-Umdar's priest sat quietly behind his desk, watching the black candle wax dripping slowly down the holder. The temple of the death god was always a quiet place; the acolytes took a vow of absolute silence, which cut out a lot of noise. Also, there were very few visitors to the temple, outside of those with family members about to join the spirits on the other side. As he sat watching the candle burn down, he wondered why they had to use black ones. There was no reason he knew of; black wasn't overly associated with death, no more than any other colour. Certainly less so than red, anyway. Besides, a little colour might improve the place somewhat, he thought.

The door opened, hinges creaking loudly in the silence and interrupting his thoughts on buying a pack of red candles just to see how people reacted. A silent acolyte entered, holding out a small scroll bearing the Chief's seal. He took the scroll, but refrained from dismissing the acolyte. "Say, what would you think to getting a few red candles for the altar?" he asked the boy. "I'm a little tired of black, I'd like to see some colour around here for a change." The boy stayed silent, only looking bemused. Not having been dismissed, however, he had to stay. A red weal on his cheek bore testimony to that lesson.

The priest opened the scroll, finding news of another death caused by the creatures known to most of the People as Lightning Demons. "The blacksmith's son, I see. The body is to be buried on Seventh day. Specifies he should be buried on the family plot, next to his mother... well, well," said the priest, rolling it back up and resting it on a small pile of similar scrolls, each bearing details of upcoming funerals. "That family doesn't seem to have much luck with the Demons. First the mother, now the son. Perhaps someone has displeased the gods. Or they may simply be cursed." He sat back, staring across the desk at the opposite wall. "You may go, boy. Oh, and fetch some red candles from the market. Bring them back to me; I want to see how they look." He waved the acolyte out. Yes, red candles alternating with the black ones, perhaps. That could look quite effective. Or I could arrange them in a pattern, a star or something, just to see how long it takes the others to notice.

Distracting himself from the vital subject of red candles versus black, the priest took up a handful of scrolls from the pile, reminding himself of who he was burying later. Two deaths from old age, one child who had died of illness, and a woman who had been staked out for heresy three nights ago. He sighed deeply, reading the details of the heretic woman. She had left four young children behind, the oldest of them only twelve summers. Why would the woman have gone around speaking blasphemies, he thought, when she had that many children to care for? Didn't she realise they would be left alone in the world when the foul Demons came for her? He picked up a quill and made a small note on the back of her scroll. He would go to check on those children after the funeral; make sure they had not been corrupted by their mother's heresy.

Kandrina walked quickly, her feet finding their own way without her conscious guidance. She knew the way from her father's smithy to her mentor's house with her eyes shut, having taken refuge there often after arguments with her father. She had crept out the back door while her father and little sister made plans for the funeral, which according to tradition should be held within the week. She had always hated funerals; they always seemed so false to her. The death priests would give a speech about how well regarded the person had been, before going into a sermon about how their life could have been extended if they had been more devout. And most of the time the entire town would turn out for the service, even if they had never met the person who had died. She did not doubt that the gods existed, there was too much evidence for anyone to seriously doubt that, but she didn't quite believe that they took a hand in everyday events, and concerned themselves with petty prayers. Remlik and his twin sister were beginning to open her eyes to some of the inconsistencies in the temples' sermons and writings.

The quickest way to Remlik's took her down a few back alleys and through the centre of the poor quarter. Her father preferred that she took a more circuitous route, but she ignored him. She had never come to harm in the poor quarter before, but Remlik had taught her a few techniques that she could use if ever she did get into trouble. Kandrina had not yet informed her father that she knew how to use a dagger, let alone carried one. Still fuming at her father's blind, ignorant faith in the temples, she barely noticed where she was until she stopped, retching. Looking up, she saw the squat, filthy slaughterhouse up ahead. A beggar man saw her pause, and took the opportunity to approach her.

"Spare a few coins for a poor old man?" he croaked, rattling a rusty can under her nose. "Pretty lady, rich lady, pity an old beggar?" He looked up at her from the hunch his aging spine had forced him into, pleading in his eyes.

Kandrina, always a sucker for those worse off than she, dug a few coppers and one silver coin from her pocket and dropped them into his can. They clanked loudly against the bottom. "I'm sorry, I don't have any more with me," she said, turning her pockets inside out.

The grubby, unkempt beggar man grinned toothlessly. "Thank you kind lady!" he cried gleefully, clutching his can close. "My family will eat tonight because of your kindness. May the gods smile upon you!" He shuffled off deeper into the poor district, leaving Kandrina to regain her bearings and continue on to her tutor's house, on the other side of town near the southern gate.

She carried on walking, breathing through her mouth to avoid the stench of blood until she was upwind of the slaughterhouse. The squalid atmosphere did not let up though; whichever way she looked she saw dirty, miserable faces and crumbling buildings. People looked back at her, some with expressions of jealousy, others with entirely blank faces. She tried not to look; not because she found them distasteful like so many people did, but because she could not bear the thought that she would have to turn them away if they came to beg for coins. Usually she was a little better prepared for her walk through the district; she would grab a handful of coppers from her moneybox and fill at least one pocket. Harndak often scolded her for 'wasting her money on wretched beggars', but she simply didn't agree with his views. During one of their many arguments on the subject, Kandrina had reminded him that his father had once been a beggar, and if a kindly stranger had not taken him in he would likely have died on the streets. Harndak had sent her to her room after that comment.

On her way out of the poor quarter, Kandrina passed a tavern called The Box, so named because it was small and square. It was, however, one of the better-maintained places in the district. The windows were all intact, and the fascia had recently been repaired. A worn brass plaque by the door informed passers by that the great Chief Morendir had been born there. Remlik had taken her there to read it for one of her history lessons a few years ago. Kandrina blinked away sudden tears; Perlak had teased her rotten about going to a tavern in the poor quarter.

Cutting through an alley between The Box and a nearby stable, Kandrina exited the poor quarter, leaving behind the filth and misery and entering a slightly more affluent part of town. Not by much, but enough to make a difference. The houses were not so crowded here; sunlight streamed down from above and warmed the cobbles beneath her feet.

She took a deep breath, clearing her lungs, and focused on the house at the end of the street, where her tutor lived with his twin sister, Remlika.

Remlik bowed his head, scrawling a few notes on a scrap of parchment next to the faded old book he was studying. Many would think it tough going –a very dry, dull text detailing the past glories and failures of the Akram tribe. He revelled in it though; enjoying every new fact he discovered, weaving together tiny strands of truth pulled from the tangle of legends often found in historical accounts, and explaining the resulting tapestry to others. In the words of his foster parents, he had been born a scholar, devouring any books he could lay his hands on from a very early age. He had apprenticed to a teacher from Astator at his adulthood ceremony, and become the schoolmaster within five years, something previously unheard of, and still a subject for discussion among the scholars of his hometown, Bewein.

He wasn't expecting any of his students until later that day, so he was a little surprised to hear a knock at the door. Knowing his twin sister was busy doing something in her casting rooms downstairs, he finished his sentence and hastened to answer the door.

"Kandi, this is unexpected," he said, opening the door and seeing his favourite pupil. She looked just the same as always, pale skin and golden hair shining in the morning sunlight. However, her ice blue eyes, usually full of laughter, were wet with uncried tears. "What's wrong?" Remlik asked, stepping back to allow her through the door.

"I needed to speak to you," said Kandrina quietly. "And I wanted a little company." She gave him a watery smile, making small dimples appear in her cheeks.

"Of course, Kandi. Come up to the study, we can talk properly there." Remlik led her upstairs, wondering what had brought her to his door so early in the day. He suspected another argument with her father; it was becoming more common as she grew older and developed a greater understanding of the world. Opening his study door, he gestured her towards her favourite seat under the solitary window. He glanced out at the view over the town, the streets just beginning to fill with people going about their daily business. It was only an hour after sunrise, so the distant hills were only just tinged a pale blue. He turned away and sat behind his desk, cleared a space and poured two fresh cups of herbal tea from the pot he always kept steaming over the fire. "Here. You look like you need it," he said, passing one of the cups to Kandrina. He leant back, sipping his own tea as he waited for her to begin.

Kandrina turned the cup slowly in her fingers, staring down at it and chewing her bottom lip. She had the look of someone who wanted to say something important, but didn't quite know where to begin. Finally she looked up, staring into his eyes. "Remlik, what do you know about the Lightning Demons?"

Remlik leant forward, placing his cup back on the desk and steepling his fingers. He knew a little about the so-called Demons, but suspected that much of what he knew was incorrect. He only had one volume that consisted mostly of fact, or at least sensible theorising, but was reluctant to reveal that he had it, even to a trusted student like Kandrina. "I know very little about them, I'm afraid. There are several tales and myths, some of which I have copies of, but from what I can tell there is very little fact in them. I could retrieve the relevant scrolls, if you wish to review them?"

The girl nodded vigorously, making some loose hair fall across her face. "Yes please," she said.

"Kandi, what's happened?" Remlik asked frankly. She was usually a calm and sensible girl, happy to allow him to direct the lessons as he wished. This morning though, Kandrina seemed agitated and edgy. "I can tell something's wrong."

Kandrina looked back down at the nearly empty cup she still held. "I want to learn about the Demons. Perlak was taken last night; I want to know why they kill us, and if there is any way to stop them." A single tear dripped from the end of her nose into the dregs of her tea. Remlik gently took the cup, handed her a scrap of cloth and covered her hand with his own.

"I'm very sorry, Kandi. Perlak was a good man." As he comforted her, he made the decision to help her find out the truth. When the girl had calmed herself a little, he withdrew his hand and went over to the shelves that lined the far wall. He took down a couple of rather dog-eared books and an old scroll, and sat back in his chair. "As I said, most of the stories you will find are pure fiction, or temple propaganda. These are a little more objective in their views, since they were written by scholars from Astator, but they aren't entirely accurate. Why don't you take them home and read them when you have the time?" he said, holding out the books for her to take.

Kandrina took them carefully. "Thank you. I'll keep them safe," she promised him, opening the smaller book at random. A small puff of dust rose from its pages, making her sneeze. "Excuse me. So, isn't there anything you can tell me? Maybe something that isn't in any books?" she asked.

Remlik thought carefully. He did know a few things that were not written in the books he had just given the girl, but she was almost certain to repeat him if he told her. If his research came to the attention of the high priest, there would be a lot of people in serious trouble, not least himself and his sister. "I do have a theory of my own, but perhaps you should study those texts and make your own conclusions," he began, before being interrupted by a loud bang from downstairs, closely followed by the sound of rushing water. The two of them glanced at each other, wondering what could possibly have happened, and ran downstairs. Remlik reached the bottom first; he stopped dead and began laughing.

Remlika, his twin sister, had clearly been practising her fire spells. It was one of the few areas of magic she did not excel in, and as such she was always trying to improve her skills. Her silver eyes, a result of her use of magic, shone brightly through the smoke and ash that hung in the air; everything else was black with soot, and rather wet. "Stop laughing and help me sort this out," she said crossly, tapping one foot in a puddle of dirty water.

Remlik stifled his giggles with difficulty and went to fetch a broom. Kandrina walked forwards, looking around at the blackened room. "What happened?" she asked. She had always admired Remlika, and at first had tried to learn the magical arts from her. She quickly discovered that she had no aptitude whatsoever though, and had settled for learning theories and philosophies from Remlik. It was proving to be just as interesting, though without the risks often associated with mages in training.

"Well, I was practising a few pyro spells," Remlika said, shuffling her feet embarrassedly, "and one of them went a bit wrong. Entirely my fault; I lost my focus and overdid the spell a little. Anyway, the place was on fire, so I cast a quick dousing spell to put out the flames. I think I overdid that one too; the room sort of flooded."

Remlik returned with a pair of brooms, laughter still twinkling in his dark, warm eyes. "Here," he said, handing one to Kandrina. "So, how did you lose your focus?" Magic required complete concentration on the spell being cast. Any slip of focus could result in a failed spell, or complete disaster. That was why mages had to be rather single minded at times. It took a lot of training, and most people simply didn't have the mental discipline to achieve it.

"I was doing fine until some idiot started banging on my window," Remlika replied, watching the two of them sweep the floor. "The gods only know what he was thinking. Looked rather intoxicated to me. So, what brings you here so early, Kandrina? I didn't think you had a lesson today."

Kandrina looked up, distracted from her sweeping. "I... There was something I needed to ask. About the Demons. My brother..." She stopped speaking, rubbing tears from her eyes with the sleeve of her dress.

"Perlak was taken last night. Kandi only just found out," Remlik said quietly, by way of explanation. "I've given her the two books from Astator." He warned her with a glance not to interfere; his sister knew about the other book, and would likely want to tell Kandrina about it before she was ready to find out the entire truth.

Remlika nodded, and crossed the room to hug Kandrina, who was trying to dry her face with a wet sleeve. "I'm sorry. I never really met Perlak, but I know you were close. How are your father and sister coping?"

"Father is burying himself in religion again; Enkarini cried when I told her, but she's helping Father with the funeral plans now," Kandrina replied, finally drying her eyes again. "I don't know if she's quite old enough to properly understand, she's only just eight summers this year." It had only been a few weeks since midsummer, when everyone was counted a year older. Those reaching their fifteenth summer had gone through their adulthood ceremonies; Kandrina's would be next year.

"Young children often understand better than you'd think," said Remlik wisely, sweeping some sooty water out of the back door and into the yard. He remembered the first time he had met Kandrina, five years ago, when Harndak had brought her for her first lesson. She had seemed quiet, with an enquiring mind that in his experience should belong to a much older child. But, he supposed at the time, she had needed to grow up quickly after her mother's death, to be a role model for her younger sister. Kandrina, when she had started her lessons, had only been a year older than Enkarini was now, and had grasped the concept of death quite well. He leant on his broom, considering his pupil. Though he had about a dozen students in Manak, Kandrina was by far his favourite. "It could just be her way of dealing with it; everyone reacts differently to news like that."

"I suppose." Kandrina resumed her sweeping as Remlika went to fetch a rag for the walls. "So, you were saying something about your own theories on the Demons, Remlik? Do you think there's a way to stop them taking people?" she asked, looking over at her tutor as she swept the remaining ash towards the front door.

Remlik watched her sweep, unsure how to respond. He knew of one possible way to defend the People against the creatures known as Demons, but it was an untested theory, and he did not want to get her in trouble if she went home spouting his ideas. "Read through the two books I lent you, Kandi. They don't tell the whole story, as I said earlier, but they'll give you somewhere to start. We can talk about it properly when you've had a chance to digest that information." Unlike the temple schools, he preferred to simply give his pupils as much unbiased information as he could, then get them to think for themselves. It helped them develop more independent minds. "Go on, you should get home before your father misses you. I'll finish helping my sister clean up."

The shaman danced around the grave, consecrating the soil in the age-old ritual. Kandrina watched quietly as Perlak's charred body was lowered into the earth and the acolytes began to cover him with soil. The priest of Fakro-Umdar incanted his prayer as the shaman completed his dance, and the other mourners filtered away, leaving the family and the Chief by the graveside. It was traditional for the Chief to offer personal condolences to the family of a Demon victim, no matter who they were.

"I am deeply sorry for your loss," Chief Jindar intoned. His dark eyes shone out from under a heavy brow. The scribe, Gondrun, hovered a few steps behind him, barely visible over the tall Chief's broad shoulders. "All of the People feel your pain, and we all pray for your son's soul to find its way to Paradise."

Kandrina bit her tongue to stop herself from saying what she really thought. As her father replied in a suitably pious manner, she bit down so hard she drew blood. This is ridiculous, she thought.

Chief Jindar and his scribe eventually left, leaving the three of them alone to mourn their lost son and brother. "Thank you, Kandrina." Harndak murmured to his oldest daughter as Enkarini patted the soil and laid a small bunch of wildflowers on the grave.

"What for?" she replied thickly, as her tongue was beginning to swell where she had bitten it so hard.

"Not speaking your mind in front of everyone." Harndak looked down at her. "I know you have your own opinions of this kind of thing, and I'm not going to try and make you change them. But I appreciate you keeping up appearances."

Kandrina nodded, not trusting herself to speak again. She was thinking of what she had read in the books Remlik gave her, wondering how much truth was in them, and what had been left out. They waited by the graveside, Harndak and Enkarini praying, Kandrina remaining quiet with her own thoughts. She ran through what had been in the scroll Remlik had lent her; not a great deal that she thought would be useful, it just seemed to sum up what was in the temple stories. Still convinced that there was a way to destroy them, she had seized on a comment in the smaller book that mentioned magical arts. But the larger, more worn book had spent almost a whole chapter talking about how the Demons weren't truly evil; meaning no harm to the People and only being curious. It didn't seem to make sense, especially not alongside the temples' stories of brutal murders and cruel tortures inflicted upon their victims.

She watched her father and sister kneeling by the graveside, wondering how they could simply sit there praying to inattentive gods. Her brother was dead! She would never again hear him teasing her, see his mischievous grin as he planned his next antic, or be able to watch him at target practice with the breeze ruffling his wavy hair; prayer wouldn't bring him back, wouldn't make the ones who stole him away suffer! The angry spark that had driven her to Remlik's after hearing the news flared up inside her, igniting a desire for revenge on whoever or whatever had taken her brother away. She stared blindly into the distance, tears running down her cheeks and her hands balled up in her pockets; silently swearing by Somri-Galin that she would discover the truth and avenge Perlak, however long it might take her.

Remlik hung back, watching the crowd of mourners from a slight distance. He was far enough back that he couldn't hear every word the death priest was saying, which gave him a chance to listen in on what certain members of the crowd were mumbling under cover of the sermon.

"It's only been, what, seven years since the smith's wife died?" whispered an old woman standing just in front of Remlik. "What a lousy piece of luck, losing your only son the same way."

"I hear the oldest daughter has been invoking dark forces; that's why the Demons keep going after that family," said the man next to her. "Right little heretic, from what I hear. Far too well informed about the old religions."

Oh dear, Remlik thought. *I knew I should have been more careful when she asked about that.* He moved around the edge of the crowd slightly, trying to see what point they were at in the service. The shaman had just begun his traditional dance to sanctify the grave; *a practice adopted from the old Wirba religion,* he thought. *If only some of this lot knew just what a hypocritical bunch the priests are, always telling us the old religions are heresy while using at least half of the old rituals.* He tuned out the priest's voice and looked around at the rest of the crowd, wishing he could push through them all and comfort Kandrina. Most of the people he could see had only come out for appearances' sake.

After a few minutes, the crowd began moving away; the service had obviously finished, most of the attendees heading for the nearest tavern to gossip about the family as they always did after a funeral like this. As much as he wanted to go forwards and see his pupil, he followed the majority. Tradition dictated that the family should be left alone by the graveside to pray for their relative's departed soul. He absently trailed after a particularly rowdy group that seemed to be heading for the Drover's Daughter.

"So whose round is it?" called a swarthy, dark haired man at the front of the group as they entered the tavern. After a moment, Remlik recognised him as the town cobbler. "Go on Amonar, you won big in that card game last night. Drinks are on Amon, everyone!"

Remlik took a seat in the corner, avoiding the general rush to the bar as most of the patrons took advantage of Amon's reluctant generosity. The cobbler and his friends parked themselves at the large table under the window, where a busty barmaid brought them drinks. He lifted an abandoned half-empty glass from the next table, so it would look as though he was simply enjoying a drink rather than trying to eavesdrop on anyone's conversation. Not that it was difficult; the cobbler was a very loud man.

"What's up with that smith, then? Not often you get two Demon victims in the same family. I reckon there's something funny going on." He took a long swig from his tankard, slopping froth down his chin. "Definitely something weird about that daughter. The older one, I mean; they say anyone with hair that pale must be demon spawn, right? Maybe the mother made a pact with the Demons, or something. Her life in exchange for a temptress of a daughter."

One of his companions shrugged, staring down into his own ale. "Probably just rotten luck, I'd say. But then, the lad was out on the plains in the middle of the night; what was going on there? No hunter I know of would take an apprentice out on a night hunt, especially not a seventeen year old."

Remlik scowled at his pilfered glass. He did not like the way people spoke about Kandrina sometimes; names like 'demon spawn' and 'devil's whore', often applied to those few who were born with rare pale hair, were offensive at best. Nobody who knew Kandrina would describe her as a temptress. But any female with a pulse was a target for the cobbler's lechery. He looked over as the man called Amonar spoke up.

"Whatever, it's still a tragedy. I'll be praying for them tonight; hope the gods show them a little mercy and kindness. No man deserves to lose a wife and a son."

"If the gods were truly kind and merciful, they wouldn't have allowed the boy to die," Remlik said, incensed by the comments. "What kind of gods do you pray to, that would stand by and watch as a family is torn apart? Maybe you should think about that, rather than spreading gossip and insulting a girl who's grieving for her brother," he said, rising from his chair.

The cobbler rose also, swaying slightly as he glared at Remlik. "Maybe you should keep your mouth shut; keep out of other people's conversations, eh? Nothing to do with you if we want to talk about the pale little whore, is it?" One of his companions, a chubby man on his left, tried to calm him; the cobbler kicked his chair back and strode across to Remlik's table. "Or maybe you're one of her customers. The little demon spawn seduced you and made you think you're in love, did she?"

"You bastard!" Remlik swung at him, only catching him on the nose because he had the advantage of sobriety. The cobbler staggered backwards a step, into a burly man carrying three glasses, which shattered on the floor. The burly man then began laying into the cobbler, which started a bit of a fight in the bar. Remlik retreated into his corner, looking for a path to the exit while trying to avoid being dragged into the brawl. He ducked as a chair leg came flying towards him, narrowly missing hitting his head on the door, which had just opened.

"What is the meaning of this?" someone shouted from the doorway. Everyone froze, expressions of guilt across their faces. The death priest who had performed Perlak's funeral service had walked in, accompanied by a servant. He pointed at the cobbler, frozen mid-swing. "You there, cobbler, explain this violence. Now!"

The cobbler stepped away from the burly man's smaller companion, and bowed his head in respect. "Holiness, that man is the cause," he said, pointing at Remlik, who had been trying to sneak out of the door. "We were all drinking quietly, mourning the smith's young lad; he walked in, boasting of copulating with Demons and spouting heresies. He threw the first punch, holiness, when I told him to shut his blaspheming mouth."

Remlik ran, not stopping to check who might be following. The priests wouldn't bother to listen to his side of the story, how the cobbler had been spreading lies about Kandrina. The temple militia would be out searching for him within the hour; his face and name would be spread around the town as that of a heretic, he would have nowhere to hide in Manak. He had to get somewhere relatively safe, send a message to his sister, and they would both have to run. She wouldn't be spared; she would also be named a heretic by virtue of the fact they were related. Rather than head south, towards the poor quarter and his own home, he went west. He had a few friends in the wild district that could hide him for a few hours, and contact Remlika for him. As he ran, taking every shortcut he knew and ignoring the shouts from behind him, he spared a thought for his students. With a little luck, they would have learned enough about thinking for themselves that they would have a chance to escape the temples' brainwashing.

Once they had finished their prayers, the family of the departed were meant to return home for personal grief and prayer. Kandrina, however, snuck out as soon as she could and went back to see Remlik. She took the books and scroll he had lent her, hoping he could clarify a few things for her, and maybe answer a few of her questions.

She arrived just after sunset, but it took a few knocks before Remlik answered. "Get in, quickly," he said, looking around feverishly and dragging her inside.

"What's going on?" Kandrina asked, wondering why her mentor was acting so strangely.

"I made a few stupid remarks earlier today," Remlik told her. "I've been denounced as a heretic, so I've had to spend most of the day hiding. Remlika's gone to lay a false trail to make it look as though we've both fled. We'll have to leave soon anyway, but we haven't decided where to go yet, and I'd rather have them off chasing a false lead than sitting right on our tails. But what brings you here at this late hour?"

"I've read through the books and scroll you lent me," Kandrina told him. "There are a few things I was hoping you might be able to clarify for me."

Remlik led her upstairs to the study. "What things? I'll do what I can to help," he said, closing the door and lighting a lantern.

"This part here," Kandrina opened a page she had marked in the smaller of the two books. "About 'the wicked Tanpèt Zèklè, commonly called Demons, will only fall by arcane means', is that true?"

Remlik thought for a moment. "If my theory is correct, it would make sense. Unfortunately I don't know anyone who has tried it, so there is no proof either way. What else was there?"

Kandrina opened the other book and flicked through a few pages to her other marker. "This." She pointed to a passage that was very faded. "It says that 'they have no intent to cause harm, and are merely curious about us, the People. We have much to learn of these strange beings, who have...'and then I couldn't make out any more. What do you think that means?"

Remlik sat back in his chair, tilting his head to the side as he so often did when thinking. After a pause, he said, "I'm not sure what to tell you, Kandi. As I say, I do have a theory; but first, what do you think?"

"I don't know. There seems to be a lot missing from these books, as though whoever wrote them has tried to avoid putting something into words. But if the Demons don't mean to cause harm, why would they kill us? Unless it's some sort of accident, maybe?" Kandrina said, still trying to gather her thoughts. The immediate shock at Perlak's death was beginning to wear off, and a kind of curiosity had started to settle in alongside her need for revenge; though she still missed him deeply, her natural desire to learn was reasserting itself. "Maybe I need to read these a little more. I think I'm missing something."

Remlik nodded slowly. "Yes, there is a lot missing from those texts." He fell silent, clearly pondering something important. Kandrina sensed not to break his concentration, but wait for him to reach whatever conclusion he was coming to. He had done this before when she asked about a difficult or forbidden subject; deciding exactly how much to tell her, she suspected. Though she always found out what she wanted to know, Remlik had never explicitly told her anything about banned topics, merely given her enough hints that she could figure out where to look for the facts. "Come with me," Remlik said at last, rising from his chair.

Kandrina followed him across to the fireplace, empty of all but a few logs, and watched him fiddle with what looked like a part of the ornamental carving on the mantelpiece. The panel at the back of the fire slid aside, revealing a dark, narrow opening. "It's a way down to our cellar," he told her.

"I didn't think you had a cellar," Kandrina said, surprised.

Remlik smiled. "That's why it's the best place for me to keep all my most precious books. Nobody knows it's there, so it doesn't get searched by the temple militia if they should ever come calling. After you," he said, gesturing towards the small opening.

Kandrina crawled in, sliding a little as it turned into a steep downward slope almost immediately. It twisted and turned, presumably down through the walls, until opening up into a large open space. Being underground, and Remlik not having arrived with the lantern yet, it was pitch black, so she moved away from the exit carefully. A small pool of light appeared on the floor, growing larger as Remlik crawled out of the passage behind her and stood up.

"There's a book down here that contains quite a lot of information on the so-called Demons; there are a lot of other names for them, you know," Remlik said, leading her forwards to a dusty shelf. "'Tanpèt Zèklè' is one of them, it's what the Astator tribe used to call them. The Tewen tribe used to think they were Angel Stars that fell to earth, and the Wirba called them Sky Spirits. Ah, here it is. I rescued this one from the temples nearly twelve years ago, when they were trying to purge the libraries of all references to the Demons." He pulled a very battered book down from the top shelf, and carried it across to a desk.

Kandrina stared as Remlik turned page after page. Some of the passages in the book were very faded, a few pages had been torn out; there was even a part of the cover that looked as though it had been set alight at some point. "What exactly did the temples do to purge the libraries, Remlik?" she asked in hushed tones.

"Sent in acolytes and the militia to gather anything that mentioned the Demons, then destroyed the ones that went against what they wanted people to believe," Remlik answered. "Most of the books like this were burnt; I managed to sneak this one away before it got thrown on the pyre. They did it in the town square, don't you remember?"

Kandrina thought back; she did sort of remember seeing a huge bonfire in the town square when she was very small, but she hadn't known what it was for. "Not really. I was only two, though; I don't think I was paying much attention at the time. So, what's in there that isn't in the ones you gave me?"

"Well, it completely dismisses the term 'Lightning Demons', for one. As I said, there are several other names for them, but the writer seems to use 'Tanpèt Zèklè' most often. He might have been from Astator, I suppose." Remlik turned pages as he spoke. "There's a lot of speculation in here, about why they came down to our lands in the first place; he thinks they were originally from much further north, but were driven out by something else."

Kandrina leant forwards, trying to read some of the faded words. "There, what was that about using magic?" A passage that mentioned a mage being taken had caught her eye.

Remlik turned back to the page Kandrina had pointed out, and read it out loud. " 'The great mage Emsudan of Pokole was one of the few to meet the Zèklè and return alive; he claimed to have been taken to a mountain to the far west of the plains, where he spoke with many of them. Weeks after his own funeral, he returned to the village, causing great distress to his wife and sons. The priests of the Creator were also distressed to learn of his return, and drove him out of Pokole, declaring his return to be a trick of the 'Demons'. Emsudan made his way to the abandoned village of Yoscar, where he remains to this day. When I travelled to speak with him, he had become quite mad from his extended solitude, but he told the strangest tale. It seems the Zèklè are particularly vulnerable to magic, though he refused to say why they are vulnerable to magic. In any case, it may be irrelevant, as I will discuss in the next chapter.' The next chapter is about why he thinks the Demons are not to be feared."

"So it is possible to kill them," Kandrina began before being shushed by Remlik. Quiet now, she could hear scuffling noises from the tunnel entrance. She doused the lantern quickly, while Remlik closed the book and hastily hid it under the desk.

A small nimbus of green light emerged from the tunnel, lighting up Remlika's face. "You didn't have to put the light out, you know. What are you doing down here, anyway?" she asked, walking over to them.

"I'm showing Kandi some of the more advanced texts on the Zèklè. Have you laid a trail?" Remlik asked his sister.

Remlika nodded. "I made it look as though we headed west; hopefully they won't follow too far. With a bit of luck, they'll think we've gone out into the dwarves' lands. We should leave soon, though; they'll probably come to burn this place down in the morning. I'm surprised they haven't been to visit already."

He sighed heavily, clearly frustrated and upset about the situation he and his sister had been thrust into. "Right. I'll start packing a bag when we're done here, then we can head out at sunrise. Do you think we could stay with your friends out in Tewen, at least for a little while? I've heard the priests there aren't quite so zealous as Manak's and Akram's lot."

Kandrina had been examining pages while the twins talked. The chapter that began shortly after Emsudan's story seemed to make sense; at least the bits that were still readable did. It said that rather than being evil spirits from another realm, the Tanpèt Zèklè were beings of another race, made of energy that came from the skies. "Remlik, what's this bit? I can't quite make it out," she asked, pointing to a large chunk of text that looked as though it had been washed off the page.

"I'm not sure; the text isn't very clear," Remlik said, squinting at the faded passage. He paused for a moment before speaking again. "Perhaps you could speak to the man who wrote it. He was exiled for heresy many years ago, I don't even know if he still lives. The last anyone saw of him, he was living rough in the hills to the north, somewhere east of the Valley. His name is Lerdran. Remlika, would you be able to scry for him?" Remlik asked his sister.

"Possibly. It would be difficult, but I can try." The sorceress rose and went back up the passage to the house.

Remlik shook his head, causing a few loose strands of black hair to fall in his eyes. "Difficult my eye; she's the best scryer I've ever known. Kandi, do you want to go and watch? If he's still alive we can head out to look for him at dawn," he suggested.

Kandrina crawled back up the narrow passageway, back into the house, and cautiously entered Remlika's rooms. She had managed to learn, during the few lessons Remlika had tried to give her, that magic was easily disturbed, so one should always proceed carefully when someone was casting. She saw Remlika standing over a scrying glass in the corner, speaking softly to it. The incantation sounded faintly musical, almost hypnotic, and Kandrina had to shake herself mentally to stay alert. She crept closer, noticing the glass had swirling colours dancing across its surface. Suddenly, the colours resolved into a crystal clear image of the grass-covered hills north of the town.

"He's still alive," Remlika murmured, almost to herself. "And in the hills. Let me see if I can get a closer look." She sang to the glass for several minutes, but the image did not change. Abruptly, she stopped, and the hills faded away. Colour swirled for a few seconds, then the glass was clear again.

"So he's still up there somewhere?" Kandrina asked quietly.

Remlika blinked and looked up at the young scholar. "Yes, but exactly where I can't tell. If you want I can help you look tomorrow," she offered.

"I'd like that," she said. "I should be getting home now though. Father will be wondering where I've gone."

"Let me," Remlika insisted. "I doubt your father would appreciate us allowing you to walk the streets alone in the dark," she said, raising her hand and casting a translocation spell.

Kandrina appeared in her father's sitting room. She stumbled a little, disoriented from the after effects of vanishing and reappearing instantaneously. "Kandrina! Where have you been?" someone shouted at her.

"What… Father," she exclaimed, clearing her head and recognising Harndak. "I was…"

"You were supposed to be in your room, praying for your departed brother," came a quiet, cold voice from behind her. "Instead, you vanish for hours and then materialise by arcane means. Who were you visiting, girl?"

Kandrina span round. The high priest of Vrenid-Malchor, the Creator God of the People, was standing in the corner of the room. "Your holiness, I needed comfort from a friend. We prayed together," she lied.

"And you did not inform your grieving father? He called me here, thinking you had also been taken by the foul Demons," the priest said in an icy voice.

"Forgive me. I had other things on my mind," Kandrina uttered.

"Assuming you are speaking the truth, girl, would you please explain how your friend managed to cast the translocation spell to bring you back here? There are precious few sorcerers powerful enough to cast such a spell. Or do you claim magic powers yourself?"

Kandrina decided it would be easier to tell the truth, or at least part of it. "My friend's name is Remlika. She is a powerful sorceress, your holiness."

The priest glared at her for several minutes. Harndak's presence was all but forgotten in the confrontation. "Remlika has a brother, you know. He was named as a heretic earlier this afternoon. You wouldn't happen to count him as a friend as well, would you?"

Kandrina shook her head, hoping her father would keep his big mouth shut for once. He did. The priest looked from one to the other as though he expected them to spontaneously confess to heinous sins.

"Very well. Go to bed, girl. As for you, Harndak, you must thank the gods for taking pity on your wayward daughter tonight." The priest turned to leave. When he reached the door, he turned back. "And may I remind you, it is your duty to report any blasphemies you hear… whoever's lips they may fall from," he said acidly, with a pointed look at Kandrina.

Harndak watched his daughter for a moment in silence. "Did you know that Remlik had been caught speaking his heresies?" he asked her quietly.

"Yes. Remlika told me." Kandrina didn't want to put her friend and mentor in danger by telling her devout father that he was still at his house.

"Why were you over there anyway, Kandrina? I know you weren't praying with her."

Kandrina looked away. "I just wanted some company. Someone who wouldn't shove prayer in my face," she lied. "Besides, I wasn't going to be there long, but Remlika was casting spells and you know how I like to watch people casting…"

Harndak held up his hand. "Kandrina, don't lie. I'm your father, I can tell. What were you really doing there?"

Kandrina lowered her gaze. She knew perfectly well that her father would not like what she was about to say, but she had to at least try to explain. "I wanted to know more about the Lightning Demons. I think there's more to them than the temples let us know. And they might not be as bad as they're made out to be."

"How can you say that? They killed your mother and brother, Kandrina!"

Kandrina tried to explain. "But, maybe they didn't mean to. Maybe they're just curious about us," she implored.

"Go to bed, Kandrina. Now." Harndak said firmly as he pushed her towards the stairs. "And after tonight I don't want to hear another word about this. You're to forget about studying the Demons. Your tutor has been exposed as a heretic, and it wouldn't surprise me if his sister were one too. Now get to sleep, and don't wake Enkarini."

Chapter Two: Punishment

Remlika appeared at the end of Kandrina's bed, just before sunrise. Shaking the girl awake, she whispered. "Are you ready to go?"

Kandrina awoke quickly, and nodded. "Can we get out the same way you came in?" she asked. She wasn't sure if it was possible to transport two people with the same spell.

"Yes. Take my hand," Remlika whispered, holding it out for Kandrina to take. "I see you slept in your clothes," she remarked before casting her spell.

"I thought it would make departing quicker," Kandrina answered when they reappeared at the crest of a hill. She could just see the first rays of the sun shining over the horizon, giving everything a grey, slightly washed-out look. A town of doll's houses sprawled out in the distance; Manak seemed so small from up here. "So where should we start looking?"

Remlika glanced around. "Pick a random direction and start walking," she said bluntly. "I would suggest a searching spell, but they are notoriously inaccurate, especially if you don't know the person you're looking for. Only to be used in absolute emergencies, really."

They started walking, always on the lookout for anywhere that could be a hiding place or shelter. The sun was well over its zenith when Kandrina finally saw something interesting. She ran across to the grey smudge she had spotted on the ground. As she approached, she confirmed that it was indeed the remains of a small fire, as she had thought. "Remlika, over here," she called to the mage, who had started to search the nearby bushes for edible berries.

Remlika walked over to where Kandrina had called from. "Looks like someone was camped here not long ago," she observed. "Keep still, I'm going to try something," she whispered to Kandrina, and began casting again. An ethereal eye appeared in mid-air and began zooming across the hillside. Suddenly, someone shouted in surprise from behind a bush.

"He's over there," Remlika declared, pointing towards the bushes. The two of them went across and pushed the greenery aside to reveal a wizen old man, with unkempt grey hair and a wild, shaggy beard.

"What do you want? I stayed away from town, didn't I?" he cried. "Why are you bothering me up here?"

Kandrina spoke first. "Are you Lerdran? You wrote a book a long time ago, about the Demons - I mean, Tanpèt Zèklè. We just wanted to ask you a few things…"

"Kandrina here is a student of my brother's," Remlika told the old man gently. Kandrina's scalp prickled slightly, and she guessed the mage was casting a subtle calming spell to help reassure the old man. "She wants to know about the Tanpèt Zèklè. Would you talk to her?"

Lerdran stared from the woman to the girl. "I suppose so. You realise the temples will have you staked to the ground outside town and left for the 'Demons'?" he said, sketching marks in the air as he said the word 'demons'.

"It's a risk I'm willing to take," said Kandrina, who was rather mature for her age and nearing the end of her girlhood anyway. "From what I've read of your book, they don't mean us any harm, so why should I fear being left at their mercy?"

The old man nodded approvingly. "You're a clever girl, you are. Keep out of the temples; they'll only try to dull your intellect. I'll tell you what little I know, and everything I suspect, about the Tanpèt Zèklè. Come, it will be more comfortable under the trees a short way away. I have food there as well." He led the two of them away to the next hill, with the blue sun glaring down on their backs.

Back in the town, Harndak was tearing the house apart looking for his missing daughter. "Where is she now? If I find out she's gone back to that mage again…"

"Father, I had a funny dream earlier," Enkarini said, oblivious to his panic. "I dreamt there was a dark lady in our room, and she disappeared with Kandrina. She was pretty," the little girl twittered.

"Who was pretty?" Harndak said, spinning around to face his youngest child.

"The dark lady. She had black hair and skin, and her eyes were all silvery and sparkling," Enkarini babbled. "She woke Kandrina up, and they held hands and disappeared."

Harndak kicked a chair. "She's gone off somewhere with that heretic sorceress, then. Enkarini, stay here. I'll ask the woman next door to keep you company while I go and talk to the priest," he told her, stalking out of the house.

After persuading the neighbours to watch Enkarini, he headed straight for the temple of Vrenid-Malchor. He needed to speak with the high priest again, to get help in guiding Kandrina back on to the right path. She'd been acting out ever since her mother's death, and now that Perlak was gone as well, she seemed to have gotten completely out of control. And those two heretics had only made matters worse, teaching her ridiculous theories and ideas about all kinds of bizarre subjects. He stormed through the market square, where a few merchants were just beginning to set up their stalls in the first rays of dawn. Lost in his worry and fear for his daughter's soul, he paid them no heed.

The towering silver spire of the Creator's temple guided him, a beacon visible from all over the town and shining brightly in the early morning sunlight. Usually it was a beautiful sight, an earthly representation of the Creator's glory, but this morning Harndak had no room in his heart to appreciate it. He turned corner after corner, making his way to the courtyard in front of the temple. When he finally reached it, he paused for a moment to catch his breath. The fountain in the centre of the yard tinkled quietly; the great marble statue of Vrenid-Malchor, his arms outstretched in welcome, almost glowed in the dawn light. Harndak, almost without thinking, tossed a gold coin into the fountain and sank to his knees in front of the statue. Closing his eyes, he began to pray. *Great Creator, where did I go so wrong?* he thought desperately, begging for an answer. *I tried to lead my children right, to teach them your ways; yet my only son fell to the Demons, and now my Kandrina is following a dangerous path of heresy. Is this punishment for some past crime? Am I being tested? Have I not been faithful enough? Surely my children have not angered you so themselves; perhaps they have been a little irreverent at times, but never sinful enough to deserve such terrible fates.*

His prayers met only with silence. The statue stood, immobile as always; the temple doors, however, had opened while he knelt there upon the cold stones. "Are you in need of guidance?" asked a priest standing in the doorway.

Harndak climbed to his feet stiffly, silently cursing his aching knees. "Yes, my daughter... I need advice from the high priest," he said. "Can you take me to speak with him? It is a matter of urgency."

"Certainly." The priest turned and led Harndak into the temple. He looked around as he entered; the great hall looked the same as it ever had, the dawn light just beginning to filter through the high arched windows, casting long, soft shadows across the floor. A pair of acolytes were tending the altar; one lighting the fat white candles at either end, the other swinging an incense burner and chanting the ritual prayer of thanks for another glorious day. The priest led him off the main hall, into a small side chamber where the high priest sat in contemplation. "Your holiness, there is someone here requesting your advice."

The high priest looked up from where he sat, cross-legged upon the prayer mat. "Ah, Harndak. Do you need further advice about your daughter?" he said, rising and waving the other priest out of the room.

Harndak sat down on one of the wooden benches, feeling slightly awkward. He knew he had been lax in neglecting to tell the temples about what his daughter had been saying, but he had been trying his best to protect her, lead her right himself. But now, with her running off every other day, he simply had no other choice. He offered a silent prayer to Aikra-Lora, the goddess of children, to look kindly upon Kandrina as he informed on her. "She has gone missing again, your holiness. My youngest child saw her leave with the sorceress, Remlika."

The high priest nodded slowly. "The sister of the heretic scholar, Remlik. We must begin searching. They may simply be hiding at the mage's house; I shall send an acolyte to check. Have you any inclination where else they may have gone?"

Uncomfortably, Harndak answered. "They might have gone to look for the sorceress' brother, your holiness. Kandrina was very upset last night; she hasn't been acting herself since... since Perlak's death, last week. She was talking about the Lightning Demons, but..." he stopped, afraid to go on. The temples taught that the terrible Demons were drawn closer by blasphemy and sin; even speaking their name could bring down their wrath. "She didn't seem to make any sense, talking about how they might not be so evil, how they might not intend any harm..."

The high priest held up a hand, interrupting Harndak mid sentence. "Has she spoken of things like this often?" he asked, watching Harndak sternly. "You must inform the temple of any blasphemy, remember. Your daughter is yet a child; her soul is still forming. But once she comes of age, there will be no more that can be done. She is fourteen summers old, yes?" Harndak nodded mutely. "A very susceptible age. If she has indeed fallen under the influence of the heretic Remlik and his sister, there may be little time left to save her. You must tell me everything, Harndak. Has your daughter been speaking of forbidden subjects?"

Harndak stared down at his hands, twisting them together in his lap; torn between protecting his daughter from the temples' wrath and letting the priests protect her from eternal damnation. Though their punishments were often harsh, the gods would punish sinners far more severely, and a small penance now would be better than eternal torture in Somri-Galin's realm. "Yes, she has spoken of the Demons before; but, your holiness, I believe she simply repeats the words of her heretic tutor. Had I known what blasphemies he taught, I would never have sent her to him. She is a good girl at heart, and I could not bear the loss of another child so soon," he pleaded, hoping the priest would take pity on him and his family.

The high priest rose from his elaborately carved chair. "We can discuss discipline when we find her. Until then, we search. She must be found before we can determine how seriously the heretics have damaged her soul. Rest assured, the sorceress will be dealt with also. Now, go home to your youngest child, Harndak. We will inform you when we find her." He swept out of the room, leaving Harndak alone in the side chamber.

Remlik yawned as he stoked the kitchen fire. He was still tired, and was willing the tea to boil quicker. He had been awake since before dawn, as his sister had woken him before she left to take Kandrina up to the hills. The sun was just beginning to creep over the horizon, bathing the town in a soft, pale blue light. He thought of toasting some bread over the flames, maybe even treating himself to a little sweet syrup poured over the top. Remlika always told him he used too much syrup on his toast, echoing their foster mother's scolding from when they were young. 'You keep eating that much syrup and all your teeth will fall out' was the usual line. He fetched some bread from the pantry, toasted it and poured on three spoonfuls of syrup, relishing the silence as he tucked in. *I don't care if it's unhealthy*, he thought to himself, *I deserve a treat now and then*. He wondered how long it would take his sister and student to find Lerdran up in the hills; though the scrying glass had given her a fairly good idea of his location, Remlika hadn't been too sure of where exactly he might be.

Remlik had just begun packing his things ready to leave later that morning, when he heard what sounded like marching at the end of the street. It was far too close to dawn for many people to be out and about, and if the army were drilling this early they would be doing it in the training grounds by the barracks, on the other side of town. He stood and looked out of the window, wondering what was going on. He saw a small group of soldiers, wearing temple tabards and led by a pair of acolytes. It only took a second to realise that they were probably heading for his place, and he dashed to the fireplace to open the passage down to the cellar. There was another way out, rarely used, that he had not mentioned to Kandrina the night before. It led around the back of the house and out into an alley near the poor quarter, where nobody was likely to report a man crawling out of a disused sewer duct. He grabbed hold of some of his most valuable texts, including Lerdran's book, and made his way out through the dank, narrow tunnel.

The temple militia smashed in the front door shortly afterwards. Remlik watched from a distance, listening to the sound of things smashing on the hard stone floor. A flickering light grew in one of the upstairs windows, probably setting fire to his study first. All those books, lost. Thankfully, he had not kept anything irreplaceable upstairs; anything one-of-a-kind had been in the secret cellar, which he doubted they would find. With a little luck, he would be able to go and retrieve the rest of the things in the cellar once the ashes had settled.

When they had gone, he left the shadows of the alley he had hidden in and went to find his sister and pupil. He would warn them at any cost.

Kandrina sat listening to Lerdran, enthralled by the tales he told of the beings he called the Tanpèt Zèklè. She had hardly noticed when the sun set, or when Remlika had lit a fire for warmth and heated up some food for the three of them.

"The book I wrote is mainly just a collection of what little fact I could find in the stories from temple dogma, and what I managed to find out from a few people who the priests hadn't got to yet," he had told her. "There's a lot more to it than that. You know how the priests say that they're evil spirits from Hell, and all the rest of it? That's all nonsense. The Zèklè are from this world, they are. They're made of lightning. That's how people die, actually. You ever been out in a storm? You know when lightning flashes down from the sky and hits a tree or sometimes an animal, and it falls down dead? That's what happens when they touch someone. I don't think they mean to do it, though."

"Like when I was little, and I found a butterfly. I caught it, to show father, but because it was so small and fragile I accidentally crushed it," Kandrina said. "You think it's like that?"

The old man nodded frantically. "That's it! That's exactly it, but the temples don't want us to think of them like that. They'd never get any offerings if people weren't scared of something."

They had all laughed at that, though it wasn't terribly funny. The old man had talked for hours, pleased to have an audience for the first time in years. At one point, Kandrina had asked him why the temples had been lenient enough to simply exile him, when they were more likely to stake people out for heresy now.

"I wasn't actually exiled, no I wasn't. They staked me out like they do with most people, but I guess they didn't tie the rope to the stakes properly, because I managed to wiggle free after a few hours. Then I ran off, I did. I've been up here for over forty summers now, and I think they know I'm here, but so long as I keep out of the town the priests don't seem that bothered." Lerdran stared into the fire for a few moments. "I see them sometimes, you know. Not close up, mind, but sort of floating about in the distance. Sometimes I think it would be nice to go up to them and talk. Then I think that they probably wouldn't understand me. I don't know if they can speak at all, let alone speak our tongue."

As the old man lapsed into silence, Kandrina shivered. Despite the fire, it was getting cold after the sun had gone down. She looked around, realising how dark it was. "We've been here all day?" she said in wonderment. "I didn't think we'd been up here so long."

"We have," Remlika responded. "I should probably take you home. Your father will be worried. Thank you for your time, Lerdran," the mage said, standing up.

"And thank you for the food, and everything," Kandrina said, preparing to be transported again.

Lerdran smiled at them both. "It was my pleasure. Feel free to visit me again, if you want. I like you," he told them before they vanished.

They rematerialised at the foot of the hills, just outside the town. "Why have we ended up here?" Kandrina asked.

"Remlik," the sorceress mumbled, looking around distractedly. "He's here somewhere, got something important to say…" she fell silent as her brother popped out from behind some trees.

"Sister, the temple militia have broken into our house. They smashed up a lot of things, I'm not sure what, and started a fire. I suspect they've destroyed most of my books and your arcane paraphernalia. Kandi, they're looking for you as well. I heard something about your father informing the high priest about some heresy," Remlik told his pupil. "Where have you been all day anyway? I didn't think it would take you this long to find Lerdran."

"It took us until well after midday," Kandrina answered. "Then we just got talking. It was dark before we realised how late it was. I suppose we should flee, if we're all wanted for blasphemy," she began to say. Lanterns blazed before she had finished her sentence though, and people began shouting. Remlika took her brother's hand and vanished, mouthing to Kandrina 'I'll come back for you'. Temple acolytes seized Kandrina and dragged her back into the town to face the high priest.

As they pulled her through the North Gate, she attempted to twist out of their grip and head down a narrow back street, but the two holding her arms seized her and held her firmly. "No back alley shortcuts," hissed one of the acolytes as they hauled her past the Sunset Tavern. Several drunken patrons filtered out, wondering what all the fuss was about. They followed the acolytes, pointing and muttering amongst themselves.

Kandrina had rarely ventured into the northern part of town; most of the people she knew lived in the lower end of Manak. The furthest she had been on a regular basis was the Market Square, when her father took her along to help him sell his wares. She was clearly being taken through the richest parts of town. The houses were much larger than those she knew, the streets much wider and cleaner. A huge silver spire dominated the sky, part of the temple of Vrenid-Malchor, the Creator God. She had always tried to avoid actually going to the temple with her father, and on the rare occasions when he had successfully dragged her along, she had spent the whole time staring at the ground, ignoring the sermons, so she had never fully appreciated just how large the spire was before.

The acolytes dragged her down another street, this one lined with shuttered shops. One sign read 'Fine Silk Garments'; another said 'Jewellers'. They turned right at the moneylender's, followed by a mid-sized crowd of townsfolk, all staring and pointing and jeering at the girl. Kandrina shook her head, allowing her pale gold hair to fall across her face, shielding her from the accusing eyes of the devout townspeople. As they passed the Chief's Halls, just before reaching the temple courtyard, the scribe Gondrun looked out of the door. He stared curiously, and withdrew for a moment before re-emerging, accompanied by Jindar, the Chief of the People. They descended the steps of the halls and joined the crowd following the girl and acolytes.

An even larger crowd awaited in the square; mostly people who had been visiting the market that day and had not made their way home yet. Harndak stood by the temple steps, looking worried and determined at the same time. The high priest, flanked by a pair of very timid-looking servants, stood framed in the temple doors, glaring down at her as his acolytes threw her to the ground by the fountain. Kandrina pushed herself up from the floor as her father spoke.

"Kandrina! What were you thinking, disappearing for the whole day?" Harndak demanded of his daughter, but was silenced by the high priest of the Creator God Vrenid-Malchor instantly.

In a heavy, preaching tone more suited to a sermon, the priest began to speak. "Kandrina, daughter of Harndak and Meradina, you have been accused of speaking heresy. You will stand trial in the temple tomorrow at dawn." He glared down at her, knowing the girl to be guilty. "After the trial, if the accusations are proven true, you will be staked out at sunset and left to the mercy of the Lightning Demons. Tonight you will sleep in the temple basement, and if you have a care for your soul you will beg forgiveness from the gods."

"I will beg no forgiveness," Kandrina said clearly, glaring back at the priest. "I do not fear the beings you call demons. And I do not believe the gods would concern themselves with my prayers, should I offer any."

There was a collective intake of breath from the watching crowd. The high priest looked as though he had been slapped. "You dare speak such blasphemy in front of me?" he hissed.

"These are not her words, your holiness, she merely repeats the words of the heretics Remlik and Remlika," Harndak pleaded, sinking to his knees in front of the high priest. "It was my mistake to send her to be educated by them, surely you would not punish the naivety of a child so severely?"

"Whether they are her own words or not is immaterial now. The girl will answer to the gods, through myself and the other priests. Unless you wish to join her I suggest you remain quiet, and pray for mercy," the high priest told Harndak, sparing him only a cold glance. "Bring her to the temple, and bind her in the cellar," he instructed his acolytes. Kandrina was forced into the temple, pushed down some narrow stairs, and tied to a rough wooden post. She was left alone in the dark, charged with praying for mercy upon her soul, but all she could think of was the mysterious creatures the priests called Demons. Bizarrely, part of her wanted to be staked out for them. She wanted a chance to meet them, even if they did accidentally take her life.

Dawn arrived unreasonably quickly. Acolytes arrived to take Kandrina up to the main chamber of the temple, where the high priest would be waiting, along with priests of Fakro-Umdar and Somri-Galin, gods of death and suffering respectively. She doubted there would be any other priests present, as there were no temples to other gods in this town. If she was fortunate there might be a travelling priestess of Aikra-Lora, the goddess of children. Servants dragged the great doors open, and she saw only three priests.

"Place her in the chair and leave us," the high priest commanded his acolytes, and they obeyed. "Kandrina, you sit before us accused of heresy and foul blasphemy. Furthermore, you spoke said blasphemy in my presence. The gods will hear your excuses through our ears," he declared, indicating the men either side of him.

"Speak your piece, child. We are listening," whispered the priest of Somri-Galin. His voice grated on Kandrina's ears like rusty nails scraping down a slate.

She took a deep breath, steadying herself for whatever might be coming. "I have no defence. I simply spoke my own mind, as I am entitled to do. If I have committed such terrible crimes against the gods, then let them strike me down themselves, for I will not explain my actions and words to pompous, self-important men like you." Raising her voice above the protests of the holy men, she continued. "I intend to discover the truth, be it compatible with your doctrines or not. If you decide to stake me out at the mercy of the Tanpèt Zèklè, whom you call Lightning Demons, then so be it. I will face them without fear." She tried to look each of them in the eye as she spoke; she would not be cowed by these men, they did not own her, and she had every right to disagree with them.

The death priest only seemed faintly amused as he looked down at her, but the other two were beside themselves with fury. "She dares such insult!" the high priest shrieked to no one in particular.

"She must answer for this, I agree," the priest of Somri-Galin declared. "However, simply leaving her for the Demons seems too kind. My acolytes are trained in the art of punishment, perhaps I could..."

"No, let the Demons have her," the priest of Fakro-Umdar mused. "If she claims to have no fear of them, and wishes to discover the truth about them, then let her."

The high priest of Vrenid-Malchor fumed in his seat. "Very well. Girl, you will be left for the Lightning Demons. Perhaps they will tell you what you wish to know before they kill you. Until then I suggest you return to your family and say fond farewells, for I doubt you will return to them alive again." He waved his hand in dismissal.

Kandrina left the temple, and decided to take the scenic route home. She was not in any great rush to see her father, after he had betrayed her to the priests. She did, however, want to say goodbye to her little sister. If it were not for Enkarini, she would have given serious thought to simply fleeing the town, perhaps out to Astator, where she had some distant relatives, or into the hills to join Lerdran in exile. She would go home for her sister, but she was in no hurry. Rather than heading southwards from the temple square, which would have led her directly into familiar territory and then home, she took the western-bound street, past the tailors and carpenter's shops and out towards what was commonly known as the 'wild district'. Having never been there, she was curious about how it got its name.

Just past the edge of the temple square, a small troop of soldiers marched across her path, heading towards the barracks near the Chief's Halls. She paused to let them pass, smiling at a few who looked her way. One young recruit near the back grinned and winked when he saw her; she vaguely recalled that he had been a friend of her brother's. She waved back, smiling to him. When the soldiers had passed, Kandrina continued her walk, noticing that the cobbled streets had slowly become more like dirt tracks lined by roughly hewn stones. Looking around at the buildings, she noticed they looked more rustic than those in other parts of town; most had thatch roofs instead of tiled, and the few that had a second storey were timbered on the upper floor. A mill loomed in the distance, its blades turning slowly in the summer breeze.

There were clear signs of old farm fields all around; furrows in the gardens indicated heavy ploughing in the past. Walking past an open patch of grass, she could see apprentice hunters being trained. Shouts echoed across the grass from the master hunters, correcting their students. Kandrina stopped to watch them. Though by no means an expert, she knew a little about hunting from what Perlak had shown her. An auburn haired young man to the right of the field seemed to be doing very well; he had hit the centre of the target five times in the few moments she had been watching. Pulling herself out of her memories, she carried on walking. It was becoming clear why people called it the wild district; it was home to several hunters and farmers who chose to live within the confines of the city rather than in the settlements outside the walls.

Rounding a corner, Kandrina immediately felt an unnatural chill settle on her skin. She wrapped her arms around herself and looked down the street. A cold, dark shadow hung over the end of the road, surrounding the temple of Fakro-Umdar, god of death. Something creaked loudly over her head. Startled, she looked up to see a sign reading 'The Black Stallion'. A sudden urge to run came over her; she turned and walked swiftly down a side street. She emerged near a stable; the smell of horse dung was strong, and oddly reassuring. A tall, thin woman standing outside brushing a grey mare saw her and nodded in greeting – one of her father's regular customers. As a blacksmith, Harndak was often called upon to re-shoe horses. It was the family's main source of income.

Kandrina was beginning to figure out where she was, so decided to head on home. She turned left, away from the stable, and made her way down the dirt track. She passed an inn whose sign showed a strong, muscled man snoozing in a chair, a bow and quiver of arrows resting beside him. 'The Hunter's Rest'; her house was only two streets away. Dirt track became cobbled road again, tiled roofs reappeared, and Harndak's smithy came into view about halfway down the street. Something was amiss though – no smoke rose from the workshop chimney. Kandrina paused outside, wondering for a second what had happened, before remembering that her father had not set foot in the forge in ten days, since Perlak's death. She sighed, exasperated, sad and frustrated in equal measure, and pushed open the front door.

"Kandrina!" Enkarini ran up to her big sister the instant she opened the door. "Did you say sorry for upsetting the high priest?" she asked, looking up at the older girl with big, sparkling green eyes.

Kandrina looked back, knowing the answer she had to give would cause the little girl's beautiful eyes to fill with tears. "No, Enkarini. I couldn't apologise for something I hadn't really done," she whispered as her sister began to cry. She knelt on the floor and held the younger girl tightly. "Don't worry, I'll be back someday. Until then I want you to always remember that there's more to this world than the temples tell you."

Harndak stood further back in the room, watching the two sisters hold each other for what he thought would be the last time. "Kandrina," he began softly.

"I have nothing to say to you, Father." Kandrina stared at him over Enkarini's shoulder. "Unless you want to take back what you told the high priest? Though I doubt it would make much difference now, after I called him and the others pompous and self-important."

"You did what? Why did you insult the priests, on top of everything else?" Harndak cried in exasperation.

Kandrina released her sister and stood up. "I told the truth, as I did last night. They are only mortal men, like everyone else in this town. If the gods have a problem with my behaviour then why don't they deal with me themselves? According to the temples that would be just the sort of petty nonsense they would concern themselves with." She pushed past him into the kitchen, heading for the back yard. It was about the time of day when she usually fed the half-dozen ibikona they kept out there, and collected any eggs. Enkarini will probably do it now, she thought.

"Don't you think you're in enough trouble as it is?" Harndak demanded from behind her. "Must you go spouting more heresy?"

"It doesn't matter what I say anymore. The high priest is staking me out for the Demons tonight." Kandrina spoke without fear or concern. She honestly did not object to being left for the Zèklè, and was more worried about what the temples were capable of doing to her father and sister once she was gone. Without her, there would be no voice of reason in the house.

The high priest arrived at sundown, with four acolytes in tow. They carried the steel stakes and short lengths of rope needed to secure someone to the ground outside town. Kandrina went with them quietly, knowing there was no point in trying to escape or fight. People stared out of windows as they passed, and the few people still in the street pointed and made comments like 'such a pretty young girl, I wonder what went wrong?' Kandrina ignored them all. They walked almost in procession, out of the western gate and through the farms, now empty of workers. By the time they stopped, the sun had disappeared completely, leaving only the stars, the small moon Eskali, and the small circle of light coming from a lantern one of the acolytes carried. Kandrina could just make out the silhouettes of the hills against the starlit sky, and the much closer lantern lights of the town, that now felt as far away as the stars.

"This will do. Girl, lie down." Kandrina obeyed, feeling slightly numb. She wasn't sure what to expect, but somehow couldn't help thinking that she wouldn't be returning to Manak. The acolytes tied rope around her wrists and ankles, one working on each limb. They fixed the ropes to the stakes and hammered them into the ground. "In the unlikely event that you survive the night, someone will come to release you at sunrise," the high priest told her.

"Pray, Kandrina. Only the gods can save you now," one of the acolytes whispered. She didn't know which one; they all looked alike in the dark. The priest and acolytes left, leaving her alone in the night. Kandrina waited, but nothing came. She recited stories to herself, ones her mother used to tell when she was very young. A few times she thought she heard something moving nearby, but couldn't turn far enough to see properly. Nothing came towards her anyway, and after a few hours she drifted into sleep.

She awoke some time later, thinking at first that the sun had risen. She blinked the sleep out of her eyes and lifted her head as much as she could. There were still stars in the sky, and Eskali was directly overhead. Frowning in confusion, Kandrina attempted to work out where the bright bluish light was coming from.

"Are you alright?" an echoing, faintly crackly voice asked from behind Kandrina's head. She tilted her head back to see who was there. When the person who had spoken came into view, she thought she must still be asleep and dreaming, because there seemed to be a beautiful, nude, glowing woman sitting by her head. Of course, she was also upside down from Kandrina's point of view. She stared, afraid to blink in case the vision vanished.

The glowing woman spoke again, in the crackling voice Kandrina had heard before. "Please do not be afraid. We mean you no harm."

"I'm not frightened," Kandrina whispered. "Are you one of the Tanpèt Zèklè?" she asked, still watching her.

"If that is what you call us, then yes." She turned to look at a nearby cluster of trees. "Are you able to free yourself? There is one of your kind hiding in those trees with a blade. I believe his intention is to kill you. Unless that is the reason for these rituals we have often observed?"

Kandrina was unsure which question to answer first. "This ritual is a little complicated to explain right now. I think I could free myself," she said, testing the ropes. The stake holding her right leg shifted a little. "Give me a minute." She pulled at the ropes, and after several moments of tugging the dry soil around the stakes crumbled. She sat up and turned to look at the woman properly. She was as attractive as Kandrina had first thought, with wide eyes and high cheekbones, and a slender yet delicately curved figure. She was almost too perfect. "Do all of you look like that? The ladies, I mean."

The woman smiled. "Usually none of us look like this. I assumed this shape because I felt it would be less disturbing for you. In our usual form we are a lot less distinct." She glanced towards the trees again.

"Would you like to come with me? You seem very different to the others of your kind," she asked.

"I would like that very much," Kandrina replied, standing up and removing the stakes from her wrists and ankles. "What's your name?" she asked, following as the woman began walking further away from the shadowy shape that was Manak by night.

The woman stopped. "We do not have names as such. Each of us is as one, in essence. You may call me Nerlarina, though. I have used the name before, and it serves as well as any other." She shimmered for a split second, and suddenly she was clothed in a sweeping garment that looked as though it was made of liquid diamond. "I recalled that your kind prefers not to gaze upon nakedness," she said in response to Kandrina's awed look. She resumed walking, and Kandrina followed after, careful not to get too close in case of accidental contact.

As Kandrina wandered into the night with Nerlarina, Remlika materialised in front of the temple of Vrenid-Malchor. She had seen her brother safely to Tewen, and persuaded an old acquaintance to take them in until they found more permanent lodgings. She had returned to fetch Kandrina, and after casting a searching spell she had transported herself to the temple. She hoped it would be accurate, but it was just as likely to have picked up an old trace from earlier in the day.

Remlika wanted a new scrying glass when she got back to Tewen. After disguising herself as an old washerwoman, she strode up the steps of the temple and knocked.

"Who calls at this time?" said a sleepy sounding priest from inside.

"I seek guidance on an urgent matter," she replied. "All I ask is a quiet place to pray to the Creator, that he might hear and take pity on a poor wretch." All Remlika needed was to get inside, so she could search for Kandrina and get out. She wished the temples wouldn't put up wards to stop people transporting directly in.

The priest opened the small door concealed in the larger one. "Enter, and be welcome," he yawned.

Remlika entered, showing proper deference to the priest as she passed him, but thinking particularly sacrilegious thoughts that she was very glad he couldn't hear. She made her way to one of the small prayer chambers off the main atrium, and began casting a slightly subtler spell of location. After a half hour she was forced to conclude that Kandrina was not in the temple, and she cursed aloud. Looking up belatedly, she saw there was still nobody around, so she made her way back outside. She murmured words of thanks to the half-asleep priest at the door, and left to begin her search anew.

She tried Harndak's house, not really expecting to find her there but wanting to check every possibility. Enkarini awoke when she heard someone walking around, and decided to start jabbering away about flowers, so Remlika made a quick exit. She checked the burnt out shell of her own house, realising sadly that all of her things had been destroyed, and Remlik's books all burnt in the centre of the sitting room. Impatiently brushing away pointless tears, she quickly looked for Kandrina but found nothing. She realised what had happened, and hung her head. "I knew I should have come back sooner," she scolded herself. Not seeing much use in trying to search the entire area surrounding the town for one girl, who was likely dead one way or another by now, she returned to her brother to tell him what had happened to his student.

Chapter Three: Search

"I like her."

Talri-Pekra shot a derisive look across the pavilion. "Of course you like her, Aikra-Lora. You're the goddess of children, you're supposed to like kids."

"I was just saying," said the diminutive child goddess, folding her arms and looking huffy. "No need to get all snippy about it."

"The girl is not the issue here," said Ralor-Kanj calmly, preventing an argument before it began. "The issue at hand is the priests, especially in the town of Manak. They are no longer paying attention to their temple duties and are concerning themselves with too many of their own wants and desires. They are harming the people they are meant to be protecting. The question is, what can we do?"

Dranj-Aria glanced up from the hourglass she was toying with. "The girl was useful. I mean, will be useful. She's one of the few people who has dared speak against the priests," she reminded the other gods. "I remember what we're going to do, since I've already done it in one sense. She goes off with one of those energy creatures, and she's learnt all about them. I send an aspect of myself to help her when she returned to confront Vrenid-Malchor's priest, and she's going to provide us with the opportunity we needed to have dealt with him."

It took the others a few moments to sort out the jumble of tenses the goddess of time had mixed up, but once they made sense of it all they agreed. "If that's what you remember is going to happen, you'd better get on with it. We're at the point when Kandrina has just gone to the city to learn about the energy creatures," Ralor-Kanj reminded her. Dranj-Aria often got muddled about what point in time they were actually at, since a lot of her mind was lost in either the past or the future. It was best not to try and work out what she was thinking about, as it tended to give anyone a headache.

"Right. If I remember correctly, I don't go down and talk to her until she leaves their city and... oh, I shouldn't say anything else. I'll spoil it for the rest of you." She grinned inanely, knowing it would irritate the others, and resumed fiddling with her hourglass.

"I don't see why we have to interfere at all," grated the voice of Somri-Galin. "They're only mortals, after all."

Ralor-Kanj replied. "We have to interfere because we are supposed to be looking after them. Besides, how can they suffer if the priests have killed them all?" he asked, knowing that would silence the god of suffering.

"I doubt Vrenid-Malchor would appreciate waking up and seeing his creations in this state," said Fakro-Umdar in a heavy, leaden tone. "Also, my domain is becoming rather crowded. We have to sort this out now."

"So it's settled. We let Kandrina learn all she can, Dranj-Aria will go to assist the girl, and with any luck this mess will be cleared up before he awakes," Talri-Pekra declared, nodding towards the throne where the Creator god slumbered. "Now the facts are settled, we ought to return to our own domains."

Slowly, the gods faded back to their own places. Dranj-Aria kept her own counsel. She knew what was about to occur in the mortal realm, and it would be far from over when Vrenid-Malchor awoke.

Kandrina stared up at the huge, glittering palace. It shone brightly against the slowly lightening sky, and as she looked closer she thought she could see lights moving around inside. "Is this your city?" she asked in wonderment.

"Yes. You are the first of your kind to see it clearly for many years," Nerlarina told her. "They walk past, sometimes, but only see a mountain."

The city seemed to flicker, and all of a sudden Kandrina only saw a tall grey expanse of rock.

"How...? Was that magic?" she asked, not knowing what else could disguise a city so large.

"No. We do not use the twisting force you call magic," Nerlarina said. Kandrina bit her lip, worried she may have offended. "Come, let me show you around," the woman continued, leading Kandrina inside as the city flickered back into view.

As they entered the sparkling city, Kandrina had to squint against the intense light that seemed to be shining from everywhere. Once her eyes had got used to the glare, she realised that the light was not issuing from the walls, but from the people. At least, she thought they were people, but whenever she tried to make out their features things got even hazier. She understood what Nerlarina had told her earlier about being less distinct. The Tanpèt Zèklè, or whatever they were really called, appeared to be amorphous clouds of light, drifting about in a diamond palace.

Nerlarina led her up a slope to some rooms that seemed to be tinted in different colours. "I understand our brightness may be uncomfortable on your eyes. These rooms should be better for you. The tint in the walls dims our light," she explained.

"Thank you," Kandrina said, lowering her hand from her eyes. "Can I ask, since you don't use magic, how do you disguise your city?"

"The same way we can change how we look. It is made from the same energy as we are, and its shape is decided by the collective consciousness of everyone inside. You are going to ask how you can walk on our floors without suffering ill effects," Nerlarina said, anticipating Kandrina's next question. "It is very simple. You are wearing wooden-soled shoes, which form a barrier between your flesh and our energy. If you were to wear wooden gloves, you would be able to touch me."

Kandrina raised her eyebrows. "Is it really that simple? I thought it would be a bit more complicated."

"Complex solutions rarely work as well as simple ones," Nerlarina smiled. "At least, that is our way of thinking. We are given to understand that your peoples' way of life is astoundingly complex. Would you be willing to teach us? We are curious to learn of your kind, that we might be able to communicate better."

Kandrina could hardly believe her luck. "I'll teach you everything I can about my kind, in exchange for everything you can teach me about your kind. Does that sound like a fair trade?"

"Fair trade?" Nerlarina queried.

"Exchange of goods or services of equal value, with all people involved happy with said exchange," Kandrina recited from one of her lessons.

"An admirable concept. Yes, it does sound like a fair trade," Nerlarina replied. "So, the ritual you were participating in before. Would you be able to explain it? We have observed it many times but cannot decipher its purpose."

"I can try. As I said, it's very complicated. See, we have temples to the gods," Kandrina began. "That's where the priests work, and people go to pray. When people don't agree with what the priests are saying, they are declared heretics, and the high priest takes them outside the town and stakes them to the ground, as you found me. People are left out all night, and then taken back at sunrise if they survive. It's supposed to be… like exposing yourself to the elements, and creatures that wander about. They say that if you survive then you must have earned the gods' forgiveness. Most people die, though. The priests always tell us that your kind are the ones who do it," she said, in an apologetic tone.

"Still? We realised a long time ago that our touch would cause your kind harm. Until now, none of us have approached one of you for several generations," Nerlarina told her. "Usually the deaths are caused by your own kind. Like the one hiding in the trees tonight, they wait until just before sunrise and then emerge to kill the one tied to the ground. They lightly burn the body afterwards. We assumed it was some kind of sacrificial ritual, perhaps to encourage favourable weather or something of the sort. Tell me, what do they call us now? There have been many names for us over the centuries; I personally was rather fond of the term 'Colourless'. But we thought that the term 'Tanpèt Zèklè' had become disused."

Kandrina smiled. "It mostly has. The priests call you 'Lightning Demons', and most other people are afraid to disagree with them. They want everyone to fear you, I think. I was lucky to have someone with an open mind teaching me." Thoughts of Remlik and his sister flooded her mind. "I wonder if they managed to escape?" she wondered aloud.

"Your teachers?" Nerlarina asked.

"Yes. Well, my teacher and his sister. They were good friends as well, and the priests are after them for teaching heresy. I hope they're somewhere safe."

Remlik paced in the dawn light. "Are you sure? You have to be sure, sister."

"She was nowhere in the town. It's likely the temples had her staked out, which means she's long gone by now. You know as well as I do that the acolytes often go out and kill people if nothing else has," Remlika replied. "I'm sorry, she was a wonderful girl, but there's nothing we can do now."

"I could scry for her. There may be a faint chance that she escaped," Braklarn cut in. He was an old friend of Remlika's, and had given the twins a place to stay in Tewen while they hid from the temples. Shaking long, straggly red hair out of his eyes, he continued. "You mentioned someone called Lerdran, who escaped many years ago. It could be that your young friend has done the same, and gone into hiding somewhere. I'm not trying to give false hope, but it's best to explore every possibility before making plans for a funeral."

Remlik could not help but feel a leaping sensation in his chest. "Yes. If nothing else, I'd like to know if she's still alive." Braklarn nodded and left the room. "It's not likely, I know. But as he said, it's possible, and we can't exactly go back to find out."

His sister shook her head sadly, and left to go shopping. Braklarn had mentioned something about a magical equipment shop earlier, and she had immediately declared her intention to visit it and replace some of the things she had lost. Remlik went to watch Braklarn scrying for Kandrina, hoping against hope that she was still alive somewhere. The sorcerer sang quietly to his glass in a corner, attempting to resolve the swirling rainbows that had appeared. "She's alive," he mumbled between incantations. "I can't seem to find where she is, though. The glass is having difficulty resolving…"

He continued to sing, watching the glass carefully for any change. A blurred picture of a mountain appeared, and then faded. Braklarn kept incanting for several minutes, but all he achieved was making the blurry mountain reappear a few more times. He looked up and saw Remlik waiting patiently.

"She lives. I'm not sure where, though. I don't understand, usually the image is much clearer," he said, scowling at the glass in confusion. "Unless it's some kind of camouflaged place. Wards or other means of disguise can confuse the glass."

Relief spread across the darker man's face. He was relieved simply to know his student was alive. Finding her was secondary, as if she was near impossible to locate then the temples would also be unable to find her. "I'm just glad she's alive. I'll let my sister know when she gets back; I think she went to get herself some more magical equipment. Thanks, Braklarn."

He went back to the small room he was sharing with Remlika while they looked for somewhere to live. Tewen seemed to be a little more relaxed towards religious beliefs, luckily. The temples were different as well. Instead of the gods of suffering and death, there were shrines to Aikra-Lora and Talri-Pekra, goddess of magic and knowledge, a temple of Ralor-Kanj, god of balance, and a temple of Dranj-Aria, the goddess of time. Of course, there was a temple to the Creator God, but all towns had one of them. At least, they had since the tribal merging over a hundred years ago, when the faith in Manak had spread and either annihilated or assimilated all the other tribes' religions. The so-called 'absent gods' were the multitude of deities that had not been accepted by Chief Morendir and his priests.

Remlik was certain that if they had had their own way at the time, nobody would even remember those gods, but as an act of peacekeeping they had agreed to keep those gods in the temple writings, but not to be worshipped. It was a great source of contention for several scholars, especially Remlik and his sister. They had managed to trace their bloodline back to an old Chief of the Bewein tribe, which had considered knowledge to be sacred. Their goddess had eventually become Talri-Pekra, goddess of knowledge and magic, but many people who could trace their families back to Bewein had a deep-seated resentment of the current temples. They seemed to be more intent on promoting ignorance than learning.

Remlika made her way through the centre of town to a shop Braklarn had mentioned, planning to buy herself a new scrying glass, along with some other materials and implements that needed replacing after the temples had destroyed them. She approached the market square, relieved that it was not market day. Still, the place was quite busy, with a fair few of the local merchants' stalls in place. Remlika kept her head lowered, attempting to deflect attention. Sellers always pushed hard to get her to buy their wares, possibly because as a skilled mage people assumed that she was very wealthy. It was one of the reasons she and her brother preferred to take lodgings in or near the poor quarter of any given city –people often judged one another on where they lived. Also, the poorer side of town was usually the more interesting.

"Buy a necklace, miss?" A young man rattled a handful of beads and chains under her nose, interrupting her thoughts. "Fine jewels, these are, and yours for just forty silver coins! How about this one? Goes lovely with your eyes, miss," he said, extricating a long silver chain from the bundle he carried.

Remlika stepped around him. "No thank you, I have plenty of jewellery already," she said, quietly but firmly. The necklace vendor protested, but she ignored him and was soon lost in the crowd. Merchants and buyers shouted all around her; haggling over prices, going through sales pitches, arguing about faulty goods. She sank down onto an abandoned crate and slowly began casting a calming spell on herself. Large, noisy crowds had always bothered her. Thankfully, she kept her concentration for long enough to make the spell work fast, reducing the crowd noise to a quiet babble, easily ignored. Remlika blinked, flicked at her hair, and stood up.

Now the crowds of people no longer bothered her, she could look around properly at her surroundings. Busy shops lined the square; carpenters, cobblers, tailors and bakers. Nothing out of the ordinary there. A large pillar rose above the heads of the crowd, pointing straight up to the sky. Wondering what it was, Remlika crossed the square to examine it. Close up, it looked weathered and chipped. Several people had carved their initials in its surface over the years. She looked around for a brass information plaque, usually placed on or near places that had some historical significance. Finding one on a stand next to the pillar, she read:

'This ancient pillar is one of the last remnants of the Tewen tribe's Sun Temple. Before the tribes of the People were united, the tribe of Tewen worshipped a god named Alch, who they believed lived in the sun. The Sun Temple is thought to have had eight of these pillars arranged in a circle, and an open roof. Another pillar can be found on the edge of Temple Square, near the library.'

Intrigued, Remlika thought about wandering over to the library to see the other pillar and check the library's books for more information. She had taken a couple of steps before realising that wandering aimlessly around the streets would get her hopelessly lost. She changed direction mid-step and kept heading towards the shop Braklarn had directed her to. She would visit the library later, or perhaps tomorrow.

Passing a smithy on the way out of the other side of the marketplace made her think of Kandrina. Like her brother, Remlika hoped that the girl had managed to escape somehow, but she was trying to be realistic about the situation. Very few people returned alive after being staked out; though some people had been known to escape, like old Lerdran, they were still rare cases. She did not believe for a second that the Tanpèt Zèklè had taken Kandrina, but more likely than not she had been attacked by a wild animal or killed by a temple acolyte. She pitied her brother's desperation to find the girl alive and well. It was plain to see that he felt very strongly for the girl, though he refused to acknowledge it himself.

She turned down a side street, lost in idle speculation, when an intoxicating aroma wafted over her. She paused, looking around for its source. A wooden sign hung over a shop just down the street, reading 'Potions and Arcana'. It seemed she had found the right place. Pushing open the door, she got a pleasant surprise. "Wordarla! I didn't realise this was your shop," she cried, recognising her friend's half sister.

The short, orange-haired woman grinned across the counter. Wordarla's father must have had dwarf blood in him, because he had passed down to his daughter a pair of deep blue eyes without whites, short stature, and the cheekiest grin in Tewen. "Tis great to see y' again, Remlika. I didn't know y' were in town, when'd y' get 'ere?" She also had a slight dwarven accent, though how she had picked it up was a mystery. It was possible that she put it on deliberately, as people were inclined to pay more for a dwarven-quality magical item or potion. They had a reputation for crafting things in such a way that they would last much longer and work better than any other.

"Only last night. It was a bit of an unexpected trip, my brother and I had to leave in a rush," Remlika told her, leaning on the counter. "Trouble with the temples, you see."

"Ah, tis becoming more common, that. Vice-chief Jindara is even talkin' about havin' a word with old Jindar about his priests. We've had a lot of y'r lot from Manak comin' over to claim sanctuary at Ralor-Kanj's temple." Wordarla beckoned the mage forwards. "I've even heard talk of goin' to war on account of the priests, though I'd ask y' not to go spreadin' that about. Tisn't somethin' that ought to be commonly known," she whispered in confidence.

Remlika nodded. "It's safe with me. Anyway, I was looking for a scrying glass, and some other items. Your brother said you might have some here," she said, speaking normally again.

"Ah yes, we've got some right good quality bits through 'ere," Wordarla said. "Scrying glass, y' said? This one's just come in, tis one of the finest I've seen in a long while," she held up a large glass framed in shining silver.

Remlika gave it an appraising look. "It certainly looks fine. How much?"

"For y'? Only a half-century of gold pieces. Though it's worth closer to one n' a half centuries, if y' ask me. Finely crafted, tis. And that's pure silver around the edge y' know, not the blended stuff y' get sometimes."

"It's not been used, has it? You know they're useless to anyone else after they've been used," Remlika said. Scrying glasses were very personal items; once they had been attuned to one particular mage they tended to resist any other sorcerer that tried to use them. She'd learnt that the hard way, after trying to use someone else's scrying glass. The after effects had made her ill for weeks afterwards.

Wordarla shook her orange head. "Tis brand new. Y' know I refuse to sell second hand goods. Y' need anythin' else?" she asked. "I've not long done up a batch of love potions, if y' like," she said, cheeky grin reappearing.

Remlika stifled a laugh. "I'm fine, thanks. I could use a few spell vessels, though." She liked to incant spells into specially prepared vessels to be used later. It saved time in emergencies, and putting basic spells like pest vanishers into vessels allowed her to sell people those spells, so she did not actually need to run around town dealing with everyone's nentila infestations.

"Spell vessels, right. I'll get y' a few from the back. Eight silver pieces each, but if y' want I'll do y' twenty for one gold," Wordarla called from the back of the room, where she was pulling small glass bottles off shelves.

"Sounds fair. So that's half a century for the scrying glass, and one for the vessels," Remlika said, checking her coin purse. "Tell you what, here's sixty gold. I think I'll take a few of these too," she told the merchant, examining some dried up berries under the counter. "They are unkerberries, aren't they?" she checked.

Wordarla nodded as she placed the vessels into a canvas bag. "Aye, they are. Y' plan to curse someone, do y'? I hope it's nobody I know. Tis my job to be fixin' curses, y' know."

"I don't think you know him. It's the high priest back in Manak. Trust me, he deserves to be cursed," Remlika said, telling the woman what had happened to Kandrina. "What happens between the armies makes little difference to me and my brother, but this ought to provide some just revenge for us."

"Ah, Remlika. I've missed y', and y'r liking for personal vendettas. Y' make sure y' curse that priest good, for the girl's sake as well as y'r brother's n' y'r own." Wordarla waved the mage out of her shop, and returned to her potions. Not only was she the proprietor of an arcane shop, she was also a highly skilled alchemist.

The high priest scowled at his acolyte. "Say that again. Without the pathetic excuses this time."

"I waited in the trees, as you instructed. The girl talked to herself for a short while, then fell asleep. I watched, and shortly before sunrise a Lightning Demon appeared and sat by the girl's head. The girl awoke, and the two of them spoke. The Demon looked towards where I hid, as though she knew I was there," the acolyte told his superior.

"She? The Demon was female?" the priest interrupted.

"Yes, your Holiness. She spoke to the girl for a moment, and then the girl pulled the stakes from the ground. They seemed to speak again, and then walked off together." The acolyte threw himself to the floor. "Forgive me, I could not follow. I feared for my own life, and the girl is likely dead by now, or taken to the Demons' Realm. Either way, she cannot trouble us again," he said.

"Get up. Go back to the temple." The high priest watched his acolyte flee back towards the town. After another look at the discarded stakes and rope, he began walking back himself. He would inform the girl's father personally, changing the story so that the girl had been killed and the remains burned away. "You, scrape up some dirt," he instructed his servant, who rushed to obey. He would tell the blacksmith that the Demons had destroyed the girl's body, leaving only ashes behind. Once his servant had a handful of finely crumbled soil, they began the long walk back to town.

When they reached the edge of the large farming community that sprawled outside the western wall of Manak, the high priest snapped his fingers at his servant. "Give me that sweet scented cloth again. I have no wish to breathe the stink of manure." The servant complied, pulling out a pale green cloth that had been imbued with the smell of aplia; a beautiful flower that bloomed once every five years, and only grew in the furthest north reaches of the Valley, the extent of the People's lands. The high priest took it, and held it to his nose as they resumed walking.

Farmhands and workers tended the fields all around; cattle and swine grazed in their pastures. Those who saw him fell to the ground in obeisance, ceasing their work and alerting the others around to his presence. The high priest looked around at them all, a clear expression of contempt showing above his aplia-scented cloth. These people were beneath him, really. It was only fitting that they should prostrate themselves as he walked by; consider themselves privileged that he had graced their stinking farms with his holy presence. He stopped abruptly, staring across the nearest field to the next pasture, where a cattle herder was continuing to watch his beasts instead of grovelling on the floor with everyone else. That needed to be corrected. "Go and fetch that man. I want to know why he is not showing me proper respect," he instructed his servant.

The servant rushed over the fields, still clutching his handful of soil, and spoke to the herder. It seemed to take a while, but the man obviously understood in the end. The high priest watched as they walked back slowly across the field, his servant seeming to lead the old herder. "Why are you not bowing before me, herder?" he demanded when they reached him. The herder did not reply. "Answer me, man!"

A trembling woman in a shapeless brown dress flung herself forwards, her long auburn hair trailing in the dust. "Please, your Holiness, forgive my father. He is deaf and blind from age; I am certain he intended no disrespect to you," she said, her voice slightly muffled because she had pressed her face so firmly against the path.

The high priest glared at the terrified woman on the ground, then looked back at the grey-haired old herder. The man was obviously blind; cataracts had clouded his eyes, making them a milky white. As to his deafness, the high priest opted to take the woman's word. His authority usually guaranteed truth from people. "Very well. I shall forgive, on condition that you provide me with transport back to the town," he said haughtily, looking down at the woman. There was no reason for him to walk any further when there was a perfectly good excuse to get a ride home.

"Of course, your holiness." The woman scurried off back across her fields, bringing a horse and small cart back within minutes. "The finest we have, your holiness. I can provide a driver, if you wish?" she said subserviently.

"My servant will drive," said the high priest, looking critically at the cart and horse. The cart itself looked old and in desperate need of repair; the horse was thin and tired. Neither looked as though they would survive the journey to Manak and back. "I will have him bring them back when I am done with them. Assuming, of course, they are still useable." He waved his servant over to help him into the cart. The woman leapt down, running over to her blind father.

The servant climbed into the front seat and flicked the reins. As the old, bony horse began plodding onwards, the high priest knelt on the floor of the cart. "I am going to meditate and pray now. Do not disturb me until we have reached the smithy," he said to his servant, who nodded in silent acknowledgement.

The rest of the journey passed uneventfully, and eventually they reached Harndak's place. The high priest, roused by his servant, collected the 'ashes' from the cart floor and approached the front door. "Harndak, I bring news of your daughter," he called up to the open window. A few seconds later, the door opened.

"What news? Did the gods spare her?" Harndak asked, stopping short when he saw the priest's handful of carefully crumbled dirt. He stared in disbelief.

"I am terribly sorry. It appears that the Demons destroyed her. This is all we could find," said the high priest, bowing his head. "Do you have something I can place her in?" he asked.

Harndak nodded, tears in his eyes, and went to fetch a bowl from the kitchen. The high priest stepped inside, looking around. Enkarini sat near the stairs, playing with a doll. She looked up when the high priest entered.

"Is my sister back yet?" she asked, with all the innocence and naivety of a small child.

Harndak returned with the most decorative bowl he could find. "She's not coming back, Enkarini. The Demons took her," he told his youngest, and now only child. "Here, let her rest in here."

The priest placed his handful of soil into the bowl. "I am deeply sorry for your loss. To lose another child so soon must be devastating," he said softly.

"That's just dirt. Why have you put dirt in Father's fancy bowl?" Enkarini asked the high priest. She had walked up to the table and poked a finger into the soil.

The priest looked down at the child. "They are your sister's ashes, child. Show a little respect."

Enkarini shook her head. "Ashes look different. I've seen ashes before, when Father puts out the fire, and they're all grey and black. This is brown. It's just dirt."

Thinking quickly, the high priest smacked his servant. "You brainless man. You picked up soil when I told you to gather the girl's ashes. I sincerely apologise for this, Harndak. I will return and collect your daughter's ashes immediately," he said, pushing his servant out of the house. "Go to the temple and get some ashes from the brazier. Put them in something, too. Bring them to me at the town gates," the priest instructed his servant. When the man had run off to the temple, the high priest walked to the gates of the town to wait. He scolded himself on the way for not realising the youngest girl, not having been fully indoctrinated yet, might recognise the soil for what it was and speak out.

"I don't think she's gone," Enkarini babbled when the priest had left. "She said she'd come back some day, and Kandrina never breaks a promise, so she can't be gone. Not really gone, anyway. Do you think she's gone, Father?"

Harndak stared morosely at his little girl. "If she was still alive, the high priest would have brought her back, not a handful of ashes. I just hope the Demons didn't burn her soul when they burnt her body." His eyes dropped to the floor. "Meradina, I'm so sorry. I've failed to care for our children properly," he whispered, praying his deceased wife would hear and forgive him.

Enkarini was puzzled. "But it's not ashes. It's dirt." She watched her father for a few moments, then lost interest and went back to her doll. "You believe me, don't you? My sister wouldn't let me down. She'll come back, and then Father will be happy again," she twittered to the little wooden figure, making it nod along with her words.

There were far fewer mourners at Kandrina's funeral than had been at Perlak's. It was well known that she had been taken with the gods' permission, rather than being the victim of a tragic accident, so people who would otherwise have turned out simply to comfort the family had stayed away. There were only a few close friends and officials who had to be there. Once the ritual had been completed, and the ashes poured into the small hole, everyone left quickly. Chief Jindar remained only to offer the expected words of comfort, and followed the others. Harndak and Enkarini were left alone in the rain.

"Father, why weren't there many ashes? There was only a little bit, and if it was Kandrina there would have been more. She isn't that small," Enkarini asked.

Harndak knelt next to the girl. "I suppose the Demons took the rest away with them. Let's just pray, Enkarini. Your sister needs our help to reach Paradise, and join your brother and mother." He bowed his head and began to whisper, begging the gods to allow his daughter's soul entry to Paradise, to forgive her naivety in repeating the words of a heretic.

Enkarini prayed as well. She asked the gods for guidance, to help her find her sister and bring her back home. She knew Kandrina wasn't really dead, because she had promised to come back. As her father whispered frantically next to her, she wondered what Kandrina had meant when she said 'there's more to this world than the temples tell you'. She thought she could go and ask her sister's tutor, if she could find him.

The next day, Enkarini decided to go out looking for someone who could help her. She knew Remlik and his sister had gone away somewhere, so she thought she would try and find someone who might know where they went. She decided to look at their house first. Kandrina had taken her there a couple of times, once through the poor quarter, and once through the town centre. She could remember the way through the poor quarter, but was a bit scared of going there alone, so she started walking towards the middle of the town. Most people knew her, from when they visited her father; so Enkarini thought if she did get lost she could just ask someone the way.

She had just reached the turning she thought was the right street when she heard a lot of noise coming from the market square to her left. There was no market this afternoon, so she wandered off to find out what all the fuss was about. Reaching the square, she found herself stuck at the back of a large, noisy crowd of people. She wiggled her way through to the front, where a platform had been set up. A young-looking woman in a long white robe stood at the front of the platform, giving a sermon about the child goddess, Aikra-Lora. Some others in shorter white robes stood behind her, clapping their hands and singing a hymn. Every so often, between the priestess' sentences, one of them would cry out 'Blessed be!' and the crowd would call back, raising their hands in praise.

"Blessed are we all!" the priestess cried. "My goddess smiles upon us today! She has heard your pleas, and sent me to banish the sickness ailing your children!" The crowd cheered, and worried-looking parents began leading their children up to the platform. Enkarini was confused for a moment - she hadn't heard about any sickness - but then remembered. There had been an illness called ibikona rash affecting some of the children she played with. It wasn't serious, causing nothing more than some itchy spots, but very catching. Both Perlak and Kandrina had had it some years ago, when Enkarini had been very small. Somehow she had avoided catching it, and when a healer had visited to deal with her older siblings he had proclaimed her immune to the rash. She watched as the priestess blessed each child who was brought up to her, and as one of the singing, clapping acolytes gave bottles of lotion to the parents.

Once all the children had been blessed, the priestess and acolytes launched into another song praising the goddess. Bored now of listening to them sing, Enkarini worked her way around the edge of the crowd and back out of the square. She had taken a few steps before realising she had gone the wrong way; there were unfamiliar houses lining the streets, rather than the shops she remembered. She jumped out of the way as a cart rolled past, and tried to figure out where she was. She looked up, remembering what her father had told her about finding the silver spire, so you could tell where you were. She saw the spire, and headed away from it. She knew the spire was part of the Creator's temple, in the centre of the city, and Remlik lived near the south gate; she'd only just left the market square, so she was still south of the temple. All she needed to do was keep walking away from the spire, and she'd end up somewhere close.

"Little girl, you shouldn't go in there. It's not safe," called a neighbour when she finally arrived at the burnt-out shell of the house.

"I'm looking for someone, they used to live here. Do you know where they went?" she asked.

The man shook his head and darted back into his house. Enkarini watched, puzzled. I wonder why he didn't want to talk, she thought. She skipped off down the road, trying to think of somewhere else she could look. She was skipping past an alley when she heard someone whispering to her.

"Psst, kid. You looking for Remlik?" the voice said.

Enkarini stopped skipping and crept over to the alley entrance. "He taught my sister. She told me something I thought he could help me with, because it didn't make much sense. Do you know where he is?"

The man in the alley shifted slightly. "Might do. You'll have to do something for me before I tell you though."

"What is it?" she said warily, still standing just outside the alley rather than getting any closer. She had been told to be careful around strangers, because some people could be very nasty to little girls and boys.

"You've got small hands. I dropped something earlier that... fell into a small hole, but my hands are too big to get it back. If I tell you where the hole is, and what to take out, can you go fetch it for me?" the stranger asked.

"I guess so. Then you'll tell me where Remlik is?"

The stranger nodded. "Of course. Now, this hole is just across town, you know where the moneylender's is?" Enkarini nodded. "Well, right behind there is a steel cover, with a little hole in it. I dropped my coin purse earlier, and it fell into the hole. Fetch it back, I'll wait here for you."

Enkarini ran off to the moneylender's, and found the steel cover behind the building. She knelt on the floor and stuck her hand in the hole. She felt lots of coins under there, but couldn't feel any purses. *Maybe the coins came out of the purse when it fell through,* she thought, and started pulling coins out of the hole. She stuffed her dress pockets full of gold and silver coins, and ran back to find the man in the alley, ignoring the shouts of 'Thief! Stop her!' that started behind her. It probably wasn't anything to do with her, anyway. She was only getting the man's coins back.

"I couldn't find the purse, but I got the coins. Will you tell me where Remlik is now?" she asked when she got back to the alley, handing the coins over to the stranger.

"Go to Tewen. You'll probably find him there," the stranger said, staring at the handfuls of gold Enkarini had given him.

"But I'm only little, how do I get there?" she asked.

The stranger shrugged. "Not my problem is it?" He stuffed the coins into his pockets and ran off, leaving Enkarini to wonder how she was supposed to get to another town without her father worrying about her.

"Why do you want to go to Tewen, anyway?" Harndak asked his daughter. "It's not much different than Manak, really."

Enkarini blinked up at her father. "I just thought it might be nice to go somewhere different for a while. Besides, there'll be different people there."

The two of them were in a trade wagon, riding across the plains to Tewen. Enkarini had come home and asked her father if they could go away for a while, giving the excuse that she wanted to see what another town was like. Harndak had agreed, being overwhelmed by memories of his lost son and daughter, so they had hitched a ride with a spice trader and left that day. The journey to Tewen wasn't too long, only three days by wagon, or two on a fast horse. They had camped out on the road for the last two nights, and were expecting to arrive by late afternoon. The scent of spice hung heavily under the canvas covering, and Harndak prayed for a small breeze in the hot summer air. None came. Father and daughter sat quietly amongst the crates of spices and herbs, lulled into a sleep-like state by the gentle swaying of the cart and the heat of the day. Insects buzzed past, and Enkarini swatted at them lazily.

Some time later, the trader driving the horses called back to them. "Right you two, this is Tewen. I'm stopping for a while to unload some of this, if you want to help me I'll forget the coin for giving you a ride." Harndak began lifting crates off the back of the wagon. "Would you like to feed my horses, Enkarini?" the trader asked her. "There's hay in my pack for them."

Enkarini pulled hay from the trader's pack and held it up for the horses to eat. She was used to horses, as her father often had them in his workshop when he made shoes for them. When she was old enough she wanted to learn to ride. "Father, when we're done here can I go exploring?" she asked as her father returned to the wagon for another crate.

"Alright, but don't go too far. I don't want you getting lost," he told her. "I'll get us a room at the inn over there; Trader's Stop, it says on the sign. Make sure you're back there for dinner." He carried the crate into the shop they had stopped by.

Enkarini finished feeding the horses and wandered off. She wasn't sure where to start looking, but she was sure someone would know something. As she left the market square, she followed a small group of children who seemed to be on some sort of trip with their teacher. They stood by a broken column for a while, which the teacher was talking about. Enkarini went closer to listen in.

"They say the Sun God Alch created the stars, to watch over us all from the sky while he slept each night. Of course, now we know they're only stories, but rather nice stories all the same. This pillar was part of the Sun Temple of the old Tewen tribe, where they would all gather to worship their gods. Let's go and see the other one in Temple Square, and then we can find out more about it in the library." The teacher and group of children walked on, and Enkarini followed, fascinated. She had never heard about any sun god, or how he made the stars. She wanted to find out more, and it sounded like the teacher was going to tell the other children about it in the library.

They looked at another column outside, in a small square that was full of bustling people, before going into a large stone building. Assuming it was the library, Enkarini went in after them. The teacher stopped by a stone carving of a slim, long haired woman reading a book, and spoke to a woman in long blue robes. The robed woman nodded, and pulled a book down from a nearby shelf. The teacher led his class over to a table, where he began to read from the book. "The Tewen built their Sun Temple on these lands about five hundred years before the tribal merging, in praise of Alch. The people of the tribe settled around the temple, and built their houses around it. They didn't have much good farmland though, so they would often trade with their closest neighbours, the Bewein tribe." As it was beginning to sound more like a dull history lesson, Enkarini snuck off, to keep looking for Remlik.

Leaving the library, she saw something shining across the street and went to see what it was. It was a small silver statue of a pretty girl, about Kandrina's age, and younger children surrounded her. There were flowers and dolls at the base of the statue, and someone had left a candle. It looked very pretty, and Enkarini wondered what it was for. She asked a short, smiling lady who was walking past.

"Tis one of Aikra-Lora's shrines," the short lady said. "Y' mean y' never come across one before? Y' must be from Manak. I hear they only got temples to the dark gods there. My brother's got a couple of friends from there stayin' with him, they got chased out by the priests."

"Are they dark people? A lady and a man, and the lady has shiny silver eyes?" Enkarini asked, not believing her luck.

The short lady nodded. "Aye, they are. Y' know them, do y'?"

"The man was my sister's teacher," Enkarini answered. "Can you tell him I want to talk to him? Kandrina said something to me before she went away that I want to ask him about."

"I'll do y' one better than that, I'll take y' to him now. That is, if y' don't have anythin' else to be doin'?"

Enkarini shook her head and followed the short lady. She seemed nice, and she knew where Remlik was. "Is it far? Only I need to be back at Trader's Stop by dinner. Father will worry if I'm not back," she said.

"Not too far, just down this road here. My brother picked a house near the library when we came to Tewen; he's a mage, y' see. Quite often goes in lookin' up spell books n' the like. Also likes to leave the odd coin at Talri-Pekra's shrine, she bein' the goddess of magic n' all that. 'Ere we are," said the short lady, knocking on the door of an old house.

After a few moments, a man with bushy red hair and yellow eyes answered. "Wordarla, how are you? Who's your friend?" he asked, peering through his hair at Enkarini.

"I'm good, thank y' very much. This young'un says she knows y'r friend Remlik, from teachin' Kandrina. Told me she wants to talk to him about somethin' her sister said."

The man pushed his hair aside and looked properly. "I'll fetch him. Come in if you like," he said, walking through the house and leaving the door open for them. Wordarla led the girl inside and sat her down. "Here she is," said the red-haired man.

Remlik came in, smiling when he saw Enkarini. "Hello again. I haven't seen you for a long time. Braklarn here says you wanted to talk to me about something?"

Enkarini looked up into Remlik's dark eyes, hoping he could help her figure out what her sister had been talking about. "Kandrina said something to me, before she went away. It was something like, 'there's more to this world than the priests say'. I wondered if you knew what she meant?" she asked.

He glanced at the others in the room before answering. "I think she was trying to warn you about some of the things the priests teach people. See, sometimes they don't quite tell people everything."

"What kind of things don't they say?" she asked, growing more curious by the minute. First the teacher talking about old sun gods, now Remlik was saying that the priests didn't tell people things; Tewen was turning out to be a very strange place. People back home just didn't talk about things like that. Maybe Kandrina had been right, when she and Father had argued about old religions and absent gods, and when she had stayed up late into the night talking about it with Perlak. When they thought she couldn't hear them, Enkarini had sometimes crept along to her brother's room to listen at the door. She'd even asked Perlak about it once, but he had said she was far too young to be thinking about things like that.

"I really shouldn't tell you. We'll both get in trouble," Remlik said. "The main thing is to just keep an open mind, and if something doesn't seem right then try to find out more. How is your father coping with everything?" he asked, changing the subject.

"He's sad because he thinks Kandrina's gone forever. I don't think she is though, because she promised me she'd come back someday," Enkarini told him. "She's just hiding somewhere so the priests don't tie her up again. Do you know where she's hiding?"

Braklarn interrupted. "We've looked for her in a magic glass," he told the child, simplifying things for her. "It told us she's alive, but all it showed us was a mountain."

Remlik suddenly jumped up. "There's something I want to check. If I'm right, it might explain why the picture was blurry, and tell us where she is." He ran out of the room and they could hear him looking for something upstairs.

"He's likely to be up there a while," Wordarla told the girl. "Why don't I walk y' back to y'r father at that inn, so he's not worryin' about y'. Y' can come back tomorrow when Remlik's done with his books," she said, leading Enkarini out of the house and back to the market square.

"Here. I knew I'd read something like this," Remlik said as he carefully placed a very old-looking scroll on his desk. He had called everyone up to the cluttered room that currently served him and his sister as both bedroom and study, to show them the scroll he had run up here to look for after Enkarini's visit the previous day. "It mentions a crystal city, full of lights, that often appears as a mountain to the casual observer. It's only a story now, but as we all know most legends have a basis in truth. This could be where Kandrina has gone."

Braklarn examined the scroll. "It would explain why the glass had such difficulty resolving the image of the mountain, too. If it is a city under some sort of glamour, or ward, that no spell can penetrate…"

"It would make an ideal hiding place for anyone who didn't want to be found," Remlika finished his sentence. "But how would Kandrina have found out about such a place? Or have been able to get in, for that matter."

Remlik continued. "That's what I was about to answer. It says a city 'full of lights'. I have also read several scrolls that describe the Tanpèt Zèklè as being formed entirely of light. What if this mythical crystal city is in fact their city?"

The two mages considered his supposition. "It's possible. We should look into it. The question is, what should we tell her sister, if anything?" Remlika asked. "We can't just tell her everything. She'd tell her father, and then the priests would know where we are. They'd also go looking for Kandrina."

"I think we ought to let her know that her sister is alive. They deserve to know that much," Remlik suggested. "We don't have to say where we think she is, or who with."

Braklarn inclined his head. "I'll talk to the child. If you two can research everything you feel is relevant, we might be able to find Kandrina and check that she's well. Wordarla should be bringing her sister back here anytime soon," he said, heading downstairs to wait.

Remlik bent low over the old scroll. "There's a surprising amount of information in here, on closer reading. It does actually specify that the crystal city is home to a race of beings called 'Colourless' here, who come from the skies to the north. Do you think it could be the same race, sister?" he asked, glancing up at Remlika.

"Could be. There have been several names for the 'Demons' over the years; Fallen Stars was always one of my favourites. I'll fetch some of your other books, see if there's any other references to the term." She left the room, leaving Remlik alone with his scroll.

"Hmm," said Remlik, mumbling to himself as he often did when studying something particularly intriguing. "These 'Colourless' do sound a lot like the Zèklè... 'stunning beings of pure light, which can take many forms'... 'often misunderstood by those less informed, as they can cause harm to living flesh upon contact. This is completely unintentional, however, merely a natural effect of the substance of which they are made'... who wrote this?" he asked aloud, scanning the fragile parchment for a name, or at least the tribe the writer had come from. "Ah, Pokole tribe. I thought the style was familiar. Probably one of their explorers from centuries back."

Remlika came back in, hidden behind an armful of books. "Talking to yourself again? Anyway, here are your other texts." She put them on the desk with some difficulty, struggling to find a clear space for them. "It's a shame these were all we managed to recover. Still, I suppose the books you had in your study are replaceable. I'll leave you to it, anyway; I wanted to go back to Wordarla's shop and pick up some potions." She left, closing the door behind her.

Remlik sat down, peering closely at the old scroll. There was something that looked like an old map reference; now what had he done with that collection of old maps? If he could figure out where this crystal city was supposed to be, they could go out there to try and find out what had happened to Kandrina. He pulled one of the books over and began combing it for any other details, anything that might help him work out a location. It would be difficult, but worth it if he could find his lost student.

Harndak walked slowly, taking in the sights. He had left Enkarini sleeping late, buried deep under the bed covers, while he went to visit the temples. The Creator's temple in Tewen was little more than a chapel, but he intended to pay his respects to another god today; the priests of Ralor-Kanj, the balance god, were known for their ability to comfort the bereaved, so Harndak headed for Temple Square, just a few streets away from Trader's Stop.

As he wandered through the streets, he couldn't help noticing the lighter atmosphere in Tewen; people seemed calm and happy as they went about their business, where back home there was always a niggling feeling of surveillance. He stopped by an ancient-looking pillar, opposite the balance temple and just outside what looked like a library - what was a library doing in Temple Square? Harndak went inside, curious. The only library in Manak was on the other side of town from the temples, near the poor quarter. Could it perhaps be a library that only dealt with the holy books?

"Can I help you find something, sir?" asked a young woman in a dark blue tunic as he entered. Harndak looked at her, immediately noting the small bronze badge she wore, bearing the emblem of Talri-Pekra's order. Two stars adorned the open book, meaning this was an acolyte who had almost earned her priestess robes.

"I was curious; I've never seen a library this close to temples before," Harndak replied, realising now that it must also be a place of worship for the knowledge goddess.

The acolyte smiled gently. "Knowledge and worship don't have to be mutually exclusive. In fact, knowledge is worship for my order. Would you like to visit the shrine?" she asked.

Harndak nodded, and followed her to a small room at the back of the library. He had not visited a knowledge shrine in a long time, and was beginning to feel slightly awkward about neglecting the other gods in favour of his devotions to the Creator. A couple of people sat on benches in front of the shrine, quietly reading books. Harndak approached the stone carving of the goddess, also reading a book, and dug a pair of silver coins from his purse. Dropping them into the box at the statue's base, he gazed up at the serene, knowing face of Talri-Pekra, and offered a very simple prayer; *please help me teach my little girl right.*

Harndak left the library a few moments later, and crossed the square to enter the temple of balance. It was smaller and simpler than Vrenid-Malchor's temple back home, but there was an air of peace and acceptance inside that had never been present in Manak's temples. He walked down the centre of the great hall, towards the gold statue of the god, which stood upon a raised dais near the pulpit. Ralor-Kanj stood straight and tall, waves of hair falling gracefully to his shoulders, gazing across the prayer hall with a benign smile.

"Do you seek guidance, my son?" a priest said softly. Harndak turned away from the statue to face him. He was fairly nondescript, grey-haired and wearing a plain yellow robe tied together with a clean but simple length of rope. Assuming he was one of the lower ranked priests, Harndak replied accordingly.

"I have recently lost two children to the Lightning Demons. I was hoping to speak with someone, for consolation."

The priest smiled, mirroring the expression on the statue. "Then speak, for I am the high priest of Ralor-Kanj."

Harndak was stunned; in his experience no high priest would ever dress so plainly. "My apologies, your Holiness. I did not realise, your simple attire confused me."

"Please do not apologise. I ask for no titles or respect beyond that you would show a common man, for we are all children of the gods and all are equal in their eyes." The priest led Harndak to a more private room, and gestured Harndak to a low wooden bench. "Tell me of your lost children."

"A son, my eldest; and a daughter. My wife was lost many years ago, I am now left with only my youngest girl," Harndak told him, memories of his wife and children bubbling to the surface of his mind. "I am beginning to doubt myself, my ability to care for her properly; I did my best with Perlak and Kandrina, truly I did, but still they were taken. Meradina, my wife, she made me promise that if anything should happen to her I would keep the children from harm. Have I failed her, holiness?" he asked, gazing imploringly into the priest's eyes.

The priest laid a comforting hand on Harndak's shoulder. "You have failed no-one. It is no fault of yours that the Lightning Demons chose to take your children, and no man can prevent their actions. But, what of your wife? It seems an odd thing to ask; one would think as their father you would have kept the children safe anyway, without a vow to their mother." He watched Harndak, a curious expression on his face.

Harndak took a deep, steadying breath as he thought back to a difficult part of his life, almost nine years ago. "It was when she was carrying our youngest girl. It was a difficult pregnancy; Meradina had a lot of problems with pains and sickness, so a healer gave her some concoction of herbs that was supposed to help. It made her hear things, voices in her mind; she would cry out in the night, terrified of something only she could hear. I stopped giving her the potion after a few days; it was obviously doing more harm than good; that's when the hallucinations started. She never told me what she saw, but it must have been something awful," he said, staring at the opposite wall, hands shaking in his lap. "I found her in the kitchen one morning, a couple of days before the birth, slashing at the air with a bread knife and screaming 'get out, you can't take my baby, leave us alone'. I calmed her down, and that's when she asked me, begged me to keep the children safe. After Enkarini was born, it all seemed to stop, but she insisted I keep my promise. She was taken not long after that." Harndak lifted a trembling hand to his eyes, covering his tears. He had never spoken about any of it before, not even to the priests back home; somehow he felt relieved to finally let it out.

The priest stayed respectfully quiet for a moment before speaking again. "I am very sorry. The gods have tested you most unfairly; to lose three family members to the Demons is unimaginable. Yet you still have one child to care for; you must ensure you do so to the best of your ability. Often parents who have lost a child will neglect their surviving offspring in their grief. Let your son, daughter and wife go, remember them fondly and allow their souls to pass on. They will be reluctant to enter Paradise if they sense you are in pain," he told Harndak.

"Alright." Harndak took a deep breath and rose from the bench. "Thank you for your time. I will try to let them go, and concentrate on looking after Enkarini from now on." He left the temple and headed back towards the Market Square, hoping his daughter had not wandered off somewhere. He wanted to return to Manak and get back to his work in the forge. It had been weeks since he had downed tools, and for the first time since Perlak's death his fingers itched to pound some newly forged steel against an anvil.

Reaching the market, he paused to watch the people bustling about, stopping at stalls and haggling with merchants. It looked like a fairly busy day, with several stallholders having come from other towns and villages. There was even a fishmonger from Astator selling his catch, probably from at least a week ago, but they had ways of preserving the fish flesh for months at a time. Harndak wandered on, stopping at a stall selling what looked like small furry blobs with tails. Curious about what they were, he squeezed through the small crowd of people to get a closer look.

"The most adorable pets in existence, these are. And easy to look after, too," the merchant running the stall was saying. "They only need a few handfuls of wheat a day, and make very little noise. They're easily house-trained, too."

"What are they?" a slim, red-headed woman asked. "And how much are you charging for one?"

The merchant smiled widely. "Only two silvers, madam. They're a newly discovered animal, from the Yoscurn Woods; I believe the man who first found one called it a gozni." He lifted a light brown one out of the box and held it up. It sat comfortably in his palm, blinking at the crowd with three small eyes. Its tail curled gently around the merchant's wrist, just as fluffy as the creature's body. "This is a young one, they do get a little bigger but not by much. Ideal pets for little kids, I'd say."

As several people dug out their purses, Harndak took a closer look at a black one with a white blob on its tail. It did look rather sweet, and Enkarini had been pestering him for a pet for quite a while.

Enkarini had, of course, wandered off somewhere. She had stuffed a pillow under her blankets and snuck out at dawn to meet Wordarla at the library. After speaking to Remlik's friend about her sister, she had followed the short lady back to her magic shop instead of returning to the inn. She had been asking all sorts of questions about the things on the shelves, and the strange potions in some of the cupboards. Wordarla didn't seem to mind, though.

"What does this do?" Enkarini asked, pointing at a strange looking paddle hanging on the wall. "Is it for stirring things? It looks like something for stirring."

"Ah, tis a special stirrer though. Y' see, tis made of a very rare wood, that gives particular properties to certain potions. Y' see all those curly bits stickin' out of the edges?" Wordarla pointed. "They get thinner n' thinner each time I use it, cause that's where the wood's not been coated. The wood gets into the potion n' makes it stronger. Twas a special gift from Remlika, years ago."

Enkarini took a moment to digest the information. "Would you show me how to mix something? Just something easy, I've never done it before," she asked.

Wordarla grinned at the girl. "Aye, I can teach y' a few basics. How about somethin' to cheer up y'r poor father? I should think he's a bit low after y'r sister bein' taken away. First, we start with a cauldron. Not just any cauldron, mind, a happy potion's got to be mixed in a copper cauldron. Tis what gives the best results. We pour in some water, which can be any old water, cause it gets cleaned in the mixin'."

Enkarini watched and listened, transfixed by the smells and colours produced by the potion as it was mixed. She helped Wordarla add things, and stir the mixture together. She was also fascinated by the woman's accent, as the dwarves had not been seen near the Peoples' towns for several years. When the potion was ready, Wordarla gave her a small flask of it. It was a bright, cheerful green, which made her smile just looking at it.

"Now you be careful with that, tis powerful stuff. Don't go givin' it to anyone but your father, twas made just for him so you make sure he gets it. Y' remember to tell him what my brother said about y'r sister, too." Wordarla waved her off and watched her down the road. Enkarini skipped away, careful to carry the potion so it wouldn't spill.

"Father, are you here?" she called when she got back to their rooms. "I made a happy potion for you." No answer. I guess he's gone out somewhere, Enkarini thought, placing the flask of potion carefully on a table and going to play with her dolls, giving one of them the same accent as Wordarla. She liked the funny short lady, and wanted to learn more about alchemy. She decided to ask her father if he would find someone in Manak who could teach her.

Harndak returned soon after, carrying something in a small wooden box. "Enkarini, guess what I bought for you," he called, placing the box on the table next to the potion flask. "Come and say hello."

Enkarini left her dolls on the floor and went over. "What's in there?" she asked, looking at the box. Something inside it was making a quiet scrabbling noise, as though it wanted to get out.

Harndak fiddled with a catch on the box lid. "It's called a gozni, and the man on the stall says they make very good pets," he said, lifting a small, black furry thing out and putting it on the table. It waved its tail gently, and blinked up at them both. "Do you like him?"

"He's so cute!" Enkarini exclaimed, picking it up and stroking it. "I'm going to call him Sooty, because he's all black like soot. Thank you Father," she said, as the gozni hummed softly in contentment.

"Well, he's all yours. Remember to feed him, though; the man said two handfuls of wheat each day, and leave a dish of water for him overnight." Harndak moved the box onto the floor, and picked up the potion flask. "What's this, Enkarini?" he asked, looking at it curiously.

"It's a happy potion. I met a nice alchemist lady while I was exploring yesterday, and she showed me how to make it, and I made some for you," she twittered. "I thought you seemed sad since Kandrina got taken away, so I made it. I hope you like it."

Harndak looked at the potion, shrugged slightly, and then drank. A warm, fuzzy feeling spread through him, and a large silly grin spread across his face. "Thank you, Enkarini. This is wonderful," he said, flopping onto the nearest chair and chuckling slightly.

"She took me to see her friends as well. They said that Kandrina's really still alive, just hiding somewhere. They think she'll come back when the priests stop looking for her," she said, taking her new pet over to her chair and tickling it.

"That's great," Harndak giggled, completely under the effects of the potion and finding everything he saw and heard completely hilarious.

Chapter Four:
War is Declared

The autumn rain began to fall lightly outside. The seasons were starting to change, trees were turning a dull yellowish brown rather than the vivid greens and blues of summer. The adulthood ceremonies were over for another year, and several young men and women had found themselves apprenticed to one craft or another. Soon the street sweepers would be out in force, keeping the busy roads free of wet leaves. A cool breeze blew across Manak, chilling the people who were out running errands or visiting family.

Gondrun stood patiently in the doorway of the Chief's Halls, waiting for Chief Jindar to finish his prayers. He glanced back out to where Jindar's daughter and Vice-Chief in Tewen waited in the drizzle for an audience with her father, and gave her an apologetic shrug. She took after her mother, both in looks and in nature. She was less pious than her father, and preferred to concern herself with more immediate affairs than the afterlife. Her pale blue eyes and brown hair that framed a long, rather plain face made her the exact image of the Chief's long-departed wife. She had, however, inherited her father's stature, making her tall and thickset.

Jindar stirred from his position kneeling on the prayer mat. "You have something to announce, Gondrun?" he asked, noticing his scribe standing next to him.

"Your eldest daughter is here. She requests an audience to discuss the... extreme behaviour of the priests," the scribe told him, hesitating before repeating the Vice-Chief's words. In Jindar's somewhat biased opinion, the priests could do no wrong, and he had been known to report those who disagreed for blasphemy.

"Extreme behaviour? I can't say I'm aware of any extreme behaviour. Go and escort her in; I'm sure we can sort this out. It's likely to be a simple misunderstanding," Jindar said, waving his scribe out of the hall.

Gondrun bowed and proceeded back out into the rain, falling more insistently now, to bring the Vice-Chief and her assistant inside. As he walked past the ancient tapestries that adorned the walls, depicting legends from the Manak tribal history, he wondered if anything going on today would be remembered in a hundred years' time; had he, or Jindar, made it into future history books?

"The Chief welcomes you into his halls, ma'am," he said, reaching Jindara's carriage and accompanying retinue. "I apologise for the delay..."

"No need. I expect the Chief was busy praying," she replied shortly. "Of course we mustn't interrupt such important business." Gondrun thought he heard a vein of sarcasm running through Jindara's words, but chose to ignore it as they approached Jindar's chair.

The Chief made a formal gesture of welcome. "Jindara, this is most unexpected. Might I know the reason for your unannounced visit?" he asked, indicating that she should take a seat.

"I'd prefer to stand, Chief. This is an official visit, after all. I have a slight issue with your priests, it seems they are scaring away your townsfolk. Many of them have decided to take up residence in my town." Jindara gestured to her assistant, who brought forward a scroll tied with blue ribbon. "This is a list of all the people who have fled Manak because of persecution by the priests. The majority of them claim to have lost innocent family members to the overzealousness of the priests, in particular the high priest of Vrenid-Malchor."

Jindar bristled. "Now, Jindara, you know it is the priests' duty to punish all heretics. It's not as though they go around randomly butchering people in the streets. All those lost have been declared anathema to the temples and punished accordingly."

"Yes, I am aware of the priests' duties. However, the people on this list have informed me that the priests are not only punishing severe blasphemy, but are staking people out for the Lightning Demons for the slightest infraction. For example, one man claims that his only son was staked out for asking a priest how prayer works. This is not reasonable punishment, Chief Jindar."

Jindar glanced at his scribe for assistance. Gondrun merely shrugged, as it was not usually his place to keep track of what the temples did. "Daughter, I cannot believe that this man is speaking truth. Perhaps he was diminishing the severity of his child's crime to ease his own pain. In any case, I will not prevent the priests from carrying out their duties. They are the voice of the gods on this world, after all, so any action they take must be sanctioned by the gods."

The Vice-Chief dropped her gaze to the floor. "Father, something must be done. If it were only one or two cases, I would not be concerned," she said, speaking informally. "But there have been over fifty people begging sanctuary in my town in the last month alone. If you refuse to deal with your priests then I will be forced to intervene. Tewen simply cannot handle any more refugees."

"Then turn them away. I cannot believe that the priests are so awful that the people will not return," Jindar told his daughter. "This will pass, like every other surge of heresy has. Now go, return to your town and deal with your people as I must deal with mine." He dismissed his daughter and leant back in his ceremonial chair. Gondrun escorted the woman and her assistants back to their carriage.

"Give your father time to process and understand what you have told him," he told the Vice-Chief. "He is a devout man, and will not believe ill of the temples unless he is forced to. I will look into this myself, and ensure he receives all the information he needs."

Jindara nodded to the scribe. "Thank you. You seem a much more reasonable man than my father." She handed him the scroll she still carried. "Look down this. There are over a hundred names here, all of them refugees from Manak. Most of them still live in Tewen; I believe some have since travelled on to Pokole or Bewein. Tironde has sent word of others arriving in Astator, as well. If you choose to look into this, I would suggest you visit the refugee camp outside Tewen's eastern gate. Several who have remained there or in Tewen itself are skilled mages; they should be able to provide some proof of the priests' misdeeds." With that, she climbed into the carriage and rode away.

Gondrun watched them leave. When they rounded a corner at the end of the street, he headed back inside. He would visit the temples later in the afternoon and take a look at the priests' behaviour for himself. He was not inclined to believe stories of the priests' cruelty, but he knew Jindara would not have chosen to visit her father unless she was truly concerned about something. The two of them had hardly spoken in twenty years, since the death of the Chief's wife.

Jindara leant back into her cushions as the horses picked up speed. She had hoped it would not come to this; her father was unlikely to ever accept the facts about the priests in Manak. Though, Onkadal had surprised her yesterday when she had spoken to him in Akram. While not so all-pervading as those in Manak, Akram's priests had become just as fanatical. Thankfully, Onkadal had seen sense and agreed to investigate his temples – which probably meant marching a troop of soldiers in and dragging the priests off their pulpits, knowing his temper. Jindara sighed wearily.

"Is something wrong, ma'am?" her squat, ruddy-faced assistant asked.

"I was just wondering if that scribe will bother looking into this. I know the Chief won't," she replied, glancing out of the carriage window at the busy market square. The people looked harried, and Jindara spotted several temple militia tabards around the square. "We cannot allow this to continue much longer," she told her scribe. "We give him a month to deal with his problem, then we involve the armies. The temples will not ignore a thousand blades outside their doors."

Her assistant looked alarmed. "Are you sure that's a good idea, ma'am? Waging war against the temples could create more problems than it solves," he warned, clearly concerned about inviting the gods' wrath.

"I am aware of that. That is why we will not wage war against the temples. If Jindar refuses to deal with his priests, we wage war against Jindar. The temples just happen to be in the way," Jindara told him. "By my reckoning, the priests will have to stand back and allow us to fight, in which case either Jindar or myself will end up as Chief of the People. Should Jindar's army win, it matters not what the priests do because we will likely be destroyed. If my army wins, I become Chief and I deal with the priests."

The assistant looked nervous. "Should I inform the soldiers to prepare to fight?" he asked.

"Not yet. My father may yet see sense," Jindara replied, closing her eyes against the sudden glare as the sun appeared from behind a cloud. "As I said, we wait. You should inform the other towns, though. Send runners to my siblings, they should be aware of this. That way they have time to decide whether to take sides or remain neutral."

She leant back into the cushioned seat, drawing the curtain across the window to block out a little of the sunlight. Hinasi and Devurak would probably come to her aid; they were just as tired of receiving

Manak's refugees as she was. She wasn't certain of her other siblings' reactions; the two youngest, Tironde and Semark, preferred to avoid conflict, and Onkadal could be very unpredictable at times. All she could say for sure was that he would likely join the fight, but on which side? He might even turn up to attack both her army and Jindar's. As the oldest son, but second child, of the Chief, he had always thought of himself as heir to the Chief's mantle; though tradition said it was the eldest child, regardless of gender, unless the Chief named another.

Of course, before the tribal merging the priests had selected the Chief of the Manak tribe, but that tradition had fallen by the wayside since Morendir. Jindara bolted upright, struck by the thought that the current priests may well be looking to revive that practice. She snapped her fingers to get her assistant's attention. "As soon as we get back to Tewen, I wish to see a scholar. One learned in tribal histories, especially that of the Manak tribe."

"Yes ma'am. I shall put out a request to the libraries the moment we arrive."

"Thank you." Jindara sat, leaning forward now, trying to work out the possible consequences of a Chief, not just of one tribe but of the entire People, who was no more than a temple puppet.

The high priest of Vrenid-Malchor tossed fitfully in his sleep. For the last few weeks he had been haunted by nightmares of burning women, and bright lights dancing around them. Suddenly, he awoke, staring around the dark room in a panic, half expecting to see lights speeding towards him. Fumbling to light a lantern, he left his room and went to the prayer hall to ask the gods what had happened to him, what he had done to deserve such torment.

Placing his lantern on the altar, he knelt on his cushioned mat and began chanting under his breath. "O great gods, creators and seers of all, I pray for your advice. I am tormented by nightmares, and seek help to rid myself of them."

"You've been a naughty boy, that's why you're getting bad dreams," said a voice from behind him.

The high priest turned, wondering who had crept in and startled him. Nobody was there. "Show yourself," he called in a rather higher voice than usual. Still no one appeared, so he stood and retrieved his lantern from the altar, intending to search the room for whoever had spoken. He had walked past the first row of seats when he heard the voice behind him again.

"You do realise you've been cursed, right?" The priest span round to see a plump, dark-skinned woman with bright purple hair. She looked about thirty summers old, except for her eyes. Her eyes seemed deeper than they should have been, and ancient with wisdom beyond that of men.

Drawing himself up to his full height, he stared at her with his usual haughty expression. "Who are you, and how did you get in here?" he demanded of her. *No woman sneaks up on me, however creepy her eyes look*, he thought.

"I got in the same way I get in anywhere," she said with a smile. "And if I told you who I am you wouldn't believe me. But I'm going to anyway. My name is Dranjari. It should sound familiar, even though we've never met before now. You won't work it out until I've left, though."

The woman is mad, he thought. "What do you mean, cursed?" he asked.

Dranjari laughed at that. "Cursed means cursed, silly. Someone has put a curse on you. I do know who, but I can't tell you, because I don't remember telling you. I don't know why I bothered saying all this, because you didn't listen. But the point is, they wouldn't have cursed you if you'd behaved yourself properly. See, you've been upsetting lots of people, and the gods aren't very happy with you either. Right, I think I'm supposed to leave now. Be seeing you." The strange woman walked away, fading as she did so.

Unsure what to make of any of what had just happened, the high priest decided it was probably just an extension of his nightmares. He mentally added purple-haired crazy women to the list of things he'd been dreaming about, so if he encountered any more he would know not to pay any attention to them. He had extinguished his lantern and got back under his covers before he realised why the woman's name had sounded familiar. Dranjari was derived from the name of Dranj-Aria, the goddess of time. Believing his mind to be playing tricks on him, he shook off the experience and tried to sleep. The burning women returned as soon as he closed his eyes.

As Dranj-Aria recalled her aspect and returned to the gods' pavilion, Talri-Pekra waited to tell her off. The goddess of magic and knowledge had watched Dranjari's visit to the high priest, and was not impressed.

"Must you play mind games with the mortals like that?" she scolded when Dranj-Aria reassembled her consciousness. "You're going to cause serious trouble some day."

Dranj-Aria smiled at the other goddess. "I know I will. If you like, I can tell you the exact time and date. But it won't be for another few centuries yet. Besides, I only do things that I remember doing anyway. If I didn't do something I remember doing, it would cause much bigger problems than messing up a few mortal minds. You know how I operate, Talri."

Talri-Pekra gave a reluctant half-smile. She preferred to deal in set facts, not suppositions and memories of things that were yet to come, which were the business of the goddess of time. Dranj-Aria was arguably the most powerful of the wakeful gods, as she knew everything that was yet to happen in every realm. Unfortunately, knowing all that is now, has been, and ever will be made her slightly insane. "Right. Can't go tearing holes in the universe for the sake of one mortal's sanity, can we?"

"Most certainly not. Besides, it's fun to mess up people's heads sometimes," the goddess of time said with a grin. "Keeps things interesting down there. If everyone were nice and sane it would get very tiresome."

As the sun set, Kandrina admired the shimmering effect of the light streaming through the walls of her room. She had learnt a lot about the strange beings that lived in the crystal city, including various names they had been known by over the centuries. Along with the names used by the tribes of the People, they had been called some very strange names by other races. Nerlarina had mentioned that she liked the name Colourless, which she said had been the name used by the dwarves until fairly recently, so Kandrina had taken to using it herself.

The Colourless had given her a small room to herself, with blue-green tinted walls. They had also produced a pair of wooden chairs and a bed for her, though she had not got round to asking where they had come from yet. She was too busy learning about their culture, and teaching them about her own. The seasons had changed outside, the days were getting shorter and the plants had mostly lost their leaves. If Kandrina returned to her own people by next summer, she would attend the adulthood ceremony, along with all the other young people reaching their fifteenth summer. She remembered her brother's ceremony, only two years past, and wondered if she would ever find out exactly what had happened to him. He had not been staked out as a heretic like she had, yet the priests still claimed his death to be the fault of the Colourless. Nerlarina entered, disrupting her thoughts.

"Kandrina, how are you this evening? I managed to obtain some interesting provisions from a nearby dwarf village." She held up a basket of odd-looking foodstuffs.

"There's a dwarf village near here?" Kandrina asked, her interest piqued. "I thought they lived further away."

Nerlarina smiled. "That's what they want you to think. As they have their own religious beliefs, some of which apparently go against yours, they decided to retreat from your priests. It seems they saw your current situation coming a long time ago. We established contact with a few of their outlying villages some years ago, and they eventually prompted us to try and make contact with your people. I'll tell you the whole story sometime."

Kandrina tilted her head sideways, imitating a habit of her old mentor. "Ah, right. Anyway, there's a question I've been wanting to ask. When I first came here, and asked about magic, you said it was a 'twisting force'. What did you mean?"

"What you call magic is a force of nature," Nerlarina explained. "We have studied it in the past, or at least attempted to study it. It is a kind of energy, which originates from the core of this world. However, as we are made of the energy originating from the skies, magic has a tendency to alter, twist, or otherwise disrupt our energy. This basically has the effect of destroying our cities and ending an individual's existence. Although we share part of our consciousness with the whole, we do have a sense of individuality. The shared part returns to the whole, but the individual is lost forever."

"You've mentioned the whole before. Is that some sort of collective mind?" Kandrina was curious. She understood that some insects operated with a hive mind, dominated by a queen, but the individuals were almost mindless alone. Though strange to the People's way of thinking, the Colourless were clearly intelligent beings with minds of their own.

Nerlarina thought for a moment. "Something similar. It's sort of hard to explain. Your people have books, scrolls, and verbal tales, to pass on facts and memories to the next generation, yes? Our kind has the whole. It's not a single, giant brain resting with a single entity, or in a single place. The energy we are made of comes from the whole, which is spread amongst the storm clouds in the sky. It contains a part of each of us, holding memories and knowledge that is shared by all, and passed on to new members of our society when they arrive. When one of us is first born, two parts are combined to make a new one."

"Similar to the way we are born," Kandrina said, thinking of a lesson she had been taught years earlier.

"Yes, we understand most races produce children in much the same way. The physical parts may be a little different, but essentially do the same thing, I believe." Nerlarina smiled. "The main dissimilarity between us and the flesh races is our lack of physical intimacy."

"I see," said Kandrina, examining a fuzzy-looking fruit. "Was there anything you wanted to ask me?"

"Actually, could you tell me a little more about your gods? There seem to be a lot of them, and I was wondering how you remember them all without getting too confused."

Kandrina put the fruit back in the basket and selected a more normal-looking one. She wasn't sure about hairy food. "It is a little confusing at first, but I can try and make it easier for you. See, we have a vast pantheon of gods, I think there's about forty something of them in all. But most of them are sleeping, or absent, so nobody really pays them much attention. I'll explain about the wakeful gods, since they're the most important." She shifted in her chair to a more comfortable position. "There's Aikra-Lora, she's the goddess of children. I think she has a small temple somewhere, but most of her worshippers pray at the shrines scattered around our lands. It is said that she grants eternal youth to her most devout servants, making her priestesses appear younger than they truly are."

"You have female gods as well as male?" Nerlarina interjected. "Many other races only acknowledge male gods, considering females to be inferior."

Kandrina raised her eyebrows. "I did not know that. We have always appreciated women equally, mortals as well as gods. Would you like me to continue?" With a nod from Nerlarina, she resumed her lecture. "Another goddess who is widely admired is Talri-Pekra, our goddess of magic and knowledge. She has no temples as such, but our libraries often have small areas devoted to her worship. Places of learning are considered to be her temples, with her priestesses organising them. We have a goddess of time as well, Dranj-Aria. She is considered one of the most powerful of our gods, as she possesses knowledge of every moment that has been, and is yet to come. She is believed to have the power to travel to any moment she wishes to.

"Ralor-Kanj, the balance god, is considered the most powerful after her. He keeps all things in balance in all realms; they say he is able to walk between realms without restraint. Then there are what some call the 'dark gods'; Fakro-Umdar and Somri-Galin, gods of death and suffering. They are brothers according to the old Entamar religion…"

"Wait, old religion?" Nerlarina interrupted. "I thought your religion had always been the same. Were there others once, then?" she asked.

Kandrina nodded. "Oh yes, every tribe once had their own religion. That's where all the absent gods come from. I'm no expert, you'd need to talk to someone like Remlik for more details, but I can tell you the basics. When the tribes merged over a hundred years ago the Manak were the most dominant, so they were in a position to compel the others to convert to their religion. They brought in a few gods from the other tribes to keep everyone happy, wrote the rest off as absent and declared the old faiths to be 'false truths'. That's supposed to mean 'these teachings, while partially correct, are not the gods' true path to Paradise' or something." She paused, sipping some fruit juice. "I can't remember many of the absent gods; I think there's a god of war, and some gods of nature and trees and things. I know some of the gods were amalgamated into one, to become the Creator."

"I have heard there is one god who is considered to be above all the rest," said Nerlarina. "Is that this Creator?"

"Yes, called Vrenid-Malchor. His priests tell us that he created the world and everything in it, and he watches over us still. However, a lot of scholars think that he, or the gods who became him, simply helped us develop from what we were into what we are. Some say that he is sleeping, but lightly, and could awake soon. Personally, I believe the scholars are right."

They talked late into the night, until Kandrina noticed the sun had long since set and the two moons were lighting up the sky. She bid Nerlarina goodnight and curled up under her soft feather quilt, content to be among friends, however strange they seemed on first impression.

Gondrun left the temple and removed his face scarf in relief. He had been attending more sermons than usual for the last few weeks, keeping an eye out for anything unusual, and had noticed that the priests did seem to be overdoing the 'damnation and heresy' a little. Attending in secret was proving to be a pain though, as the temples were always warm, which made wearing a disguise inside very hot. Gondrun wished he had learned to use magic, that way he could change his appearance without resorting to heavy scarves and wigs.

"Better report to Jindar," he muttered to himself, rolling up his scarf and tucking it into his pocket. Wending his way through the packed square, he absently noticed the presence of several more soldiers than usual. He thought nothing of it, as it was market day and people often came from other towns to buy goods from Manak manufacturers. The cries of the merchants rang loudly in his ears as he walked past their stalls.

"Luxury silks, spun right here in Manak! Only twelve gold coins a bolt!"

"Fresh vegetables, get your fresh vegetables! Ten carrots for ten coppers!"

"Pets for sale! Hunting hounds, cat companions, and for those with limited space, we have bowl-dwelling fish! Simply feed them once a day, and watch them thrive!"

There seemed to be a large crowd around one stall, such a dense mass of people that Gondrun was forced to stop while he looked for a way through. Curious about what drew such a large amount of people, he listened in to the sales pitch.

"The finest smith in Manak is back in business! From delicate trinkets to tempered steel armour, the quality is great and the prices are better! Buy here from Harndak of Manak, the best smith in the land! Special discounts for soldiers!"

Gondrun pressed closer. "Harndak, it's good to see you're back in the forge. I'm going to assume you've heard the rumours about an upcoming war?" he said, once he got close enough to talk to the man behind the stall.

"I certainly have, my good man. Wait, you're the Chief's scribe, aren't you? Can you tell us anything more definite about this war? Like who we're supposed to be fighting, for instance," Harndak asked. The crowd went a little quieter, hoping to hear something semi-official about the rumoured war.

Staring around at the rapt faces of the market-goers, Gondrun answered carefully. Tact and diplomacy would be vital here. "I can't really go into details, but there has been a difference of opinion between Chief Jindar and his eldest daughter, the Vice-Chief of Tewen. We are hoping to resolve the dispute without resorting to all out war," he said, raising his voice slightly so the people at the back could hear. He reasoned there would be no harm in giving the public a little information, just to stop ridiculous rumours flying about and causing panic.

"What's the argument about?" called an anonymous voice from the back of the crowd.

"I really can't say. It is a private matter between the Chief and his daughter," Gondrun replied, as he finally managed to squeeze his way through. "Excuse me, I must be on my way. Important business, you know." When he finally reached the other side of the square, Gondrun turned off and headed back to the Chief's Halls. He expected to find Jindar deep in prayer at this time of day, but was surprised to see him in council with his youngest son.

"Gondrun, there you are. Come here, and take notes for me." Gondrun nodded and retrieved parchment and quill from his desk in the corner as Jindar continued to speak. "My son has informed me that Jindara plans to make war on us unless I deal with my priests. Go on, Semark."

Semark, the chief's son, cleared his throat. He was a thin, reticent young lad, whose eyes were permanently obscured by the thick lenses he wore to correct his poor vision. Jindar had put him in charge of the small, outlying village of Wirba, to ensure he never had any more trouble than the occasional wild predator troubling the outlying farms. "Jindara sent runners to every town and village, Father. She was quite clear in her message, telling us her reasons and plans, and saying that she does not expect the rest of us to get involved. She has given my siblings and I the option of remaining neutral, or joining on either side." He blinked nervously, twitching his head slightly and making his light brown hair flop across his lenses.

Jindar stood, towering above both his son and his scribe. "So. My daughter plans to make war upon me, over some emotional peasants who tried to run from the gods' will. So be it. We shall prepare the army, and march upon Tewen."

The boy upon the floor shook his head vigorously, dislodging his lenses. Retrieving them from the floor, he spoke to his father. "That would not be a good idea, Father. Jindara has many more soldiers now, since gaining the support of Hinasi and Onkadal, and I am sure you know that many alchemists and mages reside in her town. If it comes to war, let them come to you. They will be on unfamiliar territory, rather than you going to fight on their doorstep."

Jindar turned to face his son, wondering how the peaceful, scholarly lad had come by such good military knowledge. "Impressive. Tell me, which book did you read those tactics in?"

"An old scroll, detailing several past wars," said Semark with a shy smile. "It explained several military manoeuvres in detail, along with suggestions of what would work best in what situation."

"You must lend my scribe this scroll some time. I should like to know what else it contains," said Jindar. He could not read himself, but was loath to admit it to anyone. "You will, of course, be joining my army?" he queried, fixing the young man with a penetrating stare.

The boy nodded slowly before making his exit. Gondrun knew that Semark would rather stay as far from conflict as possible, but the Chief had left him little option. He stepped forward. If the Chief was planning to roust the army, there was little time left to explain what he had found out in the temples.

"My Chief, before you tell the soldiers to begin polishing their blades, perhaps you would hear my report on the priests' behaviour," Gondrun began. "I took it upon myself to look into the matter, as I believe your daughter would not have travelled to speak with you personally unless there was something seriously worrying her."

Jindar expelled his breath in aggravation. "Very well. What is your report?"

"I have visited several sermons over the past few weeks, and the priests are preaching damnation and heresy a lot more than usual. I have, of course, read the holy books, and there isn't nearly as much on the subject in the texts as the priests are telling everyone. Perhaps this whole thing could be solved if you would speak with the high priest of Vrenid-Malchor, and ask him to be more patient with the less serious cases. I'm sure Jindara doesn't really want to start a war with you, she is your daughter after all," Gondrun said, playing on the chief's affection for his children.

"And why should I tell the priests how to conduct their sermons? They receive the words of the gods, and pass them on to the rest of the People. The holy books were written many years ago, Gondrun. Perhaps the gods have changed their opinions in the intervening years, and are telling the priests to be stricter on blasphemers."

Gondrun considered this. "Perhaps. But still, is it worth warring with your own kin?"

Jindar looked his scribe in the eye. "This war was not my idea. My daughter declared it, not me. Now cease pestering me about the temples and inform my soldiers that they have battles to prepare for."

Sighing deeply, Gondrun bowed and left for the barracks. He would do his duty to the Chief, as he must, but he would also write a message to Jindara and send it by fast runner. Nobody really wanted this war to happen, but Jindar's stubbornness and blind devotion to the temples would keep him from preventing it. He also wanted to organise a visit to Tewen before everything kicked off, to talk to a few of the people on Jindara's list of refugees. Perhaps they could provide something that would convince

Jindar to stop this war before any bloodshed occurred.

"Have you heard? We're going to war!"

Remlik jumped, spilling the ink bottle he had just dipped his quill into. "What? Who with? And why?" he asked, ignoring the black mess spreading over his papers.

"Vice-Chief Jindara has just announced it, the army marches out tomorrow morning," Remlika told her brother. "She's declared war against her father, and by extension Manak, because of the way the priests have been acting."

"Have they called you up yet?" When war was declared, any mages on both sides were called up to serve with the soldiers. The more powerful mages, such as Braklarn and Remlika, were usually called first.

Remlika shook her head. "Not yet. As far as I know no mages have been called yet, but it's only a matter of time. Have you found anything?" she asked.

Remlik had been practically locked in his study for weeks, obsessively researching the 'crystal city of lights' in every scroll and tome that mentioned it. "I think so…" Remlik turned back to his scrolls and noticed they were soaked in shining black ink, making them unreadable. "Ah."

"I can fix that. It's not dry yet," said the sorceress, casting a short spell to siphon off the excess wet ink. "So, what did you find?"

"I think I've managed to piece together where the city might be," Remlik said, picking up a piece of paper covered in his own writing. He and his sister had taken to using the term 'Colourless' since reading the old scroll from Pokole; it seemed more acceptable than the old tribal names. "These are the notes I've made, taking bits from all that lot that seem to correspond with each other." He indicated the large pile of scrolls and books that covered his desk.

Remlika glanced down the scratchy notes her brother had made. "So you think the city might be somewhere to the west of the plains? That's heading into the dwarves' territory. Or maybe not... how far, do you think?"

"Not far, I'd say. Far enough that people wouldn't get close too often, but in reasonable walking distance from the priests' staking ground. Remember, we scryed for Kandrina the day after she was taken, and the glass showed us the mountain then."

Before Remlika could respond, there was a knock at the door. "If they're calling me to fight, say

I'm not here. I'd rather not go, if I can avoid it, and if we're going to look for this city then you'll probably need me to come along and keep you out of trouble."

Remlik opened the door to see the sandy-haired scribe from Manak. "Can I help you?" he asked, peering through the small gap between the door and its frame. He wondered if Jindar, or possibly the high priest, had sent him to look for those who had fled Manak.

"Remlik, isn't it? I'm here on my own initiative; don't worry about being jumped by any priests. In fact, that's what I wanted to talk about. I'm sure you've heard about the war, and I'm looking into the priests' behaviour that has caused it. Jindara suggested I talk to some of the refugees," he said.

Reluctantly, Remlik let the man in. The twins had managed to find themselves a small abode on the outskirts of the town, and had only finished moving their things across a week ago. "So what did you want me to tell you?" he asked when the door was closed.

"Exactly what the priests were accusing you of, and how true or otherwise the accusations were. I'm trying to make Jindar see sense and put a stop to this war before it gets too far," Gondrun said quickly, as though he had to say the words before he lost his nerve. "If I can make him see that the priests are going over the top, he can talk to them and sort this out before people start dying."

Remlik tilted his head. "So you believe the priests are out of line?" The scribe indicated yes. "Very well. I was accused of heresy, as were most people who have run here. The comments I made were a little blasphemous, I suppose, but the priests are supposed to understand the doubts of people grieving for lost friends. All I said was, in response to someone's comment about the gods' mercy and kindness, that if the gods were truly kind they would not have allowed an innocent, gentle young man to be taken from his family." He left out the part about punching the town cobbler on the nose in defence of his student; it probably wouldn't go down well and wasn't really relevant to the purported blasphemy he had been accused of.

Gondrun nodded in understanding. "A reasonable statement. Certainly not one that warrants being chased out of town on threat of death. What about your sister?"

"Remlika was never accused of anything. People simply assumed she was guilty because of me," Remlik told the scribe, seeing his sister watching from the doorway. He knew his sister agreed with his views on the gods, and temples, but there was no point making the situation worse. "That is part of the problem, the priests often assume that entire families are demon-worshipping heretics just because one member, sometimes only a curious child, asks a question they don't like. The child is killed, and the family feel threatened and persecuted, so they run."

"The priests don't actually kill heretics, simply leave them staked at the mercy of the Demons," said Gondrun, puzzled.

Remlika stepped forwards into the room, her eyes shining silver in the dimming light. "You should report this back to your Chief, Gondrun. People who are staked out for the so-called 'Lightning Demons' are often killed by wild animals, which the priests cover up by scorching the remains. And there have even been people killed by temple acolytes, on the priests' instruction. Again, the remains are scorched to cover up the manner of death. Nobody looks too closely because they are scared to disagree with the priests, in case they are accused of heresy in turn."

Gondrun looked shocked. "How can you possibly know this? The temples teach us that the bodies are burned as a result of a Demon's touch."

"I have seen the bodies as they are brought back, and unlike most I look closely. Many of them bear unmistakeable signs of beast attacks, or dagger wounds. Unless the Colourless use blades and claws, which I doubt as they consist of lightning, this means that the people are killed by mortal means. And before you ask how I know acolytes kill them, rather than anyone else, I have seen acolytes sneaking back out of the town after staking people out, only returning after daybreak. They most often have smeared blood marking their robes," Remlika said, her tone as icy as the snows that would soon blow up from the frozen south.

Gondrun nodded stiffly; clearly still stunned by the revelations the dark-skinned twins had given him. "I will report back to Jindar immediately. Thank you for your time." He got up to leave, pausing at the door. "One thing, do you have any way to prove any of this? The Chief will refuse to accept such things unless I bring him solid proof."

"I can distil my own and my brother's memories into a vial. Will that be enough proof for him?" Remlika asked.

"I should think so." Gondrun waited as Remlika began casting intricate memory spells, to copy what she and her brother had experienced of the priests' over-enthusiasm. As she handed him a glass vial of swirling liquid rainbows, he thanked her and left.

Remlik turned to his sister. "We have to leave now. The chief will know where we are once he sees those, and he is sure to inform the priests. Shall we head to the city of the Colourless?"

"Yes. If you want to gather any scrolls you think you might need, I will collect some essentials and send a message to Braklarn. I think he'll want to come with us," said Remlika, going to fetch a few things she thought she might need.

Harndak sat at his table, checking the takings from the last week's markets. "Five hundred gold pieces, along with at least a century's worth in silver and copper. Looks like we'll be living in luxury for a while now, Enkarini. Especially with this war going on," he told his daughter, who was curled up in her favourite chair by the fire, half asleep. "There'll be lots of soldiers needing new armour and swords over the next few months. If this keeps up, I'll be able to afford those alchemy things you wanted."

Enkarini was suddenly wide awake. "Really? That sounds great! I can start practising then, and make lots of nice potions for everyone," she cried excitedly.

"You can. I just hope I don't get called to fight. I don't think I will, I'm getting too old for the battlefield now. But if it goes on for too long, they'll start recruiting older people," Harndak said, suddenly worried about what would happen to his last child if he got called off to war. "Maybe we should go away for a while. I can still work, and send my wares by caravan to be sold to the armies. Does that sound like fun, Enkarini? A little holiday away from here?"

Enkarini nodded, not really paying her father any attention anymore as she curled back up and gazed into the fire.

Father and daughter left town the next day, Harndak taking his tools and hiring a caravan containing an itinerant forge, so he could work on the road. They headed east, towards the Golden Coast, planning to spend the last of the autumn by the sea before heading over the hills to the Farm Valley, where it would be warmer, for the winter. Enkarini chattered all the way there, mostly about alchemy, but she occasionally mentioned Kandrina, who she insisted was still alive. On the journey, Harndak began to come to terms with her absence, and part of him believed Enkarini when she said she dreamt about her sister being in a glittering place, with lots of shining light people looking after her.

"You think that's what Paradise looks like, then?" he asked her when she told him about dreaming it again. "A glittering place, where everyone shines like lights?" It sounded pleasant, if not quite what was depicted in temple books. He wondered where his children had got their imaginations from; both Perlak and Kandrina had made up little worlds in their heads, where nobody else could intrude. *Probably got it from Meradina's side of the family,* he thought. A vision of his wife, glowing like a brilliant jewel, popped into his mind, and he smiled widely.

"No, Paradise is like a pretty meadow with lots of flowers, that never gets cold or rainy. The glittering place is somewhere else," Enkarini replied. "It's somewhere near a lot of short people, I'm not sure where though. I'll try and find out next time I dream about it."

Harndak nodded absently. "You do that. Look, there's the sea now. Can you see the sunlight reflecting off the water?" he pointed up ahead, to where he could see glinting lights on the horizon.

Enkarini stood up to see over the horses' harness. "I see it, I see it! We're nearly there, can I play on the beach when we stop, Father?"

Harndak laughed. "Of course you can. Don't go in the water though; it's too cold this time of year. Remember when Perlak caught that nasty cold after going in the sea in autumn?"

"I know it's cold. I won't go in the water; I just want to make a castle out of sand. I can make one that looks like the place I see in my dreams, and you can look. It won't sparkle like the real one, but I'll try and make it the right shape."

They stopped on the grass bank before they hit sand, and Enkarini ran off to make her castle. Harndak unhitched the horses and they wandered off to graze a short way away. Dragging the tools out of the back of the cart, he began setting up a temporary shelter for them to sleep in. They had stopped at several farms along the way, and had stayed in Wirba last night, so they hadn't had to use the heavy canvas tent yet. It would be strange, living out in the open for the next few months, but if it kept him out of the war and with his only remaining child, it would be worth it.

Remlik and his sister materialised a few miles west of Manak, closely followed by Braklarn and Wordarla. "Is this the place?" asked Remlika.

Remlik examined the map he held, double checked the reference against his notes, and nodded. "I think so. Somewhere very close, anyway. There should be what looks like a massive mountain right about... there. In that empty space." He tilted his head to the side and stared around. "I don't... oh, come on, it should be right here. It's a massive great mountain, it couldn't have got up and walked off."

"Tis a big mountain from a little person's view, maybe not so big to y'r eyes. Were the scrolls y' studied so hard written by men, or dwarves?" Wordarla asked shrewdly.

Remlik stared at his notes, then smacked his own forehead with them. "Gods, how could I have been that stupid? I should have recognized the style of writing," he exclaimed. "I'm sorry, I appear to have got my measurements all wrong."

Wordarla grinned at the despondent scholar. "Tis no worry, twas an honest mistake. Simply re-figure y'r measurements, tis all. These two can wait, n' I'll help y' convert the numbers." She examined the notes and map for a few moments. "Ah, I see. All y' done is forgotten to change dwarf units to human units. Tis only a matter of addin' another eight miles to our distance."

"That's simple enough. Shall we transport, or walk?" Braklarn asked. "Personally I'd rather transport, it looks like it's about to rain," he commented, glancing up at the thick black clouds in the sky.

Remlika nodded in agreement. "Transport it is." She took her brother's arm as Braklarn took his sister's, and the four of them disappeared again. Reappearing eight miles further west, they stared up at a huge grey mountain.

"Now that's a big mountain," Remlik said in awe. "This is it, it has to be. Any real mountain would have some foothills around it, even if they were only small ones." As he spoke, a few small hills seemed to rise up around the mountain.

Braklarn stared. "What? It's like someone heard what you said and changed things to fit your expectations," he stated. "But who could be listening? We're the only ones around here for miles."

The sky rumbled, and lightning flashed down right in front of them. Nobody spoke, but they all heard a voice that seemed to echo down from the clouds. 'Why are you here' it seemed to say. Remlik was the first to regain his composure.

"We come seeking a friend of ours. Her name is Kandrina. We wish to know if she is well," he shouted towards the clouds, above the noise of thunder. The noise quieted, and the storm seemed to drift away a little. The towering grey mountain flickered, and disappeared, revealing a stunning palace that seemed to be carved from pure diamond. An opening appeared in front of them, and a beautiful shining woman left the city. She wore a flowing dress that appeared to be made of pure light, and watched the two magic users with a wary eye.

Stopping a short distance away from the group, she spoke to Remlik. "You seek Kandrina?" she asked him in a crackling voice, still cautious of the mages waiting behind.

"I do. We all do, really. I was her mentor, and a close friend. My sister is also a friend to her, and these others are friends of hers," he told the glowing vision in front of him.

The woman seemed to consider his words. "If you are friends to Kandrina, then you must be good people. I will tell her you are here," she said, and went back inside. They waited in silence, gazing up at the sparkling city in front of them until Kandrina came out of the doors, followed by the glowing woman.

"Remlik!" she cried, running over to him with a wide smile on her face. "I'm so glad you're safe. And Remlika, and... who are you two?" she asked Braklarn and Wordarla, who introduced themselves.

"Have you been here all this time?" Remlik asked his former student. "We've got so much to talk about. There's a war going on back in Manak, and your sister wants to learn alchemy. They're both safe, by the way, your father and sister. It seems they decided to leave town just before the soldiers arrived, and are staying by the coast. Remlika scryed for them just before we came to find you," he explained.

"War? Over what?" Kandrina asked, concerned for her friends back home.

Remlika interrupted. "Can we talk about that in a minute? I'd like to know who your glowing friend over there is," she said, pointing to the woman who waited near the city doors.

Kandrina smiled, and beckoned the woman over. "This is Nerlarina. She's one of the Colourless, and she's been taking care of me for the last few months. Nerlarina, this is Remlik, my tutor, Remlika, his twin sister, and these two are Braklarn and Wordarla."

"Tis a pleasure to meet y'. N' don't worry about these two usin' their magic against y' n' y'r kin, they're keen to learn about y' rather than destroy y'," Wordarla assured the Colourless woman.

Kandrina nodded in agreement, confirming Wordarla's assertion. "As you said, we have a lot to catch up on. So, tell me about this war," she said to her mentor, as they headed back into the city.

"Well, it seems that the Vice-Chief Jindara has got tired of people flooding into her town begging for protection against the high priest in Manak," Remlik began. "She... Wow, that's bright." He raised his hand to cover his eyes as they went through the gates.

"Come up to my room, the walls are tinted to make the light dimmer," Kandrina told the others. "Don't cast anything, though. From what I've learned, even if you don't cast spells at them, it still disturbs their energy," she warned the two mages, leading them quickly up to the tinted rooms.

"How much have you learned about them?" Remlik asked from under his hand.

Kandrina smiled back at her tutor and his friends. "Quite a lot. Also, don't touch the walls. The city is made of the same energy as the Colourless themselves. You know, they really are fascinating. And in a lot of ways, they're not so different from us. I'll tell you all about it if you like. Nerlarina has been teaching me about their culture and things, and I've been teaching them about us."

"That is true. Aside from the obvious differences, many things seem similar in our daily lives," Nerlarina said from behind. She was following the five humans up to the next level of the city. "We are hoping to reach some kind of arrangement with your leaders, so our peoples can live in harmony with each other instead of constant fear. I understand much of the fear your kind have of us is inspired by your priests."

Braklarn snorted. "Seems like the blasted priests cause a lot of trouble. They're the root cause of the war we're having," he told everyone. As he looked around at the tinted room, he sighed in relief and lowered his hand from his eyes. "This room is much better. Your city is very bright, Nerlarina."

"The Colourless are bright, the city simply reflects and amplifies their light," Kandrina said. She noticed a basket of foodstuffs had been left on her table. "Why don't we have something to eat, then we can start talking properly."

"Sounds good to me," Remlika said, taking a haunch of meat from the basket and tearing a chunk from it. "Mmm. This is delicious; what kind of meat is it? It doesn't taste like anything I've had at home."

Kandrina shrugged. "I'm not sure. Nerlarina says they get food for me from a nearby dwarf village, maybe she'll know," she said, turning back to the door, but Nerlarina had vanished. "Oh, well, we can ask her later. So, what's going on back home? You said something about the priests causing a war?"

"That's not the official reason, but everyone in Tewen knows they're behind it," Remlik said, perching on the edge of the bed. It was surprisingly comfortable; obviously the Colourless kept their guests in luxury. "Officially, it's a difference of opinion regarding the leadership of the Chief. Jindara has already marched her army out; I heard some of her siblings are joining them on the plains, too." He lapsed into a thoughtful silence, tilting his head as he looked around the room.

Braklarn nodded, chewing a mouthful of food. "From what we've heard, the priests are stirring things even more; they're talking about 'Demon worshippers and evil heretics corrupting our lands'. They're trying to convince the population of Manak that everyone outside the city is untrustworthy and evil, from what rumours have reached us."

"Speakin' of Demons," Wordarla said, peeling the hairy skin off a green fruit, "what's been happenin' 'ere? I'm guessin' y' know more about these Colourless than the priests do, n' what y' know is true. Y' feel like teachin' us a bit?"

Kandrina smiled, pouring herself a cup of fruit juice. "I could certainly do that. I'm still learning myself, but I can tell you what I know so far." She sat down next to Remlik before continuing. "If you wanted to stay a while, I'm sure Nerlarina could explain it all better. She says they've got plenty of space here, if you wanted a room or two," she said, looking mainly at her tutor.

Remlik's eyes lit up. He had been interested in the 'Demons' for many years now, and had always longed for a chance to study them in person. "I'd love to, if you're sure there's enough room." He glanced over at his sister, who nodded slightly. "Let's ask when Nerlarina comes back. It would be great to learn about them first hand."

Chapter Five: Turnaround

The armies gathered, facing each other across the plains just south of Manak. The red and white banners of the Manak army flapped in the breeze, hanging loosely from poles. The Tewen army had only brought one banner, fixed firmly to a standard, and the blue and silver almost shone over the soldiers' heads. The skies poured rain down onto the plate and mail armour, causing many warriors to glance down, concerned about rust. The front lines began to call taunts through the rain, goading the other side to attack before the heralds announced formal beginning to the battle.

Gondrun, meanwhile, ran towards Chief Jindar's tent carrying vials of memories in a small bag, given to him by several refugees in Tewen. If he could just convince Jindar to look at them, this whole war could be called off. "Chief, I have something important you must see now," he panted, pushing the tent flap open.

"What is it, Gondrun? I have to finalise tactics for this battle," Jindar said impatiently, standing over a map of the local terrain.

"Proof that this whole thing is unnecessary. I visited Tewen and spoke with some of the refugees, and obtained these memories," he said, pulling out a couple of vials. "All you need do is uncork these vials and pour the contents onto a flat surface, and watch."

Jindar glared at his scribe. "Not this again. I have told you, I will not interfere with the temples..." he was interrupted by Gondrun leaning over and pouring the memories over his map. The liquid seemed to evaporate, and hang in the air as the events unravelled. There were several things there; a woman begging for mercy as her child was dragged away by the militia, a man whipped bloody by a black-robed acolyte, a priest watching from behind a tree as someone on the ground was attacked by wild dogs. Jindar watched, turning pale. "What is this? Can this be true?"

"Everything you see is a memory from people who have been wrongly accused by the priests," Gondrun whispered. The memories finished, and dissipated into nothingness. "Do you believe now, Chief Jindar?"

The chief nodded shakily. "I have to speak to my daughter." He left the tent and headed for the field. He made his way blindly through his own soldiers and onto the stretch of grass between the two armies, "Say nothing. This battle will not happen," he said as he walked past the brown-clad herald, who was on his way to announce the battle.

Jindara watched from her tent behind her lines, hoping that even at this late hour her father might see sense and stop this whole thing. She turned to her sister, Hinasi, who sat in the corner of the tent picking at a slice of bread. "I wish there was another way to make him listen. War is such a waste; nothing really gets solved. Where is Onkadal, anyway?"

Hinasi shrugged. "I believe he has gone to lead his troops. You know Onka; he always did enjoy a fight. Say, did you hear Semark joined our father's side in this? Apparently it was his idea to wait until we reached Manak's gates before marching their troops out."

Jindara raised her eyebrows in surprise. "Semark? I thought he'd be the least likely to get involved. We'll probably find the Chief pressured him into it," she said, pausing as the tent flap opened.

"Jindara, your father is approaching your lines. He is alone," said a soaked messenger girl, running in from the field. "I think he comes to parley with you."

Jindara smiled, adding a little beauty to her otherwise plain face. "Allow him through. He may have seen sense after all," she told the messenger, who saluted and ran back to pass the Vice-Chief's message to the others.

The Chief of the People arrived shortly after, dripping rainwater across the floor. "Jindara, Hinasi, my daughters. Please, withdraw your armies. I have seen proof that what you told me of the priests is true, and can only beg forgiveness for not believing your word alone."

"I forgive you, father. I understand it is a hard thing to accept, that holy men could be so unkind," Hinasi told him. "Even I was unwilling to accept it at first. Will you speak to your priests? It would only be a matter of asking them to be a little more lenient."

Jindar nodded. "Yes. I will hold a council with them all this afternoon. And it may be worth speaking to the priests in other towns and villages. Perhaps this problem is more widespread than we know," he said, wondering how such things had gone unnoticed for so long right under his nose.

"It is possible, of course. I have already had the priests in Tewen investigated, and a few have been dealt with. Come, we must tell the soldiers to put away their swords," Jindara said, smiling at her father and leading him out into the pouring rain. "Do tell me though, what exactly prompted such a sudden change of heart?" she asked.

"My scribe brought me some memories, given to him by some of your refugees. Memories cannot be falsified, as you know, so after seeing them I had to accept the truth, unpalatable as it is." Reaching the Tewen army's ranks, he bowed to his daughter. "I will go ahead and tell my soldiers to withdraw. Again, my sincere apologies for taking this so far." He turned and strode back to his own army.

Jindara watched him go. "Right, warriors! It seems my father has come to his senses and called off the battle," she called across her lines. "We rest here today, then begin the march back home at dawn." She turned to her sister. "We should find Onka before he charges the town gates," she said, raising her eyebrows. They both knew his temperament quite well, having put up with his aggression throughout their childhood.

"Quite right, we don't want him starting a war when we've just managed to avoid one. I'll go and look for him," said Hinasi, turning and heading off through the assembled ranks of warriors towards the fluttering flag of Akram, which had just been raised above everyone's heads.

Jindar rode at the head of his army, leading them back to the barracks in Manak. The soldiers marched behind him, a small cavalry unit followed by the infantry. Semark had begun leading his own warriors home to Wirba as soon as Jindar had announced the change of plan, looking very glad to be avoiding a battle. As they approached the gates of Manak, Jindar turned to his scribe, riding next to him. "Gondrun, ride ahead and send a message to the priests of all three temples. I wish to speak to them in council in one hour; I shall bring them to task over this, and discover why they have acted so poorly. Men of the gods should not push tensions to the point of war," he said angrily.

"Certainly, Chief." Gondrun bowed in his saddle, and rode on ahead towards the Chief's Halls.

After marching back to the barracks, the rain seemed to have lessened slightly. Jindar dismounted his horse and instructed his soldiers to dry off their armour and go back to their families. He visited his own chambers first to change out of his ceremonial armour, and then went to the council hall to speak to the priests. The three highest-ranking priests in the town waited, the high priest of Vrenid-Malchor sitting presumptuously in the chieftain's chair.

"What is this about, Jindar? We have important temple business to be about," the high priest said. He sounded weary, as though he hadn't been sleeping properly.

Jindar stood facing the three holy men. "Certain things have been brought to my attention that I wish to discuss with you. I am confident the temples' business can wait for a short while," he told them, more nervous than he wanted to let on. "And I think you will find that is my seat, high priest."

"Very well." The high priest stood slowly, scowling at the chief. "What do you wish to discuss?

Bearing in mind that anyone whose mind has been poisoned by heresy will be punished according to the gods' will."

The priest of Fakro-Umdar chuckled softly. "Let the good chief speak. You'll have him thinking we're irrational zealots," he told the high priest. "Besides, it could have something to do with those nightmares you've been having."

Glaring daggers at the death priest, the high priest moved to another chair to allow Jindar to take his seat. "I told you not to mention those," he hissed under cover of the scraping of chairs.

"I have been told that you have all been punishing minor crimes far too severely," Jindar began. "I do not wish to interfere with the gods' will, but I cannot accept the unreasonable punishment of curious children, whose only fault is naïve innocence. Several such incidents have come to my attention, and I wish to hear an accounting of them from your lips." He listed a few names Gondrun had mentioned.

The priests glanced at each other. Somri-Galin's priest spoke first. "Chief Jindar, the people you have named were all found guilty of serious blasphemy. Whoever you have been listening to is clearly misinforming you, trying to turn you away from the gods."

"Serious blasphemy, you say?" Jindar cried. "Four of those I just named were less than ten summers old, how can they have been guilty of anything?"

The high priest gave a significant look to the other two. "Perhaps I can explain things a little better for you," he said, leaning forward as the others left surreptitiously. "It is by the gods' will that we do these things. I suggest you keep quiet, lest you incur the wrath of the Demons, who even now are coming closer to our lands. They are called here by words of heresy, you see. You deal with the everyday running of this town, and let us handle the more important tasks. Because even a Chief can be taken by Lightning Demons." He stood and swept out of the room after the others, leaving Jindar to consider the veiled threat he had just delivered.

The caravan rolled through slush, swaying in the wind. Harndak and Enkarini were moving on, northwards through the hills, hoping to clear them and reach the Valley before the heavy snows started blowing in. They had found a winding trail leading through the hills, which Harndak had taken, rather than trying to drive the horses up and down over rough ground for several miles. In the back, Enkarini sat by the bags, hugging Sooty and trying to keep warm. She was getting tired of living outside, and wanted to go home, but Harndak wouldn't go back because of the war.

"Father, why can't we go home yet? Maybe everyone has finished fighting," she whined, as a freezing wind flapped the canvas open. "Can't we just go to a village and see if there's any news?"

Harndak reined in the horses. "I suppose it wouldn't hurt. I think there's a little farming village somewhere close by, why don't we go there? We can pick up a few supplies while we're there, too." He turned the caravan around and set off west, looking for the village.

They arrived at a village just after sunset, and Enkarini immediately jumped down from the cart with Sooty. "Please can we stay here, just for tonight? I'm bored of sleeping in a cold tent."

"Alright, we can stay the night. But if the war is still going on we'll have to move on again," Harndak told his daughter. "I'll get us a room, and see what news there is. Would you feed the horses while I sort that out?" He walked across to what looked like the local inn, leaving Enkarini to dig through the bags and find something to feed to the horses. The buildings around the square looked odd in the semi-darkness, and there were very few lanterns around. The large moon Teklir cast a bluish light over everything, making long shadows on the ground; Eskali wouldn't be up for another few hours yet. Harndak pushed open the door of the inn, and entered the dimly lit bar.

"Well now, whut can Ah do fur you, stranger?" The man inside spoke with a rolling, slightly twangy accent. It was rather pleasant, if somewhat unusual to Harndak's ears. "Don't git many visitors in these parts this time o' year. Ya from the south, aintcha? Ah can tell from them togs ya dressed in."

"I'm travelling north, with my daughter. We were hoping to get a room for the night," Harndak told the man.

"Sure, we got a room ya can use, if'n ya tell us yur story. We don't have much use fur coin round here," the man told him. As he lit another lantern, Harndak noticed his skin was pale, with a slight green tinge to it. His hair was hidden under a large hat, but his violet eyes seemed to sparkle with an inner light. "Yur gal waiting outside, is she? Call her in, Ah'll have the missus put a pot o' stew on an' git mah boy to stable yur horses." He turned and walked into the back room.

Wondering at the odd man he had encountered, Harndak walked back to the doorway to call his daughter inside. "Enkarini, come in now. I've got us a room, and the people here will look after the horses now." The girl patted the horse she had just fed, tucked Sooty into his box and skipped inside.

As Enkarini went inside, a plump, smiling woman stuck her head through an archway. She seemed to have midnight blue hair, though Harndak assumed it was some trick of the light. "Bless mah buns, what a darling lil' girl! Whut's yur name then, cutie?"

"Enkarini. What's yours?" she asked politely.

"Ah'm Mala, an' it's a pleasure to meet ya. Ah hope you two strangers like beef stew, cause Ah've got a whole pot brewing out the back here," she told them, retreating back into the kitchen.

Harndak looked down at his daughter. "I know they're a little odd, but they seem nice enough."

"Father," Enkarini said quietly. "I think they're elves. They talk like elves, and they look green."

"Don't be silly, Enkarini. Elves are just stories, they're not real," Harndak told her, sitting down at one of the roughly hewn tables. His own parents had told him tales of elves and dragons when he was a boy, which he had told to his children years later. Many of them had involved fantastic magic and heroic rescues, which had captured Enkarini's imagination in particular. Harndak had even had a special elf doll made for her, which was still one of the girl's favourite toys.

The man came back, smiling at the two of them. "Mah boy's stabled yur horses, an' the cart's with 'em," he said. "So, whut brings ya all this way so close to the winter?"

"We're on our way north, keeping away from the war. Do you know anything about it? It's been a while since we heard any news from home," Harndak asked him.

"War? Oh, the war that wasn't, ya mean. Yeh, we had news a fair while back," the man told them with a laugh. "Turns out yur chief called it off at the last minute, figured he'd be best off wi'out the killing that goes with a fight like that. Ya been running from an imaginary war all this time, have ya?"

Harndak turned red and stared at the table. "It sounds like it," he said embarrassedly. He had assumed there would be a long, drawn out war; both Tewen and Manak had strong armies, and neither Chief Jindar nor his daughter were known for changing their minds. Though he was glad to be wrong; it meant he and Enkarini could return home sooner. He was beginning to miss his comfortable chair and warm bed.

"So we can go home tomorrow?" Enkarini asked. "Not that I don't like it here, but I miss my own things," she added, talking to the strange man who owned the inn.

"Here comes stew," called Mala from the kitchen, carrying a large, steaming pot that issued a wonderful aroma of beef. "Ah hope yur feeling hungry, Ah made a lot."

The four of them tucked in. It was the best stew Enkarini could remember tasting, and after her second bowlful she asked the man, "Are you elves?"

As Harndak spluttered over a mouthful of stew, the man smiled. "Why yes, we sure are. Ah had no idea any o' yur people still knew about us," he said. "Ah'm Krin, by the way, pleased to make yur acquaintance." He tipped his hat to the little girl, who giggled.

"Really? I always thought elves were mythical... not that I mean any offence," Harndak said.

Mala winked at him. "No offence taken, sweetie. We've kept out o' the way o' yur kind fur a fair few years now, suppose it's to be expected we'd end up as kids' tales."

"Never had much to do with each other, even back then," Krin cut in. "Diff'rent ways o' living, kept us pretty separate. So tell us, how're ya doing with them Demons o' yurs? Yur scholars figured 'em out yet?"

"I'm not quite sure what you mean," Harndak said. "If you're talking about the Lightning Demons, we do our best to avoid them. The priests tell us they're evil spirits," he explained, wondering how these elves coped with the Demons. It seemed to be quite a small, isolated village; if anything ever did happen up here, it would take a fair while to get any help from anywhere.

A pointy-eared, dark-haired boy of about Enkarini's age laughed in the doorway. "They ain't evil spirits, just diff'rent from any o' us lot," he said nasally. "Yur priests got it wrong, mister. Or they ain't telling ya straight. Either way, ya shouldn't take their word on it. Whut we got fur eating, Pa?"

"Yur Ma's beef stew, son," Krin told the boy, who cheered and ran to the pot to fill a bowl. Noticing Enkarini's head beginning to droop, he turned back to Harndak. "Looks like ya girl's getting tired. Ah'll show ya to yur room," he said, leading the two travellers up the stairs.

Once they were settled, and in their beds, Enkarini murmured to her father. "I think that boy was right. We should talk to someone besides priests about the Demons when we get home," she said, before drifting into sleep.

Harndak thought. "I suppose it wouldn't hurt to find out a little more. We'll find a library on the way home," he said, then rolled over and fell asleep himself.

The next morning, they were awoken by a loud clattering noise, followed by a joyful shout. "Ma! Pa! It's snowed!" Enkarini recognised the nasal tone of the boy from last night. She opened the window and looked out at the thick blanket of white that had fallen on the village overnight.

"Can I go out and play in the snow? Please?" she asked her father excitedly.

Harndak sat up and rubbed his eyes. "Snow?" He rose and looked out the window. "Oh. Yes, you can go out and play. Just make sure you keep warm, and if anyone throws a snowball at you, you throw one right back." He smiled, knowing his daughter was likely to be the one starting a snowball fight.

Enkarini got dressed quickly and ran outside, immediately gathering a handful of snow and throwing it into the midst of a group of children across the street. The group scattered, and snowballs began flying in all directions, accompanied by high-pitched giggles. Harndak shook his head and went downstairs himself.

"Morning, mister," called the young boy. "Yur girl just went out to play, Ah'm off to join her. Ma's cooking ya some breakfast out back," he said before running out the door.

"Well then, looks like ya gonna be spending winter with us, unless this here snow decides to melt," Mala said as Harndak entered the kitchen. "It'll be nice to have some diff'rent faces about for a while. Ya know, Ah think mah boy Falp likes yur girl. Mustn't push 'em though, either way. Ya try an' keep 'em apart, they'll be all the more inclined to git together," she told him, flipping over a pancake.

Harndak nodded, not really listening. He sat at the kitchen table, wondering when he would be able to get home now, since the snows were unlikely to clear until springtime, which was still four months away. He thought to make the best of the situation, and set up the itinerant forge he had in the caravan. May as well work while I'm here, he thought, inhaling the smell of cooking. And the food's good too. Not such a bad place to be stuck for winter.

Remlik gazed through the walls at the falling snow. Though he knew it to be treacherous stuff; cold and wet, and slippery to walk or ride on, it looked incredibly beautiful when seen through the tinted walls of the Colourless' city. Though Braklarn and Wordarla had gone home before the winter settled in, he and his sister had remained with Kandrina, learning of the strange beings of light. He was waiting for Remlika to return, as she had gone a short distance away to contact Braklarn and find out what had been happening since they last spoke. They had all found out what had happened a few months earlier between the two armies.

From the last news they had heard, Jindar had been closeting himself away from everything for no apparent reason, Gondrun had disappeared, and the priests in Manak were practically running the town. At least half of the army had been transferred to the temple militia, and set to patrol the streets regularly. The high priest had been holding trials of 'heretics' at least four days a week, and many of them had been staked out, whipped almost to death, or had fled the town. Somri-Galin's acolytes had reportedly raided the libraries, destroying anything they found that referred to the old religions, the Colourless, and even some of the old explorer's journals about the lands beyond the People's villages. They were both interested to hear what Remlika found out this time round.

"Isn't she back yet?" Kandrina asked from behind him. She had spent most of the afternoon sat on her bed, writing down some notes about the Colourless.

Remlik turned to face her. "Not yet. I shouldn't think she'll be much longer," he said. He paused a moment, admiring the way the blue-green walls cast the light over his ex-pupil's face. It complimented her eyes beautifully, and made her hair sparkle. "Kandi, I've been thinking. Maybe we should go back to Tewen soon; I'm sure your father and sister would like to see you again, and since you've learned so much about the Colourless you can teach others. If people knew more about them than what the temples say, perhaps they wouldn't be so easily manipulated."

"Maybe. We'd have to wait until spring though; travelling through this snow would be lethal. Wait, is that Remlika?" Kandrina pointed out through the translucent wall.

Remlik turned to look, and noticed a figure wading through the deep snowdrifts towards the city. "I think it is."

A few moments later, Remlika entered the room. "It's freezing out there; the snow's up to my waist," she said unnecessarily. She began drying herself by the heated rocks Nerlarina had brought in earlier in the day. "You remember that scribe, Gondrun? He's turned up. At least, his body has. They found him out in the snow, halfway between Manak and Tewen. Braklarn reckons he was trying to get out, and warn Jindara what was happening, and the poor man froze to death. And he's worked out why Jindar's been hiding, too."

"How?" Remlik asked.

"Jindara's assistant, you know, that little fat man. He received a message from Jindar, mostly in pictures it seems, but he reckoned it said that Jindar was threatened by one of the priests. From what Braklarn said, the man reported it to Jindara first, then went around all the taverns in Tewen blabbing about it. The Vice-Chief is furious with him, apparently." Remlika turned slightly, warming her other side. "She's making plans to storm Manak and rescue her father, though I don't think she'll go through with it. One bit of good news though, the curse I put on the high priest seems to be holding up."

"What curse?" Kandrina enquired.

Remlika smiled. "Before I found out you were still alive, I put a revenge curse on the high priest. He's been haunted by nightmares ever since," she told the girl. "When we found out you hadn't been killed, I did think of removing it. But he's caused so many deaths over the years, I decided he deserved it."

Kandrina laughed. "You wicked sorceress. Though I don't blame you, considering the trouble he and his fellow priests have caused."

"Kandi and I were just talking about going home when the weather gets better," Remlik told his sister. "I think it would be a good idea, since the priests are getting far too bold. I mean, militia patrols, burning books, threatening the Chief, and public floggings; it's not right. Maybe if we return we can start educating people, about the Colourless and the priests."

"Perhaps that would be a good idea," came a crackling voice from the entrance. Nerlarina had approached soundlessly. "When you return to your town, may I accompany you? As a sort of representative. Your people might be more accepting of us if they can put a face to our people, rather than thinking of us as anonymous demons.

Also, I would enjoy seeing your town as you have seen our city," she said.

"That could be interesting. I'd like to see the high priest's expression if you walked into his temple," Remlika said. "So, if we head out when the snow clears? It shouldn't take long to walk to Tewen from here, maybe five or six days if we stop along the way."

Everyone agreed. "That's a plan, then. Was there any news of Father or Enkarini?" Kandrina asked. "I'd have thought they would have returned by now."

Remlika shook her head. "Neither Braklarn or Wordarla had heard anything. That doesn't mean you should worry though," she said hastily, seeing Kandrina's eyes tighten. "It's probably just that they've gone back to Manak. Braklarn doesn't hear about everyone that enters or leaves another town, especially not in this snow. I'm sure they're fine. I'll see if I can scry for them next time I go out."

Kandrina nodded. "Thank you. I'm probably worrying about nothing, like you say."

The high priest stood patiently as his servants adjusted his formal robes. He was preparing to give a public sermon, on a very important matter. The quality and quantity of offerings to all three temples in Manak had severely declined over the past month, and he felt he should warn the townsfolk that the gods were becoming displeased. The priests of death and suffering were giving the sermon with him, to further emphasise the importance of giving sufficient offerings.

"All weady, mathter," lisped a servant. That particular servant had earned a broken jaw early in his service, and ever since had spoken with a speech impediment.

The high priest dismissed the servants, and left the temple. It had stopped snowing for a while, and though it was still cold, a fair few people had braved the wind and frozen streets for the first time in several weeks. Everyone he passed dropped their gazes respectfully, some even pausing with heads bowed until he had passed. As it should be, he thought to himself, pulling his thick winter cloak tighter as a particularly fierce gust of wind blew snow up from the ground to swirl around him.

Emerging into the town square, he saw the low wooden podiums waiting in the centre of the open space, and the other two priests deep in conversation next to them. He walked across.

"Shall we begin? It's far too cold to stand around for much longer without freezing over," said the death priest. "Devoted as I am, I would rather serve my god in the mortal realm for a while yet."

"Quite right." The high priest shivered slightly as he stepped onto the centre podium to begin declaiming. "People of Manak, hear the words of the gods! Your devotions at the temples have been lacking recently, and the gods are becoming dissatisfied." A small knot of people who were within earshot stopped, and went closer to listen.

"The high priest speaks truth!" cried the death priest, visibly shivering in his thin dark red robes. "My god has spoken to me, and wishes more substantial offerings placed upon his altar! Four pieces of cattle rump will not placate death, nor keep him from your doors!"

Somri-Galin's priest needed do little more than fix a few members of the crowd with a malevolent stare to convince them that they did not want his god visiting their houses. He noticed a plump, dark woman near the back of the crowd, and stared at her as well. She grinned back at him, and winked. Confused, he tried to see what she looked like under her headscarf, but she turned and seemed to fade away into thin air.

"The gods ask for very little, beyond your faith and your offerings. I urge you not to incur their wrath by ignoring your duties to the temples!" Vrenid-Malchor's high priest shouted.

"Our family can't give any more than we already do!" said someone in the crowd. "We have no gold or silver, and if we offer any more of our food to the gods our children will starve!"

"Give to the temples, and the gods will provide for you," the high priest replied. "To neglect your devotions to the gods constitutes heresy and invites Demons to your family's door. The Chief's scribe was taken only last week, for spreading lies and blasphemies. What do you think almost caused a war between father and daughter?" he asked, neatly blaming the Demons for the man's death, and the dead man for the trouble.

A short, mousy-looking woman near the front shuffled her feet nervously, whispering something to her husband. He called out, "I heard different; that Jindara got tired of people begging sanctuary in Tewen, at the balance temple."

"You see?" cried the high priest, gesturing flamboyantly in the man's direction. "Even after the scribe's death, his heresies live on! You must pay no heed to the rumourmongers spreading these lies. Trust in the gods, devote yourselves to the temples; it is the only way to keep the foul Demons away!"

The death priest threw an odd glance at him across the podiums. "Quite right. You must remember your duties to the gods, to ensure the gods will remember you in times of need. Never forget, my god is the one who will judge your soul, to be sent to Paradise... or to the Hells below," he said, making a shudder run through the crowd that had little to do with the cold. Priests of death and suffering were the only ones who could speak of the twelve Hells without fear; their gods' realms were considered the first and second levels, before the Demon Lords' domains began.

"Yes," the high priest said, slightly uneasily, wanting to move away from discussion of the Hells. "The gods are the most important part of our lives, and must be treated as such. We shall be expecting better offerings from now on, at all of our temples. The gods' patience is waning, and shall not last forever!"

The listening townsfolk murmured between themselves, most nodding but a few simply watching the priests, sceptical expressions on their faces. The wind blew harder, fresh snow beginning to fall; a few stragglers at the back turned and hurried away. The death priest turned to the other two.

"I'm done; there's no way I'm standing around in the snow." He stepped down from his podium and, teeth chattering, walked swiftly back towards his temple.

The small crowd began to disperse, people rushing back to their houses or into shops; the other two priests decided to follow their colleague's example, and headed for their own warm temples.

Enkarini jumped behind a snow-covered bush. If he found her, she'd be the next one up, so she had to be very quiet. Hearing someone running near her hiding place, she dared a peek between the leaves. A small spider fell off a leaf, landing on her hand and making her scream.

"Ha! Found ya!" shouted Falp. "Yur Up now! Ya gotta count to twenny with ya eyes closed, and no peeking!" The other children all popped out of their hiding places, grinning because they hadn't been found.

The girl groaned. She was never any good at finding people; in fact she was forever losing things. "Alright. One, two, three…" She heard the others run off, to find other places to hide. "…Nineteen, twenty! I'm coming to find you!" She crept through the snow, looking around for the slightest movement. The elven children had introduced her to a new game they called Hide and Peek, which she was finding to be a lot of fun, even when she was Up.

Someone snickered as Enkarini walked past an old barrel. "You're in there!" she cried suddenly. "Come out! I found you!" She knocked on the barrel lid.

Smiling at her, Falp popped his head out. "Guess Ah'm Up again. One, two…" As he began counting, everyone ran to hide again. Enkarini decided to hide at the side of an old outhouse, promising herself that she would stay quiet even if a really big spider dropped on her. Falp finished counting, and started looking. She moved further into the shadows, and bumped into someone. She looked, thinking it was someone else hiding, and saw it was a grown-up lady, with funny purple hair.

"Shh, I've got a secret to tell you. I know where your sister's hiding," she whispered. "She's in a big, sparkly palace, west of your home town. I can show you the way, if you'd like."

Enkarini nodded. She wanted to find out where her sister was, but needed to keep quiet so that Falp wouldn't find her again. The purple haired lady said something that sounded strange, but pretty, and a map appeared in the air. "I've been having dreams about a sparkly palace, is it the same one? Where is it?" she whispered.

The lady smiled. "You know, I think it is the same one you've been dreaming about. It's right here; I'll mark it with a circle," she said, and a circle appeared around a mountain near the right of the map. "Now, this is where you are now. The quickest way to get to where Kandrina is, is to go through the hills on this trail here." A cross appeared in the hills, and a line snaked its way through the hills, going from the cross to the circle.

"Can I keep the map?" Enkarini asked. "I don't think I'll remember all that by myself." Across the square, she heard Falp find another of the children.

"Of course you can. Tell your father that it's a gift from Dranjari, and that he should make his way there before the end of winter. The trail I showed you will be clear," she said. "Go on, I think your friends are looking for you." The lady smiled again and disappeared.

Falp stuck his head round the corner. "There ya are! Wonder'd whur ya'd got to. C'mon, Ma's calling us all in. Says it's getting too cold to be playing outside," he told her, pulling a face that clearly said 'parents don't know what fun they're spoiling'.

The two of them ran back inside, waving to the others as they went. "Git in here, you two! Go on, take off them there wet things and warm yurselves up by that fire," Mala scolded as they came in, damp from playing in the snow all afternoon. "Ah'm making spit roast chicken fur dinner tonight, so Ah hope ya worked up an appetite playing yur games." She bustled off into the kitchen, leaving the children to dry off and warm up.

"Who was ya talking to behind that outhouse, then?" Falp asked, pulling off his wet gloves and warming his hands by the fire. "Heard ya talking away to someone."

"Just a funny lady. She gave me a map to give to Father," Enkarini told the elven boy, sitting down on the hearthrug next to him. "She said it shows a way to where my sister is," she said, taking the map out of her pocket before throwing her overcoat to one side.

Harndak overheard. "What funny lady? Enkarini, I've told you not to take things from strangers," he told her. "Show me this map she gave you."

Enkarini handed the rolled paper to her father. "She said to say it was a gift from Dranjari, and that we should go there before the end of winter. She said that trail would be clear," she told him, wondering what it all meant.

"Dranjari?" Harndak raised his greying eyebrows. "It couldn't be... What did she look like, this lady?" he asked, examining the map.

"She was dark, but not quite as dark as Remlik and his sister. She had purple hair, and weird eyes. She was a little bit fat too, like the old baker woman back home," Enkarini babbled.

"Weird eyes?"

The girl nodded. "Like, eyes that could see too much. Why, do you know her?"

Harndak lowered the map slowly. "Not exactly, but I know of her. Did she say exactly when we should leave?"

"No, but I can tell you now," said someone from behind him. "This week, before sunset on the sixth day. Kandrina's alive, Harndak, and she'd like to see you again."

As Harndak turned, the two children caught a glimpse of something purple in the air before it vanished.

"Whoa, did ya see that!" Falp shouted. "That lady just appeared, and vanished, just like that! Is she some kind o' magician from yur town?" he asked excitedly.

"Cool it son, ya cain't go shouting the roof off ev'ry time ya see something strange," called Krin, coming down the stairs. He was still wearing his hat, and Enkarini wondered if he ever took it off. "Likely to be a friend o' our guests, Ah should think. Why don't ya go see if yur Ma wants a hand out there?"

Falp stood up and dragged his feet into the kitchen. Krin watched him go, and then looked back at Harndak. "Ah must apologise fur mah boy, he has a habit o' sticking his nose in whur it don't belong. Yur private business is none o' ours," he said, adjusting his hat.

"No need to apologise. We don't mind," Harndak replied. "Tell me, will my horses and cart be ready to go by sixth day? Our friend passed us an urgent message, and it seems we have to be on our way sooner than we thought."

"Ah don't see why not," Krin said, rubbing his neck. "Ya gonna have trouble with snow, though. Unless yur magic friend's clearing a path fur ya. Ah'll see yur cart's ready to go by sixth day."

Harndak inclined his head. "Thank you. It's been a pleasure staying with you, and I'm sure once the weather improves we can come back and visit. Something tells me our two kids would like that," he said with a smile.

Krin smiled back. "Ah'm sure they would. And it's been our pleasure having ya stay."

Enkarini beamed at the elf man, and turned back to the fire. She'd had a lot of fun with Falp and the other children, and was looking forward to telling her friends back home that she had spent the winter with elves.

Ralor-Kanj stood in the pavilion, watching the throne intently. The Creator God had begun stirring restlessly, as though he was about to wake. "Dranj-Aria," he called softly.

The goddess of time appeared in front of him, twirling a stick between her fingers. "Yeeeess?" she drawled.

"Drop the eccentricities for a moment, please," the balance god sighed. "I'd like to know what is about to happen, whether Vrenid-Malchor is waking. Can you tell me?"

Dranj-Aria shook her head. "Not yet. I remember telling you after I first speak with Kandrina. You'll all find out soon, anyway," she told him.

"You really are infuriatingly vague, Dranj-Aria," he replied, with a small smile. "I suppose I can't argue with you though. Should I inform the others that he is becoming restless?"

"Probably. Then you can all worry about it together," she answered, and promptly disappeared again.

Ralor-Kanj rolled his eyes in exasperation, and went to visit the other gods' domains to tell them of the Creator God's stirrings. Alone among the gods, he could walk between the separate domains of the others without invitation. It was occasionally a necessity, as his task was to keep balance between all things in every realm, which sometimes meant interfering in another god's domain. He thought it would be easier to visit Talri-Pekra first, as she was likely to be the most rational about things.

The goddess of knowledge and magic inhabited what at first glance seemed to be a gigantic library, with shelves of books stretching up and back for miles. It was in fact a library of sorts, but there was so much more than books contained there. Everything that was known about the entire world was within the goddess's library, including things that the mortals who worshipped them had not yet discovered. Talri-Pekra herself was usually found in her favourite high-backed chair, reading one heavy tome or another, and that was indeed where Ralor-Kanj found her.

"To what do I owe this pleasure?" the knowledge goddess asked as he entered her presence.

Ralor-Kanj inclined his head in respect. "Vrenid-Malchor is stirring. He may be waking soon. I decided it would be best to inform all of you, so that we can form a plan to resolve the issues in the mortals' realm."

Talri-Pekra narrowed her eyes. "And if this plan is not brought to fruition before he wakes?"

"At least we have a plan, rather than being undecided on what action to take," Ralor-Kanj replied.

"Very well," the goddess said, closing her book emphatically. "I shall return to the pavilion to watch, whilst you inform the others. I will call Aikra-Lora back and tell her myself; she is visiting the mortal realm at this moment." She faded away, leaving Ralor-Kanj with a rather unpleasant choice to make.

He decided to visit Fakro-Umdar before the god of suffering. Even the realm of the dead was preferable to the torture chamber Somri-Galin called home. On entering the cold, dark mist, he called out to the death god, breaking the heavy silence. He did not wish to go any further into this realm than he had to. As he waited, the anguished cries of unsettled souls rang through the still air.

Fakro-Umdar appeared, materialising from a drifting shadow. "What do you want?" he asked lazily, as though he couldn't really give a damn about what the balance god had to say.

"I came to tell you that Vrenid-Malchor is stirring. He is about to wake," Ralor-Kanj said shortly. "Talri-Pekra is at the pavilion, once everyone has been informed we will be formulating a plan to deal with the mortal priests. You wouldn't happen to know what Somri-Galin is doing right now, would you?" he asked, not wanting to walk in while an unfortunate soul was being punished.

Waving his hand vaguely, the death god replied, "Torturing some poor unfortunate soul, I should imagine. Why don't you go and see? I'll join Talri-Pekra at the pavilion." He faded back into the shadows.

Thankfully, the god of suffering wasn't being actively sadistic when Ralor-Kanj appeared. "Ah, Ralor-Kanj! Come to watch the show? You're a little early, but I suppose I could start now."

"Actually, I have some news. The Creator God is stirring, ready to wake. We are convening at the pavilion to discuss how to deal with the mortal priests," Ralor-Kanj said. A piercing scream cut the air.

"Fine. I hope it won't take long, though. My subjects have got used to the schedule here, and I'd hate to disappoint them." The two gods faded back to the pavilion to join the others.

Chapter Six: Divine Oddness

Jindara paced up and down her halls, fretting over her father's fate. "Tell me again. I want everything clear in my mind before I do anything," she said, halting to look at her scribe.

"Ma'am, your father is safe, but practically imprisoned within his own chambers. We received word at the beginning of winter that the priests had threatened him," the stocky scribe told her. "The few people who have managed to get here have confirmed this, and have passed on news of the priests controlling every aspect of the town. There has also been word that unfair trials and excessively harsh punishments are becoming more common in Manak."

"There will always be room at my temple for those in need," said the high priest of Ralor-Kanj softly. "But it would seem my brothers are becoming too fanatical in their beliefs. Should you choose to confront them, I will stand at your side."

Jindara resumed her pacing. "Something must be done. What exactly is my father's state? Has he retreated voluntarily, or is he being forced into solitude by the priests?"

Her scribe answered. "It would seem he has chosen to hide away in fear, rather than being forced anywhere. Poor leadership, but not overtly the fault of the priests."

"So staging a rescue would be unjustified, since there seems to be nothing to rescue him from but his own cowardice. What of his scribe?"

"Dead, ma'am. In attempting to reach Tewen so that he could warn us of the situation in Manak, he froze in the snow."

Cursing, the Vice-Chief flung herself into her chair. "So there is no way to get a message to Jindar without raising the priests' suspicions." She sat in brooding silence, trying to think of a way to deal with the problem without being blamed for causing trouble.

The balance priest cleared his throat. "Perhaps you could enlist the help of a sorcerer, Jindara. There are many in Tewen who are capable of sending a message by arcane means, or even transporting directly into Jindar's presence."

There was a moment's silence as Jindara raised her head to gaze at the priest. "Why didn't I think of that?" She took up quill and parchment and began drafting a declaration. "If it is written in my own hand, they will realise it is a matter of utmost importance. Here, paste this on the board in the town square," she said, completing her proclamation and handing it to her scribe.

"Yes ma'am." He bowed and hurried out of the hall.

As her assistant left, followed by the balance priest, Jindara sat back in her chair and sighed. She had sent messengers to her siblings at sundown two days ago, and expected at least two of them back by evening. Devurak and Hinasi, Vice-Chiefs of Pokole and Bewein, were her closest siblings both by location and relationship. She expected their responses to her request for advice to be considered and thoughtful, in stark contrast to what she expected from Onkadal, Vice-Chief of Akram and the Chief's oldest son. Onkadal had always been reckless and quick to act, without stopping to consider the consequences of anything he did. Jindar had put him in charge of the scattered villages of Akram; partly to keep him busy so he wouldn't get bored and start a war, and partly because the Akram villages were fairly close to Manak, so Jindar could keep a close eye on him. Tironde and Semark's replies would likely take a while longer, as they had to come from the furthest east parts of the land. Though, Tironde of Astator would probably send her reply by mounted messenger, along with word from her most trusted advisor in Entamar. Since the Chief had only had six children, Entamar was being run by a committee of advisors until a grandchild was born, and came of age.

As Jindara sat wondering which of her brothers and sisters would contact her first, a breathless runner came through the double doors, stopping just short of the raised dais where her chair rested. Snapping out of her reverie, she gestured for a servant to bring water for the exhausted boy. Once he had gratefully drunk his fill and regained his breath, he bowed to Jindara. "My thanks, lady. I bring news from Vice-Chief Hinasi of Pokole, who bid me come with the greatest of haste." The boy rummaged for a moment in his messenger's satchel before extracting a loosely furled scroll, which he handed to her. "Lady Hinasi also asked me to inform you that your runner is resting in her halls, and should be returning to you tomorrow."

Jindara smiled faintly to herself. While her sister Hinasi was educated and sensible in many areas, she had never been able to resist any opportunity of seducing and bedding any young man in sight. "Of course. Feel free to rest a while yourself before returning; my servants will be on hand to provide food and water."

The boy smiled, bowed and retreated from the main hall, accompanied by a serving girl. Jindara watched them leave before opening the scroll that bore her sister's seal. She skipped through the first part of the missive; it was merely the flowery, overdone greeting that Hinasi always insisted on writing. The rest of the scroll was far more intriguing:

'Sister, this news of the priests in Manak is nothing new. Manak's priests have always oppressed the masses, since before the merging of the tribes. However, the idea that they have become so fanatical as to dare to threaten our father and Chief means that something must be done. As an aside, my small village has also been swamped with refugees, such that I find it hard to believe that anyone still resides in Manak proper!

'On a more serious note, though, the people in Bewein are becoming increasingly unsettled by the news coming in from Manak. As I'm sure you remember from your history, the Bewein were never overly keen on the Manak priests anyway, and though the tribes have intermingled somewhat in the last few generations, there is still a lot of ill feeling around here. My assistant tells me that some are talking of rebellion, splitting the tribes up again and returning to the old ways. I'm sure much of it is idle tavern talk, borne of ale and easily forgotten by next day. I will be keeping an eye on those I think are most serious, though.

'So, to business. I have, of course, sent runners to Devurak and Tironde; I believe they will be most useful in any confrontation that may be approaching. This situation requires tact, something not possessed by Onkadal. With his militaristic temperament, he would march his soldiers right into the prayer halls! And while I am fond of our little brother Semark, he is not particularly good with conflict. As for what I think best, it is my opinion that we should wait. I assume you have also asked advice from the rest of our siblings, and we should of course consider all opinions before acting. Also, I have been hearing vague rumours of scholars who are seeking information on certain forbidden subjects, in order to break the priests' control.

'I do wonder, though, what dear Mother would have made of all this. She would have put those pesky priests in their place by now, would she not?

'Yours in all sincerity, Hinasi.'

Jindara reached the end of the letter and rolled it back up. Hinasi's thoughts had been almost exactly what she had expected, but the part mentioning disillusioned townsfolk talking about tribal secession worried her slightly. She frowned at the scroll in her hand for a moment before pushing the thought to the back of her mind. One problem at a time, she told herself. She left Hinasi's letter on her side table and sat back again. Turning her mind back to the request for a mage to get a message to her father, she began to wonder how many sorcerers would answer. She closed her eyes, and a familiar face popped into her head, one with amber eyes and an untameable mess of dark red hair. She wondered if her old friend and sometime lover would come to demonstrate his magical skills.

By that evening, the Vice-Chief's declaration had been read or heard by almost every citizen of Tewen. Wordarla carried the news to her half-brother, realising he had hardly left his house for almost a month.

"Brother, have y' heard about the declaration from the Vice-Chief? Tis all over town that she's after a mage to send a message to her father," she called, opening the door. "Y' should take her up on it, twas only the other day y' said about wantin' to help out with the priests."

Braklarn ran to the top of the stairs. "Never mind that. Remlika's just been in touch, she says they're coming home soon. They're heading out as soon as the snow clears, and they're bringing Nerlarina with them!"

"Tis good news indeed, that is. So, y' goin' to speak with Jindara? If Remlika n' t'others are on their way back, I think they'd like to come back n' find the priests sorted out, or nearly so."

"Yes, I'll go and speak to her now," Braklarn said, gathering his cloak and scarf. "Would you stay here, in case Remlika calls again? You know what to do with the device," he called to Wordarla as he ran out the door. As he ran through the streets of Tewen, he wondered if Jindara would remember him. It had been a fair while since they last spoke, and he was sure she would have moved on since then. When he reached the outer doors, he caught his breath and spoke to the servant outside the Vice-Chief's chambers. "I have come to speak with the Vice-Chief, regarding her request for a mage," he told the thin man by the door.

"You and half the population of Tewen, it seems," said the servant as he opened the doors. "She's speaking to everyone, but you'll have a long wait." He bowed as Braklarn walked past him into the hall.

On entering, Braklarn saw an entire room full of sorcerers, some of whom he knew and others he did not recognise. He noticed Jindara and her assistant at the far end of the halls, accompanied by the high priest of Ralor-Kanj. They were speaking with a young mage, who was quickly dismissed. Seeing an acquaintance of his on the other side of the hall, Braklarn made his way over to greet him.

"Dekarem, how are you? I'm guessing you're here to see what this declaration is about," he said, grasping the other man's hand. "How long have you been waiting?"

Dekarem ran a hand over his shaven head. "Couple of hours. I don't know what some of this lot are doing here, to be honest. Most of them have only just started learning; they're nowhere near skilled enough to send messages to Manak. How's Wordarla?"

"Well enough. Still running her shop, and making a tidy profit from what she tells me. And your wife? Separated yet?" Braklarn joked.

"She's on her way out the door, or so she says," Dekarem said with a laugh. "She's been threatening to leave me since the day we married, though. What about those two friends of yours from Manak, have they come back from their trip yet?"

"I had a message from them earlier, they're coming back as soon as the snow clears. Unless things change, anyway." The two men continued gossiping for a while, until Dekarem was called to speak with Jindara. Braklarn found an empty chair and took it, thinking that he had a while to wait yet. The mages that had been dismissed didn't hang around, and nobody else seemed to have arrived for the past hour, so the hall was slowly emptying. Eventually, he heard his name being called by the Vice-Chief's assistant, and he walked across to her chair.

"Presenting the renowned sorcerer Braklarn, of Tewen," the chunky assistant announced.

Braklarn bowed to the Vice-Chief. "I am ready to carry out the wishes of my Vice-Chief," he intoned formally.

Jindara smiled at him. "I believe we can drop the formalities, Braklarn. I consider you as more of a friend than a subject. However, I will try to be impartial," she said, remembering her past encounters with the bushy-haired mage. "So, how developed are your skills these days? Would you care to demonstrate a few things for us?"

Smiling back at his occasional lover, Braklarn began casting delicate spells to demonstrate his skill in the areas required for subtle message sending. The balance priest and scribe looked impressed, and he was asked to wait in a side chamber with a handful of others who had demonstrated equal skill.

"I can't say I'm surprised," said a familiar voice when he entered the smaller room. "You're easily one of the best mages in this town."

"Another of the best being you, right?" Braklarn replied, turning to see Dekarem again. "So we just wait here for more instructions, do we?"

The bald magician nodded. "I don't think we'll have to wait long, the hall should be almost empty by now. How many others were out there when you came through?"

"Not many. Maybe a dozen or so," Braklarn answered him. "Nothing else to do for now, then. Fancy a game of cards?" He conjured a pack of playing cards out of thin air, shuffled and began dealing for a round of Kan-Kara, a game popular in taverns across the People's lands.

As they wound their way through the surprisingly clear trail, Harndak and Enkarini wondered why the goddess of time might be helping them find their lost relative and get home.

"Maybe she heard our prayers and has decided to help us," Harndak said. "The gods listen, and are sometimes kind."

"I think she's just being nice," Enkarini replied.

"It's possible. Either way, it looks like you were right all along," Harndak told his youngest daughter. "How did you know Kandrina was still alive?"

Enkarini looked up at her father. "Like I said, Kandrina promised she'd come back some day." She suddenly sat up straighter, staring into the distance. "Father, look! It's the sparkly place I keep dreaming about!" She pointed ahead at the large mountain that had become visible as they rounded the last hill and the trail levelled out onto the plains.

Harndak looked where the girl pointed. "That's only a mountain, Enkarini."

"No, it's a beautiful sparkling city," she insisted. "Can't you see it? I can see it, that's where Kandrina is."

Squinting, Harndak could see some sort of haze around the edge of the distant mountain, but couldn't make out anything sparkling. "All I see is a mountain. But it's where the map leads to, so we'll head over there," he said, snapping the reins to spur the horses on a little.

They sped across the frozen plains, past slowly melting drifts of snow, towards the mountain. As they approached, they saw four figures standing around. Two were tall and dark-looking, one was slightly shorter and pale, and another seemed to be shining. Once they were near enough, one of the figures turned and saw them, exclaiming to the others.

"Kandrina!" Enkarini squealed in delight, jumping down from the cart and running to her sister. "I knew you were here, I've been dreaming about you. Who's your pretty friend?" she asked, staring at the glowing woman.

Kandrina smiled at her little sister, pleased to see her again. "This is Nerlarina, she's a friend of mine. You mustn't touch her though, alright?" the little girl nodded. "I'm assuming Father is still in the cart. Why don't you go tell him it's okay to come out?"

Enkarini skipped back to the cart, calling out as she did. "Kandrina's here, Father, she says it's okay. The sparkly lady is her friend," she said, looking back over her shoulder.

Harndak stared over at the four of them, recognising Remlik and his sister, their dark hair and skin making them stand out clearly against the white snow, and Kandrina, facing the cart and looking expectant; yet the bluish-white, strangely glowing woman drew his attention. She was beautiful, tall and slim with fine features; almost too perfect, no real woman had ever looked like that, surely? He climbed down from the cart slowly, watching the shining vision closely. The temples had always warned that the Demons would take an attractive form to lure people closer.

Kandrina smiled as he approached. "It's good to see you again, Father."

"I'm glad you're alive, Kandrina," Harndak replied, embracing his older daughter while keeping a wary eye on the glowing woman standing just behind her. "Tell me, how did you convince the Lightning Demons to spare you?" he asked, burning with curiosity.

"Firstly, they're not demons," Kandrina told him. "They call themselves Shcal'csh, which means People in their tongue. But Nerlarina here says they are happy with the name 'Colourless' which is easier for us to pronounce," she said with a smile.

"Kandrina has told me a lot about you," Nerlarina said, shining brightly even in the weak winter sunlight. "It seems there are many things that we still need to learn about each other, but we hope to begin relations on good terms. The first thing I wish to make clear is that we intend no harm to your kind," she told him.

Harndak was puzzled. His daughter had clearly been well cared for while she stayed with them, but the priests had constantly maintained that the Demons were evil creatures that killed anyone they touched. This, and the comments from the elves they had spent the winter with, gave him pause. "I... I admit to being confused. I don't see how our priests could have been wrong about your kind for so long, but clearly they are, else Kandrina would not be here," he said to her. "Maybe it would do us good to learn about each other."

"I'm glad you're finally seeing sense, Father," Kandrina said, winking at Nerlarina.

"And I'm glad you're all back together again," said a voice from somewhere behind Remlik. They all turned to see who had spoken.

Enkarini smiled at the strange woman who had appeared. "Hello again. Thank you for helping us find Kandrina," she said.

Looking from her sister to the strange woman, Kandrina asked, "Do you know each other?"

"Sort of. She gave me a map, which I gave to Father, that led us to you," Enkarini told her older sister. "She's called Dranjari, and she's nice."

"Thank you," said Dranjari, smiling at the little girl. "I'm sure most of you have heard of me before, though I don't think you two quite believe in me." She looked at Remlik and Remlika, who were standing back watching the scene unfold, unsure what to make of the odd woman who claimed to be the aspect of a goddess.

Kandrina was also flummoxed. "Meaning no disrespect, but why have you come down here? I've always thought that the gods took a rather distant approach to the goings on here," she said.

"Kandrina, show a little reverence," Harndak scolded. "You are speaking to a goddess."

Dranjari giggled. "I don't mind. It's always been pleasantly refreshing talking to you, Kandrina. You're right, of course, usually we don't interfere," she told the group. "However, there was a major problem with some of your priests that we had to sort out. I mean, there is a major problem. And we're going to need people like you to help, because you're one of the only few with the courage to speak out. Plus, we like people who don't pester us with every little difficulty in their lives," she said with a wink.

Completely befuddled, Harndak kept his silence. Here was the aspect of a goddess, whose sole purpose was to listen to and sometimes answer prayers, according to the temples. But she had just said that she and the other gods preferred not to be constantly pestered by people asking for things. What with that, and the supposed Demons obviously having looked after his daughter; doubts began to creep into the corners of his mind. Did the priests really know the truth of the world, and if so, were they telling people everything?

"Anyway, before I get sidetracked, I should be telling you that you can't go home yet. There were a few things you need to do in the dwarven villages first," Dranjari continued. "I think you're supposed to give us all a ride in that cart of yours, Harndak. Shall we proceed?" Without further ado, she sauntered across to the cart and hopped into the back. Thoroughly perplexed, the others followed her, Harndak climbing up to the driver's seat with his two daughters either side.

Jindar sat upon his bed, staring vacantly out of the window at the snow-covered plains. He had hidden himself away all winter, uncertain of his priests but unwilling to confront them again. At heart, he was a simple man who preferred the old tribal ways of the People, and he could not quite grasp the concept of a bad priest. They had always led him right, given good advice; except for one instance, the illness that his wife had succumbed to many years past.

The high priest had told him that prayer would heal her, and medicine would not work on her sickness. In his faith and devotion to the gods, he had believed them and refused to seek the help of any healers, ignoring the pleas of his now-deceased brother, and oldest children. When she had died, Jindara had been unable to forgive him, blaming him for her mother's death. They had hardly spoken since, and the estrangement played on his mind quite often. He had no idea how to go about repairing their relationship, though; he had always hated having to admit being wrong.

As he sat in contemplation, the last thing he expected was a man with bushy red hair appearing in front of him. "Chief Jindar?" the man asked. "My name is Braklarn. I've been sent here by your daughter, to check on your well-being and give you a message."

Jindar stared for a moment. "My daughter? You mean Jindara?" He gathered his thoughts. "What message do you have?"

"Jindara plans to confront the high priest of Vrenid-Malchor, and put an end to the fanatical behaviour of the priests in this town. She also wishes to ask for any help you can possibly provide," Braklarn told him.

The Chief considered the mage's message. "I regret that I am not in a position to provide much help. Though, she may do well to contact some of her brothers and sisters. They may be able to assist her better than I," he said. He paused for a moment, wondering if perhaps it was time to try and heal the rift between them. "Would you also tell her that I am sorry for causing her so much grief and pain? She will know what I mean." He met the mage's gaze, a spark of understanding passing between them.

Braklarn thought he knew what the Chief spoke of, but said nothing. "I shall pass on your words, Chief Jindar. Farewell." He disappeared back to Tewen, leaving the chief alone once more.

Jindara looked up as he rematerialised in her chambers. "Well?"

"Your father is well, though he refuses to leave his rooms. He says he cannot help, though some of your siblings might be able or willing to do so," Braklarn replied. "He also wanted me to tell you that he is sorry for causing so much grief; that you would understand what he meant." Their eyes met.

The Vice-Chief sighed sadly. "I have no secrets from you, Braklarn. Do you believe him to be sincere?"

"I do. I believe your father has finally realised his error in judgement, and wishes to make amends."

"That is good news indeed," Jindara replied, rising from her seat and gazing out of her window at the setting sun. "If my mother is watching from Paradise, she would be glad, I think."

Braklarn approached and gently embraced her. "I think you're right." She turned in his arms, and pressed her lips to his.

Night was fast approaching, and almost everyone in the cart was dozing off. Except for Dranjari, who feigned sleep to blend in with the others, and Nerlarina, who had no need for sleep. She watched the others drift slowly into unconsciousness, wondering what the purpose of such a state of being could be. Clearly something important, as the humans seemed to do it every night, for several hours at a time. They had spent the last week travelling across the plains, crowded into Harndak's tent at night and the back of the cart during the day. To save room, and to ensure that nobody came to harm in their sleep, Nerlarina had returned to the whole every night. She was about to do the same tonight, when Kandrina suddenly asked a question.

"So why do we need to go to the dwarven villages anyway?"

Dranjari's eyes flickered open. "Partly so that Enkarini can learn about alchemy and magic. That reminds me; Remlika, you should be sending a message to your friends to let them know where you were heading," she told the mage.

"Right, I'll find a place to cast when we stop." She shook her head slightly, rubbed her eyes, and glanced out of the back of the cart. "We're almost there, aren't we? I think those hills are near the first village, if I remember those old maps correctly."

Harndak replied sleepily. "I think we're close. There's a few lights flickering over there," he pointed towards a large shadow in the distance, where the others could indeed see a few pinpricks of light.

The shadow grew steadily larger, and more lights became visible as they approached the village. They were stopped at the village gates by a pair of spear-wielding sentries. "Halt, strangers. What be y'r business 'ere?" one of them asked sharply, holding his spear across the path.

Lacking a comprehensible answer, Harndak and the others looked back at Dranjari. "Business of utmost importance. We seek a meeting with your leaders on the matter of the human priests," she told them.

The sentries glanced at each other, still holding their spears across the path. It was clear that they were reluctant to trust humans, which was unsurprising considering the state of relations between the two races. They were about to ask another question when Nerlarina drifted down from the back of the cart.

"These people are honest. I can vouch for them," she crackled.

They exchanged another glance before the darker-haired sentry nodded emphatically. "A'right, if y' say they be worth trustin'." He raised his spear and opened the gates to allow the cart through. "Not many of y'r kind been about f'r a bit, tis good to see one of y'. Enjoy y'r stay."

"Thank you very much." Nerlarina drifted along after the cart, which had rolled on ahead through the open gates.

"How did you get them to do that?" Remlik asked her curiously when she caught up with them.

"We have been friends with the dwarves for many years now. They trust us, and our judgement," she explained. "They are not so trusting of your kind, as you may have guessed."

They rolled up to an inn, the sign showing a bucking horse, and Harndak stopped the horses. "Let's see if we can get a few rooms here for the night," he said, jumping down and stretching. It had been a long journey. He wandered into the building, Nerlarina following behind in case she was needed.

"I'd better go. I think I hear Talri-Pekra calling me," Dranjari said. "See you all in the morning." She faded away.

Remlika watched her disappear. "She is one strange woman. Right, I'll catch up with you all in there after calling Braklarn." She meandered off down the street, searching for a quiet place to cast.

"Let's get in there. It's freezing," Kandrina said. Gently, she picked up her sleeping sister and followed her father into the inn. The second she walked through the door, she caught a glimpse of something flying towards her, and quickly ducked. A bottle smashed above the door frame. "What...?" she cried, inaudible above the noise in the bar.

Remlik entered after her, stooping to avoid the low ceiling. "Looks like someone started a bar brawl," he shouted to her. "I can see your father, he's in that corner," pointing over the dwarves' heads to an upturned table in a corner near the stairs. They made their way across the room with difficulty, Enkarini miraculously still sleeping, and ducked down behind the table with Harndak.

"This was going on when I came in," he yelled above the ruckus. "I don't know where Nerlarina went, she seemed to vanish just after I opened the door."

A blinding light flashed through the room, then everything went dark. "Will you lot calm down now?" came a crackling voice in the dark. Silence fell, and someone lit a lantern. Smashed bottles and broken chairs littered the floor, and a few dwarves stood frozen in the midst of hitting one another.

"That's better." A glowing cloud coalesced in mid air, which resolved into Nerlarina. "Now, my friends would like to get a room for the night. Harndak, talk to the bar lady."

As the patrons sheepishly returned to their usual pursuits of drinking and card games, Harndak approached the kindly woman behind the bar. "Hello. I'd like to rent a couple of rooms, if you have any," he said with a nervous smile. The dwarf woman smiled back, and they arranged two rooms for the group.

Kandrina took Enkarini upstairs while Remlik helped clear up some of the mess. "How did you manage that?" he asked Nerlarina. Yawning, he reconsidered. "On second thoughts, tell me in the morning. It's getting late," she said.

"Alright. I shall return to the whole until morning, I think. You should all be fine now." Nerlarina replied, before transforming back into the cloud and floating out of a nearby window.

Remlika entered shortly after, and looked around at the remaining mess. "What happened in here?" she asked.

"Twas nought but a simple disagreement over cards, to begin with," replied a surly looking dwarf near the door. "T'only became a fight after everyone else involved 'emselves. Didn't 'elp when all y' tall folks started walkin' in…" his voice trailed off into disgruntled grumbling. Remlika walked across to the table her brother had just righted, and the dwarf returned to his beer, occasionally throwing a baleful glance towards the humans who sat in the corner.

"So how are Braklarn and Wordarla?" Remlik enquired, ignoring the muttering, staring dwarves.

"Quite well. Wordarla seemed excited when I told her where we are, she says she's going to head out and join us," Remlika replied. "Has Harndak managed to get us some rooms?"

Remlik nodded. "Kandi and her sister went up already. I'll head up myself in a moment; I just thought I'd help clear up a little first." He glanced around the room, and decided to leave the dwarves to deal with the rest of the mess. "You coming?" he asked his sister as he headed for the stairs.

"Certainly. After a week sleeping in that freezing cold tent, I could do with a decent night's rest," Remlika yawned as she followed him up.

Dranj-Aria appeared in the pavilion, still wearing the guise of her aspect. "You called, Talri?"

The goddess of knowledge frowned at her. "Yes, about half an hour ago. What took you so long?" She raised a hand as Dranj-Aria began to explain.

"Forget it, it doesn't matter now. The Creator awakes."

"Ah." The goddess of time stepped back a little, to watch from behind the other gods as Vrenid-Malchor slowly opened his eyes. A small smirk crept onto her face, as she knew the others were about to get a serious telling off for neglecting the mortals.

"What are you all staring at me for?" He looked to the right, to check his vision orb that showed an overview of the mortal realm. A few moments of silence ensued, then – "What have you all been playing at while I slept? The mortals are in complete disarray! My high priest has become a fanatical lunatic! They're all being killed arbitrarily, and in our names! Tell me you have done something to stop this," he said.

"We do have a plan," Ralor-Kanj said quickly. "We're all going to appear to our respective high priests, and tell them that their actions are unacceptable…" His voice trailed off. Now he had to explain it, it seemed like a rather feeble plan.

"That's pathetic!" Vrenid-Malchor exclaimed. "You honestly think they would listen to you now? With the attitude I can see they've taken, your aspects would most likely be executed. I sincerely hope you can come up with something better, or will I have to deal with this myself?"

"We could always leave them be," Somri-Galin suggested. "I for one am rather enjoying…"

"We are not leaving them in this state," Ralor-Kanj said, cutting him off mid-sentence. He frowned slightly, clearly thinking hard. "I suppose we could do things the old way; you know, a bit of smiting here and there, maybe some grand demonstration of displeasure…"

The Creator actually banged a fist on the arm of his throne. "I am not orchestrating another Great Melting! Why do you think I've been asleep for so long? I expected better than this; if I'd known you were going to let things get this bad I wouldn't have left you in charge! And what are you giggling at?" he shouted, glaring over the other gods' heads at Dranj-Aria, who had just stuffed her knuckles in her mouth to stifle her laughter.

Dranj-Aria stepped forward, still grinning but attempting to control herself. "Actually, while this lot have been up here making useless plans, I have been in the mortal realm working towards a solution."

They all stared at her. "Alright then, enlighten me. What have you been doing down there?" the Creator asked her.

"I have been helping the girl Kandrina – you should be able to see her in your orb – to learn some of the truth about the world outside of the

People's lands. She was – will be extremely useful to us in dealing with the priests," she explained. She always made an extra effort to control her tenses when speaking to the Creator. "She is staying with the dwarves at the moment, and come sunrise I will be heading back down to help her convince them to assist the People. She has also made contact with the energy beings, and they have begun to teach her their ways."

Vrenid-Malchor looked impressed. "Very well, I shall observe your solution. As for the rest of you, return to your own domains and get on with your own business. Dranj-Aria and I will deal with this situation from now on." He sat back and glared at them until they faded away.

Enkarini awoke at first light. At first, she wondered where she was, because when she fell asleep she had still been on the cart. She pushed the blankets out of the way, and climbed over her sleeping sister to look out of the window. Twitching the thin curtain aside, she looked down and saw several groups of short, slightly odd-looking people making their way through the streets. Guessing they must be dwarves, she crept out of the room and quietly went down the stairs, to take a closer look through a downstairs window.

"Y' be out of y'r bed early, young'un," came a gruff voice from her left. "I was always giv'n to thinkin' y' tall folks slept late."

She turned to see an orange-bearded dwarf watching her from a seat by the door. She couldn't quite see, but it looked like he was smiling. "My father and sister are still sleeping. I usually wake up before them," she said. He had very dark brown eyes, with no whites, just like Nerlarina had told her on the journey. His beard was long and fuzzy, but he had very little hair on top of his head, making it look as though his head was on upside-down. Enkarini smiled back at him, thinking he looked friendly.

The dwarf's beard twitched. "Aye, tis the same with our young'uns. They always be up with the dawn birds, watchin' the sun as she rises." He took a pipe from his pocket and snapped his fingers, producing a small flame that he used to light his pipe.

Enkarini was fascinated. "Are you a magician?" she asked him.

He chuckled. "Nay lass, twasn't magic I used. Tis alchemy," he told her. "We c'n use magic, unlike y'r lightnin' friend, tis just that we prefer not to. Y' interested in such things, are y'?"

"I'd like to learn, yes. I know a lady at home, Wordarla I think her name is, and she's shown me a few things already," she babbled excitedly, remembering the short lady she had met on her trip to Tewen last summer.

"Wordarla, y' say? Well I'll be. There's a name I haven' heard in years," said the dwarf. "Y' say she's livin' in y'r lands, then?"

Enkarini nodded. "Do you know her too?"

"Aye, though she doesn't know me. Tis likely best all round if things were to stay that way," he said sadly. He stared glumly at the floor for a few seconds before changing the subject. "Y know, if y' care to learn alchemic arts, y' might do well to stick around 'ere for a bit. There be many more teachers 'ere than back in y'r lands. N' if the lightnin' folk trust y', so do we."

"Really? That would be great," she exclaimed. "I'll ask Father as soon as he wakes up."

Upstairs, Kandrina rolled over in her sleep. She was dreaming that she was out on the plains near Manak, playing mock hunting games with her brother as they had often done as children. Someone kept calling her name though, and when she turned to answer them the dream faded.

"Kandrina, wake up. We've got things to do, though none of them will work. But we should try," said a voice, getting clearer as Kandrina reluctantly awoke.

"What things?" she asked, rubbing her eyes. She worried for an instant where Enkarini had gone, until she heard a giggle from downstairs. "What's she doing down there?"

"Your sister is beginning her alchemy lessons," Dranjari replied, smiling. "Don't worry, she'll be perfectly safe here. So will the others. You, Nerlarina and I have to meet with the dwarven council elders, so look smart. We'll wait outside for you," she said, tossing a dress onto the bed and leaving the room.

Kandrina threw the blankets off and dressed quickly, wondering when Dranjari had organised this meeting. She dragged a brush through her hair, and slipped her shoes on before heading downstairs. Noticing Enkarini ensconced in a corner with a dwarf, who appeared to be producing flames from thin air, she crept out of the door quietly so as not to disturb them.

"How are you this morning?" crackled Nerlarina.

"Sleepy," Kandrina yawned. In the distance, she could see a rather impressive building. It looked like it had at least ten floors, something unheard of in the People's towns and villages. Many of the shops and houses they passed also had several floors, and Kandrina couldn't help staring at them, wondering how they stayed up rather than collapsing under their own weight. There were also glowing globes outside some of the doors, and similar globes on posts down the side of the street. Kandrina wondered what they were, and decided to ask someone when she returned to the inn. "So how did you persuade the council to meet with us, Dranjari?" she asked as they began walking up the street.

"I didn't. But I knew they weren't busy this morning, so we managed to get in and speak to them," she replied. "Like I said, they decide not to help in the end anyway, but we should at least try. It would look really weird if we'd come all this way just to get your sister some alchemy tuition." She skipped ahead a little, whistling an old tavern song about an ancient Chief, who had been convinced he could control the sun.

Nerlarina looked puzzled. "Are all of your gods this... peculiar?" she asked quietly.

"I don't know," Kandrina answered. "She's the only one I've ever met."

They continued walking, attracting a little attention from the dwarves they passed on the way. Some smiled and nodded or waved at Nerlarina, others merely looked quizzically at Kandrina and Dranjari. Kandrina smiled amicably at those who caught her eye, wondering what exactly they thought of her. She knew from her history lessons that many younger dwarves had never actually seen a human; it had been almost seventy years since the two races had been close. They had gradually drifted apart since then, the respective religious leaders becoming more uncomfortable with the subtle differences between the faiths. Thirty years ago, the human priests had actually threatened to execute the remaining dwarves if they remained in the People's lands.

They reached the council halls surprisingly quickly. As they approached, the doors slid aside into the walls. "They're called electric doors," Nerlarina explained, seeing the bemused look on Kandrina's face. "Something we taught them, how to generate energy to power things."

"Oh. And the globes of light outside use the same energy, I assume?"

"Yes. Most of the dwarves' lights work in the same way, that's how I was able to affect the lights in the inn last night."

The entrance hall was simply decorated; panelled walls and a stone floor, lit by a larger version of the light globes in the street. A few portraits hung on the walls, presumably of celebrated councilmen and women; Kandrina could see small plaques under them that seemed to have names on. There was a polished wood desk in the centre of the room, between two wide, curving staircases that led up to the next floor. A young dwarf sat behind it, immersed in paperwork. She glanced up as the three women approached. "C'n I 'elp y'?" she asked politely, looking mainly at Nerlarina.

"We'd like to speak to the council, please," Dranjari said. "Very important business, and I know they're not busy today. We're happy to wait a while."

The dwarf behind the desk flipped through a few diary pages before nodding. "Well, y' c'n go on up then. Y' might be waitin' a couple of hours, but y' should be in before midday. Tis on the seventh floor, main room. If y' get lost, just ask someone to show y' the way."

They thanked her and headed up one of the staircases. Since the halls had been built for dwarves, it wasn't far to the seventh floor. They got up there quickly and took seats in a small waiting room with about half a dozen others. Dranjari closed her eyes and seemed to enter a meditative state, while the other two made conversation with the others who were waiting.

At length, they were called into the council chambers. They were escorted by a couple of well-dressed assistants into a large room, with several windows. The sunlight streamed in, quite bright for the time of year, and made more so by the remaining snow scattered around outside. Three elderly, but still robust dwarves waited around a large square table.

"Take a seat, ladies. We hear y' be havin' some important business to talk about?" one of them said enquiringly. He had steel-coloured hair and jade green eyes, that reminded Kandrina of her sister.

"We do. We're here to request some help with a situation," Dranjari said. "It will probably take a little time to explain, but if you can help it would be greatly appreciated."

They began telling the dwarves what had been happening in the People's towns, each of them adding points they felt the others had missed. "So, will you help us?" Kandrina asked after nearly an hour.

"Maybe. We'll be needin' to talk with t'other village councils, mind. Y' say y' be stayin' at the Buckin' Horse?" the steel-haired dwarf asked. "We'll send y' a messenger there once we decide. Til then, y' enjoy y'r stay here." He smiled, and called the assistants to escort them back out of the halls.

They made their way back to the inn, noticing the streets were a lot busier than earlier. They passed several groups of dwarves clutching tankards and singing songs. When they reached the inn, they found the bar full of dwarves, making a lot of noise. Kandrina spotted her old tutor and his sister in a corner, playing a strange game with pointed sticks. She went over to join them, as Dranjari and Nerlarina both seemed to disappear.

"What game is this?" she asked, raising her voice so Remlik could hear her.

Remlik paused in his throwing. "They call it 'darts'. What you've got to do is throw these things at that board over there, and try to hit the small circle in the centre," he said, pointing at a wooden board on the wall that had different coloured circles painted on it. It looked a little like a smaller version of the archery targets Perlak had practised with. "You get fifty points for the centre circle, forty for the next one out, then thirty and so on. Here, have a go." He handed Kandrina a dart.

She threw it, missing the board entirely and putting a small hole in the paint on the wall. "I think I need more practice," she said, raising a few laughs from the dwarves who were watching.

"Good evening, Talri," said Dranj-Aria as she appeared in the pavilion.

The goddess of knowledge glanced over the top of her book. "Good evening Dranj-Aria. Is there something I can help you with?"

"Yes, there is. I need you to speak to one of your acolytes," Dranj-Aria said, smiling. "Her name is Crenkari, she lives in the small village called Pokole."

"Would this have anything to do with your solution to the mortals' troubles, perchance?"

Dranj-Aria winked at the other goddess. "It most certainly would. See, your acolyte and one of my priestesses were incredibly helpful to young Kandrina and her friends, so we need to go and speak to them so they can be in the right place to have met each other."

"Where exactly is the right place?"

"The town of Tewen, in the alchemist's shop. She needs to be there on eighth day, two weeks from now. Would you speak to her?"

"Very well," Talri-Pekra agreed after a moment's deliberation. She located her acolyte and sent a vision to her.

Crenkari jumped as a warm hand brushed her arm. She had thought she was alone in the library, and had been tidying the shelves. "Hello?" she called, wondering who had crept in without being noticed. A tall, slender woman stood next to her, watching her intently with unfathomably deep brown eyes. "Are – are you looking for something?" she asked, suddenly very unsure of herself.

The woman smiled. "Actually, I was looking for you, Crenkari. I have an important message for you."

The question of how this strange woman knew her name seemed to die on Crenkari's lips. Instead, she asked, "What message?"

"There is someone you need to meet. A young woman named Kandrina. Travel to the town of Tewen, and be in the alchemist's shop on eighth day, two weeks from now."

Crenkari nodded mutely, and the woman disappeared. "Wait, who are you?" she called.

"I think you know that already," the woman's voice echoed.

The young acolyte brushed a few loose strands of fiery red hair away from her face, and left the library to prepare for a long journey. She wondered how long it had been since Talri-Pekra had last appeared to anyone.

As Talri-Pekra recalled her mind to the pavilion, she noticed Dranj-Aria had vanished again. She shook her head and returned to her book.

The goddess of time had gone back to the mortal realm, to visit her high priestess in Tewen. "Yantrola," she exclaimed, making the plump old woman leap into the air in surprise.

"Ah! What…? Oh, hello," the priestess said. "You startled me. So, what causes your sudden appearance in my humble temple, my lady?"

Dranjari smiled. "Just a quick message. Kandrina will be arriving back here next week, and it's about time the two of you met up."

Yantrola smiled back at her goddess. "Of course. Anywhere in particular?"

"I'll be sending her here, accompanied by myself and a few friends. Be seeing you," Dranjari said, before vanishing back to the dwarven village. She reappeared in the Bucking Horse inn just before the council messenger arrived.

Remlika was the first to realise she was back. "Where did you disappear to?" she asked.

"Here and there," Dranjari replied cryptically. "We should be receiving a messenger in a moment. Is Nerlarina back yet?"

"Yes, she's upstairs with Kandrina and Remlik. I'll go and fetch them," Remlika answered, standing slowly to avoid bumping her head on the ceiling. As both she and her brother were quite tall, they had to walk stooped while inside the dwarves' buildings. The others were all that little bit shorter, so low ceilings did not trouble them so much.

Kandrina led the way back down a few minutes later, just as the messenger arrived in the bar. "What's the word?" she asked him.

The ruddy-faced dwarf cleared his throat. "The councils 'ave decided they can't 'elp y' with y'r priests, but should y' manage to sort 'em out, we'd gladly foster a friendship with y'. Sorry to be the bearer of bad news, lass," he said.

"That's quite alright," Dranjari told him. "We've found a few friends back home who can help. I'm sure by this time next year it will be sorted."

The messenger grinned through his bushy beard, saluted her, and left the inn.

"You've been up to something, haven't you?" Kandrina said, watching Dranjari closely. She received only a smirk in reply.

Chapter Seven: Truths Revealed

As the last of the snow melted, Wordarla approached the dwarven gates cautiously. Though she had always known herself to be part dwarf, she had never visited their lands, and was unsure of the reception she would have.

"'ello there," she said to the sentries when she reached the gates. "I be lookin' for some friends of mine, tall folk all. Said they got 'ere a week or so back, y' seen 'em?"

The white-haired sentry nodded. "Aye, we've all been hearin' about 'em. Word is they be stayin' at the Buckin' Horse. Tis simple enough to find, y' just follow the main street til y' reach the sign. If y' get lost, just follow the noise," he said with a grin.

"Thank y' very much," Wordarla replied, as he opened the gates for her to ride through. She reached the Bucking Horse quickly, and dismounted outside. After tossing a coin to the young boy who came to lead her horse into a nearby stable, she entered the busy inn.

Remlik was the first to spot her. "Wordarla, over here!" he called, beckoning her over to a table near the dartboard, where most of the group were sat.

"How was the journey? I'm guessing the snow has mostly gone by now."

"Tis all melted; I think we'll be gettin' some warmer weather comin' through now," she told him. "So, what have y' lot been up to since last time we spoke?"

"Well, my sister has begun learning alchemy," said Kandrina. "And we spoke to the village council four days ago, they said they couldn't help us with the priests but they're happy to start a friendship once we've sorted it out."

"That reminds me, we ought to be heading back to Tewen at the end of the week," Dranjari cut in. "There's some people you need to meet. I'm Dranjari, by the way," she said, introducing herself to Wordarla.

The orange-haired alchemist smiled. "Aye, Remlika told us about y' when she called. Surprised to have met y', I think. So, where's the young lass?" she asked. She was curious how Enkarini was getting on; Remlika had mentioned something about the girl starting to learn some basic alchemy from the inn's proprietor.

"Over by the stairs, I think. Father's with her, watching her lesson," Kandrina replied.

Wordarla wandered over to the stairs to see what the lesson was about. She had noticed the unusual talent the girl had shown when they made the joy potion for Harndak, and had considered taking her on as a student herself.

"So y' see lass, tis a simple matter of balancin' out y'r materials. Once y' get that right, the rest's easy as pie. Go on, 'ave a try," said the bushy-bearded dwarf as he handed her two leather pouches.

Enkarini took a pinch of yellow powder out of one pouch, and a pinch of white powder from the other. Wordarla stood and watched, as the little girl dabbed a little of each onto finger and thumb, and snapped them together to produce a spark. She giggled in delight, and did it again to show her father, who was also standing by to watch.

The dwarf teaching her smiled beneath his beard. "Y'll make a fine alchemist some day, lass. It'll be my pleasure to teach y'." He looked over to where Wordarla stood. "Seems y' got y'self an audience, too. Come to watch the lesson?" he asked.

"Aye, she be the sister of a friend of mine," she replied, watching the little girl producing sparks from her powdered fingers. "I'd been thinkin' of teachin' her myself, back in Tewen. Showed her how to mix a joy potion last summer. Y' have anywhere y' can teach her that sort of thing?"

"There be a back room 'ere, we'll use that. I be Worrald, owner of this 'ere inn. Y' say y' live in Tewen?"

Wordarla smiled. "That I do. Name's Wordarla, I run a magic n' alchemy shop back there. Tis a pleasure to meet y', Worrald."

"Oh, hello Wordarla," Enkarini interrupted, having run out of powder on her fingers. "I'm learning to make fire by clicking, though I haven't got past making sparks yet. When did you get here?"

"Only a few minutes ago, lass. Y' seem to have a knack for the art, if y' don't mind me sayin' so."

As Wordarla chatted with the little girl, she didn't notice Worrald staring at her in disbelief. He had always known he had a daughter, with a human woman he had known and loved deeply over thirty summers ago, but had taught himself not to think about her over the years. He had been forced to abandon the woman days before she gave birth, and due to circumstances had been unable to return. Initially he had cursed the humans' priests for forcing the two races apart, but had eventually convinced himself that perhaps the child was better off without him around, as he thought of himself as a rather unsuitable parent. Now it seemed that the daughter whom he knew only by name had come to him, and he was completely uncertain of how to act.

While she chattered to the young girl, he made a hasty decision to act casually.

"So, y' plannin' to stay long? I can show y' around if y'd like," said Worrald. "Tis a fine little village 'ere, n' I be sure I can find y' a room."

"Y' know, I might just stick around for a while. Twould be good to explore these lands a bit." Wordarla glanced around the bar. "N' there's a few 'ere I'd like to meet, if I get the chance. My father comes from around 'ere, or so I been told. Never met him though, he had to leave Mam before I came along."

"You two look a lot like each other," Enkarini remarked. "And your names are similar too. Are you related?"

Harndak intervened. "Enkarini, you really mustn't ask personal things like that. I do apologise, she can be a little nosy at times."

"Why not? Besides, Worrald said he knew Wordarla anyway," she whined, completely unaware of her new teacher's embarrassment.

Wordarla, however, was looking carefully at the older, bearded dwarf. "Now y' mention it, there is a likeness 'twixt us. Y' ever visited the People's lands, Worrald?"

He fidgeted in his chair. "Aye, a long while back. Before the troubles began," he said. "Y' know all about that, I guess, from y'r history. Y' must understand, though, there was those what didn't want to leave. I be certain y'r father would've stayed with y'r mother, if he'd been given a choice in the matter," he implored as Harndak led Enkarini away quietly, to leave the two dwarves to discuss things privately.

"Aye, I'm sure he would. Me mother told me about him, n' I reckon he's a good man," Wordarla replied. After Enkarini's remark, she suspected that she was speaking to her father, but wanted to be sure, so she threw in a leading question. "Tis a terrible thing, bein' forced to leave the woman carryin' y'r unborn child. If it were y', would y' ever return to see her, if y' had the chance?"

"I'd like to, but I don't reckon I'd be a good father. Maybe y'd be better off wi'out knowin' me, lass," he said without thinking. A few seconds later, he realised what he had just said and bit his lip apprehensively.

"Well, maybe we should get to know each other before we start sayin' things like that," Wordarla said kindly. "Mam always said y' were too modest for y'r own good. Tis nice to finally meet y', Dad."

Worrald looked long and hard at the woman who had sat down next to him. She was smiling, which was good. "Y' don't carry a grudge 'gainst me f'r abandonin' y' n' y'r mother, then?"

"Course not. Tis not as though y' snuck off in the dead of night, I know the history of what was goin' on back then, n' why y' all left. N' besides, I'm in no place to be lecturin' y' about it. I could've come to find y' any time, but always been too shy to do so. Still, tis no matter now. The past is past, n' we're here now. C'n I get y' a drink?"

Worrald grinned. "Aye, n' get y'self one too. Y' c'n tell me all about y'r shop," he said, looking forward to finally getting to know his daughter.

Birds chattered outside the window, causing Jindara to stir. She turned, half asleep, and snuggled closer to the warm presence next to her. An arm crept around her shoulders and held her closely.

"Ma'am, I regret disturbing you so early, but you must awake," an irritating voice shouted as the chamber door was flung open. It banged against the wall, making Jindara and her bedmate start. "There is news from your father," her stout assistant said, flinging open the heavy curtains and allowing the dawn light into the room.

The Vice-Chief grudgingly sat up, dragging the bed covers with her to cover her modesty. "Very well. Kindly leave us to dress, we will receive the news in a few minutes," she told him shortly. The assistant bowed, and left the room. Jindara sighed. "Well, it looks as though we have to get back to business. Will you sit in on this morning's council, Braklarn?"

The mage pushed his hair out of his eyes. "If that is what my lady wishes," he said with a roguish grin. He leant over to kiss her before getting out of the bed and picking his robe up from the floor, where he had thrown it the night before in a fit of passion.

They left Jindara's personal chambers a few minutes later, ignoring the disapproving look from her assistant, and proceeded into the main halls to receive the dawn news. Jindara took her place on the decorative chair that rested upon a raised dais, leaving Braklarn and her assistant to stand either side. She gestured to the young man waiting patiently with a scroll in his hand, and he began reading from it.

"Urgent news from the Chief of the People. My sons and daughters, it seems the People are in jeopardy. Not from the Demons, or the wild predators that roam the plains, but from within our own temples. My own blindness has allowed this situation to become so dire, and I make no excuses. I cannot act against them, on fear of death, but I ask of you this; find a way to unite the People, and prevent any more needless deaths in the names of the gods. Do right by our People, and learn from my mistakes." The young man rolled up the scroll and waited for a response.

Stunned that her father had actually admitted that he had been wrong about something, Jindara blurted out the first thing that came into her mind. "The Chief has a new scribe, then?" She shook her head. "Forget that bit. Tell him that I will do my utmost to help the People through this situation. Are you running to the other towns and villages?" she asked the lad.

"I will be shortly, Vice-Chief. Was there anything else you wanted to add?"

"No, that will be all, thank you," she replied, dismissing the messenger. He bowed and left, running to his next destination. "Is there anything else that needs my attention this morning?" she asked her assistant.

He consulted a short scroll on a nearby table. "Nothing vital, just a few disputes between shop owners and the arrival of several more refugees from Manak," he said. "Oh yes, and the arrival of an acolyte of Talri-Pekra from the village of Pokole. Apparently she has taken up residence in the library in the town centre, on the instructions of the goddess herself. As I said, nothing overly important."

"Good. In that case, I shall return to my bed for an hour." She rose from her chair and swept down the dais, turning at the door to her chambers. "Are you coming, Braklarn?" she called back.

The bushy-haired mage grinned, and went after her. The stocky assistant by the chair scowled at them as they left.

"Father, stop fretting about me, I'll be fine," Kandrina told Harndak as she climbed into the cart and settled herself between Dranjari and Nerlarina. "I've got this lot to look after me. Stay with Enkarini, she'll need you more, and it wouldn't be fair to drag her away now."

The little girl smiled up at her big sister, green eyes shining in the sunlight. "Come back soon, so I can show you more alchemy," she said.

"I will. I'm sure you'll be very good at it when I see you next," Kandrina replied. "And take care of Father, you know what he's like," she added with a wink.

The others said their goodbyes to Wordarla. "Are you sure you won't come back with us?" Remlik asked for the umpteenth time.

Wordarla grinned up at her friends in the back of the cart. "I be sure. Tis too interestin' 'ere to be goin' back there. Though I'm sure y'll have y'r fair share of excitement," she said with a wink. "Y' go ahead, we'll be meetin' up again soon. N' tell my brother that he's to take care of my shop while I'm 'ere," she called to Remlika, who was sitting next to her brother in the front of the cart.

Remlik snapped the reins to get the horses moving, and they headed back towards the village gates. The dwarven sentries opened the gates as they approached, and waved them through. For the next week they rolled steadily across the plains, chatting about nothing in particular and watching the animals that came out to play in the spring sun. When they passed the Colourless' city, Nerlarina decided to go back there for a while, promising to meet them in Tewen's library in a few days.

On the last day of their journey, they stopped for a meal next to a large dip in the earth. Kandrina stared into it, lost in memories. She had helped to dig that hole six summers ago, along with her brother and several other children. They had been out on the plains playing, and Perlak had got the idea in his head that there were untold riches lying in a cave below the plains, so all the children had got together to dig down and find the treasure. They had never found it, of course, but the pit remained, filling with grass and flowers over the years.

"Kandrina, come back," Dranjari snapped her fingers by the young woman's ear. "We're moving. We'll be in Tewen by nightfall."

Kandrina blinked and looked around. "Oh, alright." She stood and climbed back into the cart.

"So, what were you remembering?" Dranjari asked as the horses reluctantly started plodding onwards. "I guessed you were reminiscing about something, you had that distant look."

"I was just thinking about my brother. We used to play together out here all the time," Kandrina replied. She looked across at the goddess' aspect, who was watching her interestedly. "You're probably the best one to ask, but I understand if you can't tell me. What did happen to Perlak? I know what the priests told us, but it can't be true."

Dranjari looked at her sadly for a moment before answering. "I can't tell you, but I can show you, if you'd like." She held out her hand. "Take my hand, and shut your eyes."

Kandrina obeyed, and felt a sudden breeze blowing her hair about. She opened her eyes and found herself floating in mid-air above the moonlit plains. She heard men's voices on the ground, and looked down to see her brother, and two other men. They were on a night hunt, clearly tracking something from the way they moved. One of the others made a hand signal, and the three hunters spread out and ducked below the long grass. They would have been difficult to spot from ground level, but Kandrina could see them easily from her vantage point in the air.

As Perlak moved forwards, she drifted after him, as though a long string connected them. He seemed to be going in a different direction to the other two, and she wondered if he had lost his bearings. They continued onwards for several minutes, Perlak creeping through the grass and Kandrina floating silently above him, and ended up quite a distance from the other two men. The young man stood and looked around, whistling softly. When he did not receive a response, he turned and began heading off towards the hills. Kandrina looked and saw a flickering light, which could have been a fire. She followed after him again.

As they got closer, they could see a couple of shadows moving around near the light. Perlak called out in greeting, thinking it was his two companions. Kandrina could see more though, and cried out to her brother in warning. The light was not a fire, but a pulsating globe of magic; and the shadows around it were inhuman. Perlak couldn't hear her though, and continued towards the light and the strange shadows. One of the things near the light had heard his shout, and was moving towards him at an alarming speed. Belatedly, Perlak realised something was wrong and turned to run, but the creature immobilised him with a spell and dragged him to the light.

The globe grew brighter, and Kandrina saw that the creatures had huge, scaly bodies and almost serpentine faces. She could see the terror in her brother's eyes, and called to him again in vain. She realised that she could not be seen or heard, as she was simply watching a vision of the past. The creatures made snarling, hissing sounds to each other, and suddenly one of them raised a clawed hand and incinerated the young man. The vision faded to darkness, and Kandrina awoke in the cart, weeping openly.

"Kandi? What's wrong?" Remlik had handed the reins to his sister for the rest of the journey, and had climbed through to the back of the cart to find his former pupil unconscious and crying.

Kandrina hugged him fiercely, and looked around for Dranjari. "I asked her what had happened to Perlak, I mean really happened, because I know now that it wasn't the Colourless. She said she couldn't tell me, but she gave me a vision of what happened and… where did she go?"

"Dranjari? I don't know, she just disappeared. What did she show you?" Remlik asked gently, handing the girl a scrap of material so she could dry her eyes.

Kandrina took a deep breath and swallowed hard. "Perlak was out on a night hunt, with two others. He got lost in the grass on the plains, and he saw a light that looked like a fire but it wasn't, it was a magic light globe. There were things around it; they looked… almost like snakes, but with arms and legs. He tried to run away but they caught him and burned him alive," she said, dissolving into tears again.

Remlik held her tightly and stroked her hair. They stayed like that for the rest of the journey back to Tewen, and by the time they had reached Remlik's house Kandrina had fallen asleep in his arms. He carried her inside and laid her on his own bed while Remlika took the cart back to a hire shop. He lit a single candle and pulled a chair up to the bedside, and watched her until he too drifted into sleep.

He awoke some hours later, when the candle had burnt down to a stub. Kandrina had thankfully settled into a deep, undisturbed sleep. He would have gone back to sleep himself, but the woman near the door caught his attention. "You have some explaining to do," he whispered, walking over to the door and gesturing her through. "Why did you show her that? Surely you could have just said her brother was killed by lizard men. She cried for hours after you left."

Dranjari hung her head. "I know. It may seem unkind, but she's a strong woman. She needed to know about them, and see for herself what they're capable of," she said. "There were things going on in this world that you don't even know about yet, and Kandrina is a part of them, or will be. Just be there for her, and she'll be fine."

Remlik stared at her for a moment before nodding. "Alright. I suppose I should trust that you know what you're doing. She'll probably have a lot of questions when she wakes up, though. Are you staying somewhere?"

"Yes. I'll be at the Chieftain's Arms, two streets away. Come along at sunrise, there are a few things we need to talk about. Goodnight, Remlik." She faded away, and Remlik returned to the chair by the bedside to sleep.

The Chieftain's Arms was a very rough tavern. The regular clientele fell into two categories; burly thugs looking for a brawl, and criminals who came to split their loot and organise their next job. As a result, there were steel gratings across the windows, and the chairs and tables were fixed to the floor with bolts. But the ale was good, and the rooms were cheap, so it also attracted the odd traveller who had never visited before. They usually learnt their lesson the first time around. Dranjari had chosen it precisely because the majority of law-abiding people avoided it, meaning anything she discussed there was highly unlikely to reach the ears of the priests.

The bar was usually empty in the early mornings, except for the occasional unconscious man left on the floor from the previous night. Dranjari and the barman were the only ones in there that morning, and she was sitting at a table in the corner when Remlik and Kandrina walked in. The barman glanced up from the glass he was wiping and sneered at them before slouching off into a back room.

"Ignore him, he's just annoyed that I woke him up so early for a drink. Come and sit down," Dranjari said, beckoning them across the room. "Did you sleep well?" she asked Kandrina as she sat down.

"After a fashion. There are a few things I need to ask you," Kandrina replied shortly. "What were those creatures, and why did they kill my brother?"

Dranjari sighed. "They are beings from the north, beyond the hills. Your kind has not yet explored that far, but you will soon, and you ought to be forewarned of what you may encounter there. Your brother was unfortunate, he simply got too close to their scouts." She raised a hand to stall Remlik and Kandrina's interruptions. "You will discover more for yourselves when the time is right. For now, you have other things to concern yourselves with; namely forming alliances with the dwarves, elves and the Colourless. You will need them in the years to come." She looked the two mortals carefully in the eye, silently convincing them to wait for the answers to reveal themselves.

"She's right," Remlik said quietly after a few moments. "We should finish dealing with the problems we have now before we go looking for others. We can find out more about these lizard men later. You said last night there were some things we needed to talk about?" he asked.

"Yes. Once Nerlarina arrives, we headed to my temple to meet one of my priestesses. She's brilliant; you two really liked her. Anyway, she'll help teach people about the Colourless, along with someone else who you're not supposed to meet for another few days."

It only took Kandrina a few seconds to get her head around Dranjari's mixed-up tenses, as she was getting used to the way she spoke. "Right. So, Nerlarina will be arriving in a little while?"

"I'm already here," crackled a voice from the doorway. "How is everyone this morning?"

"Fairly well," Remlik answered. "Shall we get going then? I'm not sure we should hang around here any longer than we have to." Anyone who had lived in Tewen for more than a few weeks was well aware of the tavern's reputation, and tried to avoid spending too much time there.

Dranjari smirked. "Alright, let's go. I'll lead the way, it's not far to walk." She led the others through the streets of Tewen to the town centre, where a handful of merchants were beginning to set up their stalls for the day's market. As it was just past sunrise, there were very few others about, so they attracted a little attention from the few who had got up early. One merchant, on seeing Nerlarina, dropped his wares and ran back into his house. Trinkets rolled everywhere, some of them falling into drains, but the man seemed not to care, merely staring out of his window until they had passed.

They arrived at the temple quickly, and found the doors had already been flung wide open for them. A nervous acolyte waited to guide them in, but Dranjari dismissed her, saying "Go back to bed, I know you were up late with that young man from Bewein." The girl blushed deeply, and ran off. They continued on to the main hall, where Dranjari greeted an old priestess with a hug.

"You must be Kandrina," said the old woman, waving to the young, pale girl. "I'm Yantrola, it's nice to meet you at last. I'm not sure who you two are though," she said, pointing at Nerlarina and Remlik.

Kandrina smiled. The priestess reminded her of her great aunt, who lived over in one of Astator's fishing villages and had only visited them once. Her single visit, however, had stood out in Kandrina's mind because of the stories she had told; several tales of the old gods, lost dragons, dark spirits and strange people from other lands across the horizon. "This is Remlik, my old tutor. And this is Nerlarina; she's here representing the Colourless. Is there somewhere we can talk?"

Yantrola cackled, showing a few missing teeth. "We can talk here; there's nobody around. Except us, anyway," she tossed her flyaway grey hair back over her shoulder as she spoke. "Come and sit down, I'll have one of the acolytes fetch us some water." She led the three of them to a bench at the front of the hall, sat down and rang a small bell that she had apparently been keeping up her sleeve. An acolyte rushed out of a door by the altar, carrying a tray of glasses and a jug of water. The young girl set her tray down and bowed deeply, first to Yantrola and the others, then to Dranjari, who remained standing by the altar with a ridiculous grin on her face.

"So, my goddess tells me you've been off learning about the Colourless." Yantrola frowned slightly. "It still feels odd, calling them that. Anyway, what have you learned?"

Kandrina began telling the old priestess her story, starting when she was staked out by the high priest. Nerlarina helped clarify a few points, explaining things about her own kind that Kandrina had gotten slightly muddled; Remlik explained what had been going on in the dwarven villages while Kandrina sipped her water. Yantrola listened with interest, and after the others had told their story she nodded.

"It sounds like we've all been misled about you for quite a while," she said to Nerlarina. "And in turn, we've been misleading others. I for one would like to start setting the record straight, so I'll teach people who come here that your kind should not be feared," she proclaimed, standing up and stretching.

"So you'll help us?" Kandrina asked.

"I most certainly will. I'd like to know more, too, when you've got the time. I'm sure we'll become great friends." Yantrola turned to look at her goddess. "Until next time, lady." She bowed as deeply as her old joints would allow her to, and watched the small group leave.

By the end of the week, spring had well and truly set in. There were flowers blooming everywhere one looked, and the livestock on the farms had begun birthing. Odd rains still fell every so often, but they were warm rains, and didn't last long. Most people were spending longer outside enjoying the improved weather, but Kandrina couldn't face the cheerful sunshine. Remlik was poring through every book he owned, and a few he found in the library, for any mention of the bizarre lizard creatures Kandrina had described. Kandrina had read through some books as well, but mostly sat by herself thinking.

On eighth day that week, Remlika was on her way across town to pick up some more supplies from Wordarla's shop. She had told Braklarn to look after it, and he seemed to be doing so, in between visits to the Vice-Chief's chambers anyway. She had practically insisted that Kandrina should come along, saying that she was tired of watching the girl mope about the house. Kandrina had reluctantly agreed, if nothing else it would give her a change of scenery and maybe take her mind off the vision Dranjari had shown her.

They ambled through the streets, enjoying the bright sunshine that warmed the cobbled roads. There were rumours spreading through the town about what had happened at the beginning of the week, when Kandrina had visited Dranj-Aria's temple in the company of a Lightning Demon. A few people recognised her, as her pale complexion and golden hair made her stand out from the crowds. She ignored them all though, as she had done so many months ago in Manak, lost in her own thoughts of Perlak and strange lizard men. She had debated asking Nerlarina if she could find anything out, but had decided against it for the moment. She did not want to have to relate her vision to anyone else if she could help it.

"Braklarn, how are you today?" Remlika called as they entered the shop. "Finally been kicked out of Jindara's bed?"

The red-haired sorcerer winked amicably at her. "Only for today. I'm sure she'll call me back later on tonight," he replied. "What can I get you today then?"

"Just a few supplies," Remlika said, reeling off a short list of items she needed. Kandrina gazed around at the artefacts and potions in the room. Usually she would be fascinated, and be asking all sorts of questions about what they all were, but today she couldn't muster the enthusiasm. She noticed a young woman, barely a year older than herself, standing in a corner watching her. Wondering who she was, Kandrina left the two mages haggling over some arcane frippery or other and walked across to her.

The young woman spoke first. "Are you Kandrina? I was told that I had to meet you here, today. My name is Crenkari," she said, stepping forwards into a shaft of sunlight from a high window. The rays caught her hair and made it shimmer like a river of fire.

"I am. Who told you we had to meet?" Kandrina asked, thinking that Dranjari had something to do with it.

"I am but a simple acolyte of Talri-Pekra, but my goddess appeared to me, in the library of Pokole," said Crenkari. "She told me that I had to be here, now, to meet a young girl named Kandrina. I have no idea why though. Do you know why?"

"I have an idea. Dranjari said there was someone else I had to meet, who would help me teach people about the Colourless," Kandrina replied with a smile.

Crenkari looked confused. "What are the Colourless?"

Kandrina's smile grew wider. "You probably know them as Lightning Demons. Apparently I'm supposed to teach the People that they are not evil spirits to be feared," she told the bemused acolyte.

"I have always wondered about the Demons," Crenkari said. "Perhaps this is a gods-given opportunity to spread true knowledge of the world, rather than old-fashioned superstitions."

"Maybe it is," replied Kandrina. "Why don't you come back with me? You can meet Nerlarina. She's one of the Colourless, and has come to help us learn about their kind." The two young women left the shop and walked back down the road, discussing the Colourless on the way.

"What do you mean, Demons in the temples?" Jindara exclaimed, frustrated at her assistant's evasive attitude. "Speak plainly or do not speak at all, man. It is not as though there are people here we cannot trust."

The squat assistant threw a pointed look at Braklarn before continuing. "I am simply passing on the rumours that are circulating through Tewen, ma'am. Rumours tend to be vague at the best of times."

The Vice-Chief sighed wearily. Her assistant had been getting more cryptic lately, and it was beginning to chafe. She liked things to be set out as clearly as possible, not because she could not deal with complications, but because most of the time they were unnecessary. "And why, pray tell, are you informing me of rumours?"

"Unlike most, these particular rumours seem to be true. Many people have reported seeing a Lightning Demon, in the form of a beautiful woman, entering and exiting both the temple of Dranj-Aria and the library in the town square. She is reportedly accompanied by a young woman with pale gold hair, and occasionally a dark-skinned sorceress." He glanced at the scroll in his stubby hand before continuing. "People have been saying the temples have become corrupt, or that the Demons are trying to seize control of our priests. I myself have heard talk of strange lessons given in the library, scholars teaching that the Demons are not evil."

Braklarn interrupted. "If I may speak, my lady?" He waited for Jindara's nod before continuing. "What your assistant is saying is correct, if somewhat mangled by the public mill. I have first hand knowledge of what is happening, and if you wish I will tell you everything I know."

"I do wish," said Jindara, sitting up straighter in her chair upon the dais and frowning at him. "Please tell us everything, and explain why you did not tell me before now."

"I sincerely apologise, Jindara, but I was sworn to secrecy by several close friends of mine. You see, this is not simply a mortal matter." He raised a hand to silence the little man standing opposite him. "Dranj-Aria herself is involved, and has been walking among us directing this for many months now. I am given to understand that Talri-Pekra has also had a hand in it. An old friend of mine, Remlika, and her brother have been giving houseroom to a being called Nerlarina for several weeks. She is one of the Colourless, commonly called Lightning Demons."

There was an intake of breath around the room, followed by muttering from the advisers and gathered petitioners. Jindara's eyes widened. "Perhaps you should start at the beginning," she said when the murmurs had died down.

So Braklarn explained everything, starting with Kandrina's punishment by the Manak priests. He told the gathered people all he had heard from Remlika while they stayed at the Colourless' city, the dwarven village, and everything that they had informed him of since. "Now, the girl Kandrina is helping the priestess and acolyte teach people about the Colourless, so that everyone can learn that they are not demons to be afraid of."

The great hall was completely silent for a full minute after Braklarn finished speaking. Jindara's assistant stared at him as though he could not believe his eyes. Jindara rose slowly and walked towards him. "I would like to hear one of these lessons," she said quietly, looking deeply into the mage's amber eyes. "My assistant will deal with this morning's business, while we visit the temples." She walked past him and headed out of the doors. Braklarn followed, leaving the hall in a state of baffled stillness.

They walked through the busy streets to the temple of Dranj-Aria, Braklarn attempting to make conversation but Jindara rebuffed him each time. She was not pleased with the way he had kept his knowledge of this secret from her. On reaching the temple doors, they could see a far larger crowd inside than usual. Jindara took advantage of her station to get close to the front, where the priestess Yantrola was standing at the pulpit declaiming.

"And so I put to you, that these beings have not been sent from the depths of hell to torment us and steal our children, but rather they are from this world. They seek not to destroy us, simply to learn of us, that we can all just get along with each other. Seek out knowledge at the libraries should you wish to learn more, but most importantly do not fear the Colourless."

Parts of the crowd cried out in praise, others looked at each other in bewilderment. Jindara turned to Braklarn and whispered: "This is an unusual turn of events."

"It most certainly is," said a plump, purple haired woman next to them. "Although, I think it's rather pleasant to have a change of pace sometimes. Say, you're Jindara, right? You should come and meet the so-called Demon they're all talking about," she said with a grin.

Jindara narrowed her eyes at the strange woman. "Who are you?"

"She's Dranjari," Braklarn answered with a stifled laugh. "The aspect of the goddess of time. I told you this wasn't just a mortal matter."

The Vice-Chief stared from mage to aspect, and then threw up her hands. "I suppose I'd better go with you then. Obviously I have very little control over the situation," she said, following the two of them out of the crowded temple hall and through a side door. They emerged into a cosy, well furnished room where a young girl sat, apparently talking to a glowing cloud. The girl looked over when she heard the door open.

"Hello Dranjari. How's Yantrola's sermon doing?"

"Pretty well. She's trying to convince them to go and visit the libraries at the moment," Dranjari replied. "Anyway, I'm supposed to introduce you both to Jindara here. Nerlarina, it might be easier for her if you could resolve into something less fuzzy for a while."

Nerlarina obliged, becoming a beautiful, shining woman. Jindara could not help staring; she had never seen anything like it. "It is a pleasure to meet you, Jindara. Have you come to learn about my kind?"

Jindara sat heavily in the nearest chair, stunned by what was going on around her. "You… are one of the Lightning Demons?"

"We prefer the term 'Colourless', but essentially yes. I am here representing my kind, so that we can establish a friendship between our peoples," Nerlarina replied.

"And you are the girl Braklarn told me about? Kandrina?"

Kandrina nodded. "Yes. I assume he's told you everything that's been going on?"

"I've told her all I know," said Braklarn. "But there's a lot that you haven't let me in on. Perhaps you should explain it. After all, she is the Vice-Chief."

Nerlarina quickly explained the situation to Jindara, Kandrina and Dranjari throwing in odd bits she had missed. "So we have been teaching people about my kind, in the hopes that it will break the high priest's hold over everyone," she finished.

Jindara thought quietly for a moment. "What can I do to help?"

"Tell your father what's happening here. And get Ralor's priest to start teaching his congregations too," Dranjari replied. "If we all work at this, we had it sorted by the end of summer."

"Alright. Braklarn, would you go and speak to my father again?" The mage nodded. "And if anything like this happens again, tell me what you know straight away. You shouldn't keep secrets from the people you care about," she scolded him lightly.

Dranjari snickered. "I don't think you're one to talk about that," she told the Vice-Chief with a smirk.

Jindara turned to face her. "What are you talking about?"

Dranjari glanced down at Jindara's belly, raising her eyebrows. "You know what I'm talking about."

"What?" Braklarn looked between the two of them for a second until it clicked. "You're carrying a child?"

Jindara blushed bright red. "I wasn't going to tell you until I was absolutely certain, but I suppose I can be sure now," she mumbled. "I am carrying your child. Let's go back to my chambers, we can discuss it there. Then you can go to my father and inform him that he is to have a grandchild soon."

She inclined her head to the three others in the room, and left with Braklarn.

Jindar stood by the window, staring out across the blue-tinged sunlit plains. He remembered his first hunt as a boy, his father watching him as he chased down a large limij buck. He found himself longing for the simplicity of those days, before he had taken on the Chief's mantle and responsibilities. Had his great grandfather, Morendir, not united the tribes under one Chief, he would only have a small village to take care of instead of the entirety of the People. Lost in speculation, he only realised Braklarn had appeared behind him when the mage spoke.

"Chief Jindar, your daughter sends another message," said Braklarn.

Jindar turned to face the bushy-haired man. "Has she decided what to do about the priests?"

Braklarn smiled. "She has indeed, Chief. It is a complicated situation, but the essence of it is that we intend to educate the people about certain things, in the hope that people will see through the high priest's fabrications once they know the truth." He thought it best to avoid telling Jindar that the Colourless were involved for the moment. "There is something else as well, unrelated to the difficulties. Jindara is with child; my child."

Jindar stared at the sorcerer for a moment before responding. "I sincerely hope you intend to marry her, then. A member of the Chief's family should not be born to a lone mother," he said seriously.

"I most certainly intend to marry her," Braklarn replied, smiling. "I would not have any child of mine born out of wedlock either."

"Well then, my congratulations to you, and to Jindara also." The Chief smiled back at him. "Finally, there is some good news amongst all the trouble. Go, take care of my daughter and grandchild," he said as Braklarn prepared to vanish again.

When he reappeared in Jindara's chambers, Braklarn checked that he was alone before beginning a complex spell. He had planned to ask Jindara to marry him when the priests were dealt with anyway, but her pregnancy brought the matter forwards a little. It could prove awkward, because tradition said that the high priest of the Creator god should conduct marriages within the Chief's family, but they would find a way around that.

He refused to pay exorbitant prices at the jewellers' stalls for a ring that was less than perfect, so he decided to make one himself with magic. By the time Jindara arrived, he had completed his crafting spell and taken a seat under the high, arched window that looked out across the town. He hastily hid the ring behind his back when she entered.

"What did my father have to say?" she asked when she saw him sitting there.

Braklarn rose from the chair. "He seems to be in agreement with the plan to teach the people," he said. "And he would like me to pass on his congratulations on your pregnancy."

Relief broke across her face. "I thought he would disapprove, since I'm not married to the father," she said, taking a seat between the window and her bookshelf.

"Well, I was hoping to amend that situation," Braklarn said, revealing the ring he had made. The gold band sparkled in the sunlight, and the clear blue gem he had conjured to sit in the centre matched Jindara's eyes perfectly. He did not need to say the words, as Jindara stood and allowed him to slide the ring onto her finger before embracing him.

"We shall hold the ceremony at the beginning of summer," she whispered into his ear. "I don't care what Vrenid-Malchor's high priest says. If needs be, we can have Ralor-Kanj's high priest perform the marriage rites."

Braklarn smiled. "I knew you'd think of a way to dodge tradition," he whispered back.

Chapter Eight: Two Parties

The crowd gasped in awe as Nerlarina moved forwards, a shimmering beacon in the twilight. A few at the back turned and ran, but most stayed, staring at the vision in front of them.

"See? There is no reason to be afraid of them," said Kandrina, taking another step forwards to stand next to her. "They have never intended to harm us, and they wish to extend the hand of friendship. We cannot allow blind fear to control us any longer. Many of you have heard the recent sermons in this town's temples. Those of you who have come here from Manak will perhaps be surprised by the open mindedness of the priests and priestesses here, but their messages of acceptance should not be ignored."

Remlik joined her at the front of the makeshift platform. "There are creatures in this world that are truly horrific," he said, thinking of the mysterious lizard men, "but Nerlarina and her kind are not to be feared. My sister and I lived among them, in their city, over the last winter; Kandrina stayed there for much longer. If they were really as bad as we have always been told, do you think we would be standing in front of you now?"

The crowd broke into confused muttering, and one man at the front called out. "How do we know you two aren't Demons in disguise?"

Remlik and Kandrina glanced at each other. They had not anticipated that question, so they had no ready answer. Thankfully, Nerlarina stepped in. "What would we do that for? Putting aside the question of how we would manage to take possession of a living being, why would we choose to possess a child and a scholar? Wouldn't it be better to use someone high ranking, like your Chief or a high priest? Also, if one of us is prepared to appear in person, why would we need to possess others of your kind?"

A few members of the audience clapped, and the man who had shouted looked down at his shoes. "I suppose…" he mumbled.

They continued speaking to the assembled group, explaining the most basic things about the Colourless and answering questions, until the blue sun had completely set, and the only light came from Nerlarina. The crowd slowly dissipated, and Remlik led the way back to his house at the edge of the town. They walked past The Chieftain's Arms on the way, noticing a couple of large men outside who seemed to be sizing each other up. Kandrina stopped, staring across the road as another figure walked out of the door. The newcomer was quite a bit smaller than the two men, and seemed to be attempting to get between them.

"Kandi, come on. You really don't want to get involved," Remlik muttered in her ear. He tried to pull her away, but she seemed frozen to the spot.

The smaller figure had successfully got in between the two men, and was talking to them. They couldn't hear exactly what the words were, but they could tell the voice was female. Remlik crossed his fingers hoping that the two men were decent enough not to hit a woman, and that the woman between them wasn't Dranjari. He was wrong on both counts.

The lighter haired of the two men took a menacing step forwards as the darker haired one took a swing. Whether he was aiming for the other man or the woman between them wasn't clear, but it didn't matter anyway. The woman raised both hands, palms outwards facing the men. Both of them seemed to slow down, as though they were suddenly moving through thick treacle, giving her time to step forwards out of the way. She lowered her hands, and both men fell forwards and hit the cobbled pavement with a loud crack. Out of the shadows, Nerlarina's light fell across her, shining on her purple hair. She smiled over at the other three before turning to check the two men were still alive. Once she was satisfied, she crossed the road to join them.

"What was all that about?" Remlik asked her.

Dranjari's smile widened. "They both tried to get me into bed. I said I wasn't interested in either of them, then they decided to fight over me anyway. I think they just wanted an excuse to hit each other," she told them. "Anyway, how have your public lessons been going?"

"Pretty well, I think," Kandrina replied. "We've just come from one, most people seemed to listen to what we said. How are the temple lessons doing?"

"Last time I checked in, Yantrola had managed to convince most of the regular congregation that they should learn about the Colourless instead of being scared of them," Dranjari said. "Crenkari's swamped with people asking for information. Ralor's priest has been talking about realigning the balance of the world, or some such thing. Very calm and collected. He seems to have accepted things quite easily; Ralor might have spoken to him about it actually."

"That makes three of your gods that are involved," Nerlarina interjected.

"Yes, three. At the moment anyway." Dranjari looked back at the men on the floor, who seemed to be stirring. "Right, I should get back inside before they come over here. You lot head back to your place, I'll see you tomorrow." She turned and walked back into the tavern, skipping over the men on the floor.

Kandrina watched her go. "What do you suppose she meant, 'at the moment'? Are the rest of the gods going to stick their holy noses in as well?" she asked indignantly.

Remlik burst out laughing. "I'm sure we'll find out sooner or later. Come on, let's get back home." He turned away from the inn and resumed walking towards the house he shared with his sister.

"Nervous?" Dekarem asked, watching his friend shift his weight from one foot to the other.

Braklarn turned, uncomfortable in his formal robes. "Just baking hot. I wish they'd open one of the windows, it's stifling in here." He looked around at the attendees; it seemed that most of the townsfolk had turned out for the wedding. "How long does it take to put on a dress?" he asked, frustrated.

The bald mage grinned. "She's a woman, she'll keep you waiting forever if she wants. Ah, your friends are here," he said, nodding towards the double doors. Remlik and his sister led the way in, followed by Dranjari and Kandrina. Nerlarina had arrived earlier, and found a spot in the rafters out of the way. Remlika waved to them as she sat down.

"You know our mothers tried to set us up once?" Braklarn said to his friend. "They seemed to think we'd be a perfect match, both being skilled mages.

The problem was, we both fell in love with the same girl," he said, waving back at Remlika.

Dekarem was shocked. "You mean she's... that way? I'd never have guessed," he said, falling silent when the double doors opened once more. Everyone stood as the bride entered.

Jindara swept through the doors, flanked by two of her lady servants. She was resplendent in a pale blue silk dress, and carried a small bouquet of summer blooms. Braklarn couldn't help but smile when he saw her. The high priest of Ralor-Kanj followed her, dressed in a robe of pure white and carrying the ceremonial staff of marriage. An acolyte trailed after them all, holding a covered cage that contained a pair of golden onai birds. They would be released at the end of the ceremony, and if the gods blessed the union the birds would sing sweet songs as they flew away. If the birds did not fly or sing, the marriage would be dogged by ill luck.

The bridal procession reached the temple dais, and Braklarn took Jindara's hands in his. "You look beautiful," he whispered as the priest gestured everyone to take their seats. Dekarem and the two lady servants took their places in the front row.

"Shall we proceed?" the balance priest asked them. When they both nodded, he began the traditional marriage rites. "We are gathered today to bless the union of two loving souls. Today they will vow to honour each other for all eternity, loving no other for the rest of their mortal lives." He rested the ceremonial staff lightly upon the couple's joined hands. A crystal embedded in the end began to shine dully. "Braklarn, sorcerer of Tewen, will you love and cherish this woman forever, until you are called to the next realm?"

Braklarn gazed into Jindara's eyes. "I will." The crystal grew brighter.

"Jindara, Vice-Chief of the People, will you love and cherish this man forever, until you are called to the next realm?"

"I will," said Jindara, smiling at the man she was marrying. The crystal in the staff grew brighter still, shining a pure white light that spread out and surrounded the couple.

The balance priest stepped back. "This light is a sign of purity; these two people have vowed honestly and with all their hearts. May the gods smile upon your union." He signalled to the acolyte carrying the birds, who removed the silk covering from the cage and threw open the tiny golden door. The birds hopped out, looking around for a moment before taking flight as one. They spiralled around each other, up to the highest rafters, where they perched and began to sing. The noonday sun shone across their golden feathers, making them seem like tiny shining statues.

A thin young man with floppy hair stood up and began to applaud. A few others copied him, and soon the entire congregation was on their feet. The balance priest just managed to make himself heard over the noise. "You may kiss," he told the newly wed couple, who embraced shyly.

"Go on, snog her!" Dekarem shouted from the front.

Braklarn shot a look at his friend before kissing Jindara. She responded passionately, and they barely heard the balance priest dismissing everyone. Slowly, everyone filtered out of the temple and towards the town square. The bakers and butchers had been working overtime to prepare the wedding feast, but their efforts had paid off. There were five long tables groaning under the weight of food. The townsfolk had brought out chairs, and someone had organised a band.

Tradition said that the newly joined couple should be the first to dance, so Braklarn and Jindara swept into the centre of the square when the band started playing. It was a strange tune, slightly ethereal sounding; Braklarn surreptitiously glanced across at the band and noticed Dranjari standing at the side of the hastily assembled platform conducting the band members. After a few minutes, the last notes faded into the still summer air, and the band began another tune. Other people flooded into the centre of the square to dance; this tune was well known and slightly more upbeat than the last.

"Congratulations, Jindara," came a quiet, nervous voice from behind her shoulder. "I wish you many happy years together."

"Thank you, Semark. I am glad you could make it here today, I understand Wirba has been experiencing difficulties with a pack of predators lately?" Jindara replied, turning to greet her youngest sibling.

The young man nodded, his hair flopping about. "Yes, the nayrim. There seems to be a large group of them to the south, we are losing cattle almost every night."

As the two of them were likely to be talking business for a while, Braklarn excused himself and went to find his friends. Dekarem had gone to stuff himself silly at the feast tables, but Remlika was standing by herself watching the dancing. He went across to her.

"Enjoying the party?" he asked, wondering who she was watching so intently.

Remlika answered without taking her eyes off a pair of dancers. "Yes, it's very pleasant. My sincerest congratulations to the both of you," she said. She stared for another moment, chewing her bottom lip, before blurting out her next sentence. "Tell me, do you think they look close? Closer than they ought to be, I mean."

Braklarn followed her gaze, and saw Remlik and Kandrina dancing together towards the centre of the crowd. "They look as though they're enjoying each other's company, but I wouldn't say there's anything inappropriate there. Why do you ask?"

"She's still a girl, for the gods' sake! He's almost fifteen years older than she is, he should be acting his age, not flirting with a child."

"She won't be a child much longer," Braklarn replied evenly. "If I remember correctly, she comes of age this summer. Besides, you've known he has feelings for her for a long while. Why the sudden objections?" Remlika did not reply, only glowered at the dancing pair. "You're jealous, aren't you?"

"Don't be ridiculous. I like her as a friend, nothing more."

Braklarn was puzzled for a moment. He had only thought Remlika was jealous of their closeness, and wanted someone of her own, not that she might be jealous of Kandrina's affection for her brother. He tried to diffuse the tension a little. "They're just dancing. Maybe we're reading too much into it. Relax, have some wine and food." He pulled her over to the nearest table and handed her a plate.

"There you are," cried a loud voice. Dekarem had clearly found the ale. "My congratulations, Braklarn. Here's to hoping your marriage is better than mine." He raised his cup and drank deeply.

"That is a very good idea," Dranjari said, appearing behind him. "It's a party, so let's all get drunk. Here's a cup for everyone," she said, producing a tray full of wine cups. Everyone took a cup, and toasted the newlyweds. "So, where has your lovely bride got to?" she asked Braklarn when the cups were empty.

"She's talking to her brother about some chiefly business," he replied. "Something about over active nayrim taking all his village's cattle. Now I think of it, it's a little strange; the nayrim don't usually start killing our livestock until the end of summer."

Remlika glanced over the top of her wine cup, just refilled. "The nayrim are hunting our cattle already? Where is this?"

"I think they said Wirba; you know, that tiny village out by the Twin Lakes. I don't know much about it, I only heard a little of what Jindara and Semark were talking about," Braklarn said. He took another cup and drank a little before continuing. "You don't think it's anything to be concerned about, do you?"

Remlika shrugged. "I've no idea. There's been a lot of strange stuff going on recently. I know my brother's been searching his books for something, but he won't say what. Unless Dranjari wants to tell us anything, we'll just have to wait and see," she said, looking over at the purple-haired aspect.

Dranjari merely smiled. "You'll find out when the time is right. And believe me, your brother most certainly needed you." She raised her cup. "To the future, and everything it held." As the others copied her, it was unclear whether she had meant the future of Braklarn's marriage, or something a little more general.

Crenkari stood behind the library table, her fiery hair ruffled in the light summer breeze that came through an open window. She had been up since dawn making copies of Lerdran's book, given to her by Remlik. People from all over Tewen had been coming in and asking for information on the Colourless, and she had worked herself to the point of exhaustion trying to provide it. Most requests had been filled, and the few people who had not been given a copy of the book had keenly sat and listened to her reading from the original copy.

"How are you doing?" someone asked her. It was a young scholar who had come in the day before to listen to her reading. He had been very enthusiastic, and asked her for a copy of his own if she had the time.

"Quite well, though I am a little tired," Crenkari replied. "Have you come back for a copy of the book?"

He shook his head. "Not entirely, though I would gladly take one if there is a spare. I have come to ask if you would like to come with me to Manak, to teach in their library. There is no shrine there, but I am certain you would be welcome," he said, smiling at her. "There are many others who can take over here."

"It would be a pleasant change of scenery," Crenkari said, thinking of what she had heard of the town. "I shall ask Remlik if someone can take my place here, and I will go with you." She smiled back at him, admiring his dark blue eyes and black hair that fell just past his pointed chin.

The young man inclined his head. "I will go and arrange a pair of horses for tomorrow, then. Do you ride?" he asked.

"I have never ridden before," she replied. "Perhaps a gentle horse, until I am used to the saddle."

"I shall find you the gentlest horse in the land," he said, smiling again. "Before I leave, might I ask your name? Such a beautiful lady as yourself must have a truly divine name."

Crenkari blushed, a delicate pink. She had joined Talri-Pekra's temple the day of her adulthood ceremony, so had never been in a situation where a young man would flirt with her. She was unsure how to react, so she decided just to politely answer his question. "My name is Crenkari. May I ask yours?"

"A lovely name indeed. Mine is Mikrald," he replied. "Shall we meet outside here, at midday tomorrow? That will give us ample time to prepare for the journey."

Crenkari agreed, and as soon as Mikrald had left she ran to arrange for Remlik to take over in the library. She had no idea why, but the young man excited her. She knew of the physical goings-on between man and woman, but although acolytes such as herself were not required to be celibate she had simply not been interested in that sort of thing. She wondered for a moment what it would be like to kiss a boy, but then scolded herself for allowing her mind to run away with itself. She had knowledge to spread, and here she was lusting after a young man she barely knew.

The following day, she waited outside the library for him. He arrived at precisely midday, riding one horse and leading another. He dismounted to help her climb onto the second horse, then leapt back onto his, a tall black stallion. He had found a brown gelding for her, and she took the reins nervously.

"Don't be shy," said Mikrald. "Just do what I do, and we'll head out slowly." He led her out of the town, teaching her as they went. She got the hang of it fairly quickly, and when they reached the road that led from Tewen to Manak she felt confident enough to try a trot. A few yards down the road she landed face first in the dust. The gelding stopped a short way off, snorted and began grazing at the side of the road.

Mikrald reined in his stallion and dismounted to help her up. "Maybe we should just keep going slow," he said, trying to hide a grin as she dusted down her loose tunic.

"Maybe we should," she said, grinning back at him. She mounted the gelding again and they continued on to Manak.

They arrived two days later, just before sunset, and stopped to leave their horses in a stable in the centre of town before asking for directions to the library. A truculent man outside the stable reluctantly pointed the way, and they proceeded down some narrow streets in the fading light. By the time they reached the library, the sun had sunk behind the hills and lanterns were being lit in houses. The streets were almost completely deserted. A stooped, jumpy old man was about to lock the doors when they walked up to him.

"Wh-what do you w-want?" he stuttered, avoiding their eyes. "L-library's c-c-closed for the night. Have t-to come back t-t-tomorrow."

"It's quite alright," Crenkari said gently. "I can look after the library for the night."

The old man's eyes flicked about and landed on the small bronze badge that Crenkari wore on her tunic, marking her as an acolyte of Talri-Pekra. "Oh. Y-you know how t-to look after b-books then. G-g-get inside, y-you d-don't want to b-be caught out at n-night. I'll l-lock the d-doors s-so you'll be safe." He ushered them inside and closed the doors, mumbling something about demons and priests. They heard a lock click.

Mikrald lit a lantern. "Looks like we're staying here for the night then," he said, attempting to sound upbeat. "What do you think could have made him so nervous?"

"He said that we wouldn't want to be caught out at night, and there was something about demons as he shut the doors," Crenkari replied. "Maybe its just paranoia from what the priests here have been saying. I'm sure we'll find out sooner or later."

The librarian shuffled through the streets as fast as he could. The high priest had asked the townsfolk to inform him of any strangers that arrived, and the librarian had no desire to be named as a heretic for sheltering strangers. He reached the Creator's temple and knocked on the heavy wooden doors.

"Who calls at this time?" said a voice from inside.

"I c-come to r-report a pair of st-strangers, arrived at m-my library just this n-night," the man stuttered in reply. The small door opened and he was escorted inside to speak with the high priest.

"Take a seat, librarian. I hear you have encountered some strangers?" said the high priest when they entered. The acolyte who had escorted the man inside bowed and left.

The librarian sat opposite the priest, rubbing his hands together nervously. "A p-pair of strangers c-c-came to my library earlier t-tonight. A m-man and a w-woman. T-the woman is an acolyte of t-the kn-knowledge g-goddess, I-I know not who the m-man is," he said. "I g-gave them shelter f-for the night, f-for fear they w-would be t-t-taken by the Lightning D-Demons." He waited apprehensively for the priest's reaction.

The high priest narrowed his eyes, watching the candle on his table. The light cast a shadow across his face, highlighting the bags under his eyes. "Did they say where they had come from?" he asked. The librarian shook his head rapidly. "They may be from Tewen. I hear that town has become a veritable nest of heresy and Demon worship. I will not have them spreading their blasphemous lies in my town. You will return to your library in the morning, and keep a very close eye on these two travellers. If they should take one step out of line, alert me and I shall deal with them. Now go home."

The librarian scuttled out of the room; glad to be going home for the night. The high priest sat watching the wax dripping down the side of his candle, praying to any god that might be listening that he would get one night's undisturbed sleep tonight. He was still haunted by nightmares, and no amount of prayer had been able to cure him of them. Silently, he begged the gods for peace.

The town square filled with young boys and girls. It was midsummer, when this year's adulthood ceremonies would begin. Most families celebrated their child's coming of age on midsummer's night, then spent the remaining weeks of the season finding someone who would take them on as an apprentice. A few preferred to find their apprenticeship first, and celebrate their coming of age at the end of summer. Without her father present, Kandrina had planned to wait until the end of summer; but Remlik had pointed out that her father and sister may be remaining in the dwarven villages for some time yet, so she had decided to join in the general festivities with the majority.

As Kandrina wandered around the square chatting with the other youths who were celebrating, Remlik and Remlika stood to one side discussing what to do next.

"I don't know what's been happening in Manak, but the last time I heard from Crenkari was over two weeks ago. You think she might be in trouble?" Remlik asked his sister.

Remlika furrowed her brow in thought. "She could be. You want me to ask Braklarn if he knows anything more detailed?"

"Could do. Hey, the ceremony's starting," he replied, nodding towards the crowd of young people in the square who had fallen silent. Jindara stepped up onto the raised platform in front of the crowd, accompanied by Ralor-Kanj's high priest and her stout assistant, who carried a tightly furled scroll.

The Vice-Chief stepped to the front of the platform to address the assembled crowd. Her pregnancy was beginning to show, and a few of the younger children pointed to her swollen belly, asking their parents what it meant. She began her speech regardless. "Young people of Tewen, today marks the end of your childhoods. At sunset today, you will no longer be boys and girls, but become young men and women. Those of you who have already found a craft, or plan to have your parents choose one, will be free to do so. If any of you wish to pledge your lives to the gods, the high priest of Ralor-Kanj will speak with you before the day is through. A few of you have already approached me wishing to become members of my staff; my assistant will now read out the names of those I have chosen to take on." She stepped back to allow her assistant the front of the platform.

As the podgy man read out a handful of names, Remlik glanced across at Kandrina. Her pale gold hair shone in the sunlight, making her stand out among the rest. He seemed to drift away from the surrounding crowd of proud parents and families as he watched the twinkling highlights in her hair, until Remlika gave him a sharp nudge. Jindara was talking again.

"Any who wished to join my staff whose names have not just been called, feel free to find another craft. Now, one last item of business before the festivities begin; my husband Braklarn has offered to teach those wishing to become mages. If you have such a desire or talent, please seek him out. I presume he will be somewhere near the wine barrels," she said sarcastically, raising a few titters from the crowd. "Let the feasting begin!"

The crowd of youngsters dispersed, moving towards the tables that were scattered around the square. Kandrina headed straight for her old tutor and his sister. "It seems I must find myself a craft before the end of summer," she said with a smile. "I wonder if there are any scholars who would be willing to take on an apprentice? I have no talent for magery, as you well know."

Remlik smiled back. "I'm certain we can find someone who would take you on. Until then, let's enjoy this wonderful food."

"Yes, let's," Remlika said, squeezing through the crowd to get a place at a nearby food table. "I think Dranjari is around here somewhere, I saw some purple hair a few moments ago," she scanned the crowd.

Kandrina shrugged. "If she's here, I'm sure she'll find us when she wants to. Did Nerlarina come out?" she asked as she filled a plate with bread and cheese.

"No, she said she'd wait back at our house and congratulate you later," Remlik said, piling his own plate high with a little of everything. As Remlika went to fetch some drinks for them all, he took a deep breath and looked her in the eye, about to raise the subject they had both been avoiding. "Have you asked her about your vision at all?"

"No. I'm not sure I want to go through it all again," Kandrina replied. She had been trying to get the details of her brother's death out of her head, and did not want to bring it all up again unless she had to. "Maybe if we can't find anything in your books, I'll ask her. But let's finish sorting out this mess first," she said, referring to the issue with the priests.

"Yes, what is it you two have been so secretive about for the last few months?" Remlika had reappeared with three flagons of ale. "It's about time you told me what's going on."

Kandrina and Remlik looked at each other. "You explain," said the young girl wearily. "I think I've just seen Dranjari over there." She left the dark skinned twins to talk, and weaved through the crowd in pursuit of a flash of purple.

"So I told him... oh, hello Kandrina," said Dranjari when she turned round and saw her. "I was just telling Baprand here about the time I..."

Kandrina interrupted. She wasn't really interested in some random guy Dranjari was flirting with. "Actually, I wanted to ask you something. Can we go somewhere and talk?"

"Sure. Don't go anywhere darling, I'll be right back," Dranjari said to the bewildered young lad before following Kandrina to the edge of the crowd. "What's up?"

Kandrina took a deep breath. "Can you tell me when my father and sister will return from the dwarven lands? Or when I might get to see them next?"

Dranjari smiled. "That's easy. You'll see them tonight, when Wordarla calls you on Remlika's calling mirror. They won't be coming back for a while yet, though. Besides, you've got a lot of things to do while they're gone." She took a sip from her cup.

"Things like what?"

"That would be telling. Go on, get back to the party. I've got to find that handsome young man again." She drained her cup and headed back into the throng, leaving Kandrina to ponder.

After sunset, when the ceremony had ended and Jindara had officially declared all present to be adults, Kandrina headed back with Remlik to his house. Remlika had remained behind, having met someone at the party. When they got in, Nerlarina waited to greet them both.

"Congratulations, Kandrina. I understand your adulthood ceremonies are very important," the Colourless woman said. "We have no such thing, being born much as we remain for the rest of our lives. In essence, we are born into our adulthood."

"Really?" Remlik was surprised. "So you have no children as such?"

Nerlarina smiled, preparing to give another lesson. "We do in a sense; that is, there are new members brought into our society from time to time. But they are born as full individuals; there is no sense of being young, or getting older. We enter this world with all the basic knowledge we need, provided by the whole. I assume Kandrina has explained to you about the whole?" Remlik nodded. "That is where we all come from, and all return to, eventually."

"So you're not immortal?" Kandrina asked.

"No. Our energy will eventually dissipate back to the whole; I suppose it is akin to the process your kind goes through towards the end of your lives. An individual nearing the end of its natural existence will become dim, move slower, and sometimes be unable to hold a form. In rare circumstances, the dimming individual will retreat to the whole voluntarily, giving itself up before it has a chance to fade entirely. I have heard that the final few hours can be quite unpleasant."

"Unpleasant how? Like, painful, or tiring?" Remlik asked.

Nerlarina stared into the distance. "Imagine yourself disintegrating; all the different parts of yourself slowly drifting away, spreading out until there's nothing left. Not painful, just uncomfortable; strange." She fell into a silence that neither of the other two wanted to break.

They were saved the awkwardness of speaking first by the calling mirror. It made a ringing sound, like a small bell. Remlik got up to answer it. "Hello… oh hello Wordarla, how are you?"

Wordarla's voice sounded a little distant over the mirror. "Well enough, ta. N' y'self?"

"We're doing fine here. The adulthood ceremony was tonight, we've just got back," Remlik replied as Kandrina came over to say hello.

"I know, tis why I called. Her father n' sister be 'ere, wantin' to say hello. I'll pass y' over." The picture in the mirror shook for a bit, then settled down. Harndak and Enkarini were in the frame now, grinning widely.

"Father, I'm so glad to see you," Kandrina said. Remlik quietly went back to the other room, leaving her alone with her family. "And you, Enkarini. How is your alchemy coming along?"

The little girl bounced up and down on her father's knee. "I'm doing really well, I can make seven different potions now." She held up seven fingers to show her big sister. "And Worrald says that I'm very good at it. You're a grown up now, aren't you?"

Kandrina smiled at her little sister. "I am, and as soon as I can I'm going to come and see you properly. You can show me all your potions," she said. The little girl nodded and scampered off, presumably to bed.

"I'm sure she will," said Harndak proudly. "Now, seriously for a minute, have you found yourself a craft? I can come back and help if you want," he said, obviously worried about his oldest daughter's future.

"Don't worry Father, I can manage. And I'm sure Remlik can help me if needs be," Kandrina said, reassuring him. "How are you finding the dwarves' village? It seemed quite rowdy compared to here," she asked.

Harndak looked to his left. "It's certainly more exciting here. There's a lot of, shall we say activity in the taverns. Plenty of work for me as well, they've got all these machines that do things for them." A yellow haired dwarf woman came into view and beckoned him outside. "Looks like I'm wanted elsewhere. Come and visit soon, won't you? Enkarini misses you a lot, and I do too."

"I'll come and see you as soon as I can," Kandrina promised. Her father waved goodbye, and the mirror went dark. She watched it for a moment, glad that her family was doing well, before heading up to bed herself. It had been a long day, and tomorrow promised to be even more hectic.

"Dranj-Aria, get up here."

She appeared in the pavilion to find the Creator staring into his vision orb. Glancing over his shoulder, she noticed it was focused on his high priest, who was giving an evening sermon in his temple.

"I've been watching you down there," he began. "Do tell me, what was the purpose of attending the wedding, and the Tewen adulthood ceremony? I thought you were down there to fix the problem with my high priest, not go to some mortal parties."

"I assure you, it's all part of the bigger plan," Dranj-Aria replied. "There are some things that needed to be set in motion now, and this was the easiest way of doing it. Besides, why can't I have a little fun?"

Vrenid-Malchor sighed. "Very well. Just don't make things any worse than they already are." He waved her out, and she began to fade back to the mortal world.

She had just dropped back into her aspect's form when she heard another call, this time from the god of balance. She drifted back up to meet him. He waited for her in his own realm. When Ralor-Kanj was not wandering between various realms, he resided in a small room where the only items of furniture were a plain wooden table and chair. Only two other things were in there; a one-handed shortsword, engraved with the word 'balance' in ancient script, which hung on the wall behind the table; and a large set of golden scales resting on the table. If all was in balance in the world, the scales would also be balanced. Should the scales tip, the balance of the world would skew. Currently, they were slightly tilted to one side, but not terribly so.

Dranj-Aria had always been tempted to tap one end of them and see what happened.

"You called me, Ralor?" she said, once again ignoring the temptation. Someone would tap them one day, but it would not be her.

He looked up at her. "I did. You told me something last time we spoke, and I wanted to ask you what exactly you meant. I have been trying to work it out, but it still doesn't make sense."

The goddess of time smiled at him. "Which bit didn't make sense?"

"All of it. Why do I have to watch Kandrina carefully, and what am I supposed to do when she meets the Li Buqu?"

"Rescue her. That's all I can tell you, Ralor. Now, I ought to be getting back. We're going to start some riots soon," she said, fading away. "Be seeing you."

Ralor-Kanj sat back in his chair, puzzling over what she could have meant. He was so wrapped up in his thoughts; he did not notice the scales in front of him twitching the tiniest bit lower on one side.

At sunrise the next day, Remlik and Kandrina were about to have breakfast when Remlika burst through the door. "Braklarn says there's big trouble going down in Manak. A lot of people have been locked up in the temple basements, some of them have been executed apparently," she said, breathless. "I don't know if Crenkari's locked up, or otherwise."

Brother and sister exchanged a significant look. "All the more reason to be on our way, then. If we leave now, travel quickly, we should be there by sunset tomorrow. I've already hired a fast caravan; we can pick it up as soon as we're ready to leave. Yantrola's meeting us by the hire place, and Dranjari says she'll wait for us outside the Chieftain's Arms," Remlik said. "Come on, we can eat on the way." He tossed some bread, cooled meat and cheese into a bag and led the women out of the door.

They diverted past The Chieftain's Arms, seeing Dranjari waiting outside the tavern. "Morning all, I hope everyone slept well." She fell into step beside them as they walked past. "Don't worry, Crenkari's fine. If I remember right, she's busy working on a plan to get the lad she went with out of his shackles. You met her outside Somri-Galin's temple, just before you all split up."

"That's a point, we don't really have a plan," said Kandrina. "Should we make one, or just take things as they go?"

Dranjari smirked. "Just wing it, you did fine."

Shortly, they arrived at the caravan hire shop. Yantrola was waiting by the cart they had hired, deep in conversation with Nerlarina. "I wondered where you'd got to," Remlik said when he saw her. "Come on, we should get moving. I've paid the hire man in advance, so we're good for a few days. It shouldn't take that long, but I thought it would be best to make sure." He climbed up into the front seat, his sister taking the space next to him. Kandrina got into the back next to the bag of food, Nerlarina drifted up next to her, and Dranjari helped Yantrola climb in before jumping up herself. Once they had all settled, Remlik snapped the reins and the horses set off.

Being just past sunrise, they were expecting the road between the two towns to be fairly empty, but they were surprised to see several caravans heading towards Tewen. "What do you suppose is going on?" Remlika asked, as one particularly large caravan rolled past. She turned back, and noticed that it was packed with crates and sacks. "Looks like a merchant's wagon. I would have thought all the merchants would be heading into Manak, not away. It's their big summer market week, isn't it?"

Remlik tilted his head. "Usually, yes. But if you say there's a lot of trouble going down they might be getting away from it. Still, it means good business for the stall holders in Tewen," he said. "Actually, we might do well to come up with a reason for visiting Manak. Sister, can you create an illusion of crates of trading goods in the back? That way we can pass ourselves off as merchants come to sell our wares at the market."

"I think I can manage that. I'll begin casting when we get nearer; Nerlarina, you might want to go on ahead if I'm going to be casting," the sorceress said, glancing back.

"I shall do that. Let me know when we are close, I will go ahead and wait in the centre of the town, most likely above the crowds so as not to create panic," Nerlarina replied.

They rolled along quietly for a while, enjoying the warm summer weather and each other's company. Remlik broke the silence. "Dranjari, has anyone managed to get to Manak and teach people about the Colourless?"

"Yes, quite a few scholars have been there teaching people. A lot of them have got the message, but they were too afraid to stand up to the high priest," Dranjari told them. "Also, nobody has mentioned that the priests have been spreading lies about the Colourless. The people just think it's new information that has come to light. You were able to use that to get the townsfolk riled up."

Kandrina nodded thoughtfully. "Maybe we can go and tell them that particular revelation; it could be enough to get them to speak up. The priests won't be able to ignore the entire town."

After a while, Yantrola drifted into a light snooze. Dranjari appeared to be examining her own hair, pulling strands of it in front of her face and frowning at them. Suddenly, it turned bright, vivid green. "I fancied a change," she said in response to everyone's stares. "I've had purple hair for ages, it's about time I did something different with it."

"Can you change anything about the way you look, then?" asked Kandrina, curious.

"I can change the way my aspect looks; usually I stay much the same as this but I can appear differently if I want to," Dranjari answered. "In fact, I've appeared to a few people looking very different." She smiled.

Kandrina smiled back, having some idea of the goddess's quirky sense of humour by now. "So, what do you actually look like? If you don't mind me asking, that is," she said.

Dranjari tapped the side of her nose, winking conspiratorially. "You'll find that out when we get there," she whispered. "Some drunken idiot is going to ask me to prove who I am. Don't tell those two though, it's supposed to be a surprise for them too." She nodded towards Remlik and Remlika, who sat together in the front.

"Right. That should be fun to watch," Kandrina replied. She settled back against the canvas, pulling a hunk of bread out of the food bag. "Want some?" she asked, offering it to her old tutor.

Remlik turned. "Yes please. Actually, we're making pretty good time here. Shall we stop for a few minutes and eat?"

Yantrola suddenly awoke. "Ooh, that sounds like a good idea. Have you got any limij steaks?" she asked, referring to the tender meat of the grazers that wandered the plains.

"I think we do," Remlika said, rummaging in the bag. "Here. Take some bread too, they're quite juicy."

They all tucked in, the horses grazing at the roadside while they ate. After a half hour rest, they continued onwards, the clear road making their journey much quicker.

As they approached Manak in the late afternoon light the next day, Nerlarina transformed into her natural cloudy shape and drifted into the sky, moving ahead of the cart. Once she was out of sight, Remlika cast a powerful illusion over the back of the caravan, making it seem like it was packed with crates of seasoned meat. She included an appearance altering spell for herself and her brother, so they would not be recognised by the guards at the town gates.

"Hold," cried one of the guards as they reached the gates. "There are new restrictions on travellers entering Manak. We will have to inspect your goods." He signalled to his partner, who proceeded to the back of the cart to check the crates.

"Inspect away, my good man," said the disguised Remlik. He appeared as a brawny, tanned young butcher. "We only come to sell our fine meats in your town."

Remlika had cast her illusion well. The crates were as good as solid, and the guard pried a few open to see, and smell, the fresh meat inside them. "They're clean," he called to his partner, who waved them through the gates.

"Why thank you sir," Remlika giggled as they rolled onwards. She had disguised herself as a thin, honey haired woman, intended to be perceived as the butcher's wife. "Right, let's get into the town square. Once we're round the corner I can drop this illusion; anyone in the town shouldn't bother us if they know we've got past the gate guards."

They turned a corner and the image of meat crates vanished. Kandrina wafted the air around. "Thank the gods for that. Did you have to make the smell so pungent?"

Remlika smiled back at her. "Don't knock it, it worked."

They rolled onwards, wending their way through the streets of Manak towards the market square.

Crenkari ducked behind the rickety old bookshelf, waiting for the two militia men to get bored and leave. They only wanted to ask her a few questions, about a woman who had been in that morning to find a book on treating some minor illness. They'd come in earlier, but she'd managed to avoid speaking to them then by saying she was busy with her devotions to her goddess, and they should return later. She knew they'd never bother to come looking for her in the dusty old archive, where she had spent many hours hiding over the last couple of weeks. Usually, Mikrald was next to her, which had made it into something more like a game. But he had slipped up and been arrested three days ago, and was currently locked in the basement of the Creator's temple, along with several others awaiting trial for teaching heresy.

"Come on, she must be some place else. We can come back later," she heard one of them say. Two pairs of booted feet marched back out of the door, and silence fell over the library once more. She breathed a quiet sigh of relief. Now she would have a few hours to figure out a way to break into the temple basement and get Mikrald out.

The two of them had been trying to explain to the townsfolk of Manak about the so-called Demons, how they were not what the temples had been telling everyone. From the attitudes they had encountered, some people were starting to have doubts about the stories the priests told, but little had been said or done outside of the taverns. Several scholars had been trying to make themselves heard over the past few months, however, which had inspired a massive crackdown by the temple militia. People were being tried and disciplined for blasphemy almost every day now; the slightest remark could see someone thrown in a cell in the temple of suffering.

Crenkari stood, brushed a cobweb off her sleeve, and crept back into the main library. She already had an idea of how to get into the temple, it was getting back out that would be the problem. The old librarian they had met when they arrived had, in his twitchy, nervous way, been trying to help her. But he seemed to be petrified of being caught himself, always double checking the doors and windows were locked before he would talk about anything with her. She could understand his paranoia, because the militia had been making a point of checking up on anyone who worked in or even visited the library. She herself had some degree of protection, being part of Talri-Pekra's order, but many did not have that luxury.

As she pulled down some old building plans of the temple, which she had carefully concealed at the back of a shelf of old almanacs, her thoughts turned to the enigmatic young man she was planning to rescue. He seemed curious about almost everything, from the details of the old tribal territories to the ancient myths of the ice giants. She had told him everything she knew about what he asked her, and what she hadn't known they had researched together. He had been quite secretive about his own life, though; she didn't even know where he came from. But she hadn't exactly told him a lot about herself, so she supposed she couldn't really complain. It just hadn't come up. Probably they would get to know each other better after the priests' fabrications had been revealed, and the dust had settled.

"Ah, this looks promising," she muttered to herself, peering at one of the old plans. There seemed to be some kind of old passageway linking the temple basement with the building next door; the schoolhouse, if she remembered correctly. That would be empty after sunset, easy enough for two people to creep out of unseen. Now if only there were some way to check the passageway was still there…

She leapt up, an idea having dawned on her. As an acolyte, she was permitted access to any temple-run building at any time; she could simply go to the schoolhouse now and check out the passageway herself. If anyone asked what she was doing there, she could just say she was researching the architecture of the period. It had been built shortly after the tribal merging, so it was a fairly important period in the People's history. That should provide enough of an excuse, and if it didn't, she could always go back at night when the place was deserted.

Chapter Nine: Revolt

They pulled into the market square and abandoned the cart near a stall. Kandrina jumped down from the back with the others as Remlik slipped the merchant a handful of gold and told him to swear blind that the cart was his if anyone should ask. "What do we do now then?" she asked once they found a secluded spot. She hoped someone had an idea how to go about starting this. The best she had come up with so far was to storm into the Creator's temple and start yelling at the high priest.

"We start assembling groups in taverns, explain who's behind all the lies, and hope they make enough fuss that the high priest pays some attention. Then we somehow convince him to listen to what we have to say," Remlik said. "There's a tavern near the temple of suffering; it's called the Bloody Soldier, I think. Maybe we should start there, then we might bump into Crenkari."

"I'll stay here, start preaching to this lot," Yantrola said, indicating the milling crowd of market goers. "It'll be easier than trying to squeeze my way through everyone. I'll meet you in that inn near the Creator's temple later," she said, waving them onwards as she clambered onto an upturned fruit crate.

Remlik nodded. "See you later then, and good luck." He set off, the others trailing behind him. Nerlarina drifted above them in her natural cloud-like form. She was slightly less obvious that way, as few of the people bothered to look up, and those who did merely saw her as a brighter patch in the still sunny sky. On reaching the tavern, she drifted downwards and took the shape of a beautiful woman again.

Kandrina looked up at the sign, creaking slightly in the breeze. It showed a surprisingly life-like armoured soldier, covered in splashes of red. "Ugh. Couldn't they have picked a better name for the place?" she asked, feeling slightly queasy.

"They had to go with something that would sit comfortably with that lot," Dranjari told her, nodding towards the temple of suffering at the end of the street. "Come on, we'd better not hang around out here for too long." She pushed the door open and headed in, the others following her.

There was a reasonable crowd in there, all talking and drinking. A few glanced up when Dranjari and the others entered, but Nerlarina attracted the most attention. The place fell silent when she drifted in, with every eye fixed upon her. The drinkers seemed frozen in place, following the group only with their eyes as they walked across to the stage where fiddlers sometimes played. The barman stared also, the glass he had been filling overflowing onto the floor, forgotten.

Remlik looked around the silent room and cleared his throat. "Good afternoon everyone. Have any of you heard the most recent lessons being given in the libraries?" he asked, his voice wavering slightly. A few people nodded slowly, still staring up at them. "Right then. I would like to introduce Nerlarina, here representing the Colourless, who we have wrongly been calling demons. If I may begin by explaining a few things, that some of you may have heard in the libraries or from travelling scholars; I then have something else to reveal to you."

As Remlik told the crowd of bar patrons a few basic things about the Colourless, Dranjari leant across and whispered to Kandrina. "See that man over there, in the brown shirt? He's the one who ends up asking very silly questions," she said, a shadow of a grin on her face.

Kandrina smiled faintly, looking over to the man. He seemed to be swaying on his stool, eyes out of focus. Clearly he had had quite a lot to drink. She stepped forwards as Remlik gestured to her. They had been through this lecture so many times in the streets of Tewen that she no longer needed to pay attention closely. "It is true. There is no reason to fear Nerlarina and her kind; they are much like us in so many ways. The deaths caused over the years have been no fault of theirs," she said.

"So whose fault were they?" the drunken man shouted out, clambering unsteadily to his feet.

Remlika answered him. "Many of those who were staked out were killed by wild beasts, and the ones who were lost under other circumstances often died in tragic accidents." She glanced sideways at Kandrina. "None of the Colourless have ever harmed us intentionally; in fact they have not approached us for generations until now."

The man took a step forwards, pointing at the group. "So why'd they come now, eh? And why pick you lot over all the rest of us?"

"Because they happened to be in the right place at the right time," Dranjari said, smiling over at him.

"And who are you then, lady? You don't seem the sort to be going around with a girl and a couple of booksy people," he said, staggering forwards again and squinting at her.

Dranjari's smile widened. "Me? I'm the goddess of time, sweetie." She waited patiently as the man stared, then began laughing raucously. A few others joined in, breaking the tension that had settled when they had walked in. She winked at Kandrina.

The drunk man managed to stop chuckling before he fell over, and straightened up to look at her. "Alright then, why don't you prove it? Surely a goddess would look more impressive than you do right now," he said, still grinning stupidly.

Remlik and his sister looked over, expecting her to refuse, or be insulted, but Dranjari merely continued smiling. "If you insist," she said softly, and closed her eyes. There was a flash of bright white light, blinding everyone in the room for a second. When the light faded, Dranjari no longer appeared plump, dark and green haired; she had become a slender woman, towering over everyone's heads. She emitted a soft golden glow, radiating an aura of power, and stood watching the drunken man with one hand on her hip and a smirk on her lips. "Believe me now?" She twirled her other hand, and an hourglass appeared, which she began playing with.

The ridiculous grin fell off the man's face, and he promptly fell over backwards, landing on the wooden floor with a thud. The others in the room either stared in amazement, or dropped to their knees in supplication. Remlik and Remlika were among those staring, while Nerlarina silently puzzled over how she had managed to change her appearance without magic, or the fluctuations in energy that her kind used.

Kandrina looked at her, smiling. "Nice. Very impressive. I'm glad you warned me though," she said.

"Told you you'd find out later. Oh, knock that off," Dranjari said, resuming her aspect's form. "Seriously, get up, unless you're trying to lick ale off the floor." The men and women kneeling slowly stood, a new respect in their eyes. "Right, this lot have something important to say now, and you're all going to listen. Then, you're going to go out and spread the word to as many people as you can find. Got it?" Everyone nodded. "Good. Remlik, continue," she said, smiling across at the stunned scholar.

Remlik shook himself a little before continuing the lesson. "As I was saying, there is a great deal to be learned from the Colourless. But there is something you should all know now. This information is not new; rather it has been suppressed for many years by the priests, especially the high priest in this town." The crowd broke out in alarmed muttering, debating hurriedly whether he spoke truth. Dranjari's presence helped to dispel any doubts they had, however. "I say we should demand the truth from the temples; they cannot keep the People ignorant forever!" Remlik cried, punching the air.

The bar patrons shouted agreement, and several of them left, presumably to carry out Dranj-Aria's instructions. A few remained, grabbing lanterns from the tavern and proceeding into the streets with Remlik and the others.

When they had got outside the tavern, Remlika turned to Dranjari. "Don't – ever – do that – again," she said, in a much squeakier voice than usual.

"But your expression was hilarious," said Dranjari, clearly trying not to giggle. "Anyway, that worked quite well. We should wait here for a second, Talri's acolyte was here soon, then we all head to different taverns to spread the word before meeting up at the Sitting Horse a few streets away from the Creator's temple. Remlik, you stormed around with one of the mobs while we went to see the high priest," she told them all.

They waited for less than a minute, and sure enough Crenkari came running around the corner accompanied by a young man with a pointed face and black hair. "Oh, you're here already. I was wondering how to get hold of you. This is Mikrald," she said, indicating the lad she was with. "What's going on?"

Kandrina quickly explained the situation. "Apparently we're all heading to taverns around the town to get a few mobs going. What about Yantrola?" she asked Dranjari.

"I'll go and look after her," the aspect replied absently, staring at her reflection in a window. "You know, I think green suits me better than purple."

"It certainly makes you stand out more," said Remlik. "Alright, let's get going. I'll take the south end; Remlika, new guy, you're with me. Kandi, you take Crenkari and Nerlarina and go round the north end of town." They parted ways, agreeing to meet up at the Sitting Horse inn after sunset.

An acolyte came rushing into the high priest's private contemplation room. "The peasants are revolting!" he wheezed, desperately trying to regain his breath.

"Well of course they are. They hardly ever bathe, and I have never seen any of them wash their clothes. I should imagine most of them are thoroughly disgusting," replied the high priest from his position on the prayer mat.

The acolyte stared blankly for a second, before he realised the mix up. "Not that kind of revolting, the other kind," he explained. "They're marching about with flaming torches, chanting 'tell us the truth'."

The high priest rose with difficulty. His knees were becoming more awkward with every passing year. "The truth about what, precisely?"

"I believe they are talking about the Lightning Demons, your holiness. Rumour has it that there have been scholars and even priests from Tewen coming here and teaching that the Demons are not so different from us, and should not be feared," the acolyte responded.

"Is that so? We must go to correct these rumours then." The high priest dusted the front of his robe and swept out of the room.

"Your holiness, there is something else," the acolyte called after him. "There is a Demon among the mobs. It appears to have befriended a small group of scholars and mages, and it has been sighted within the walls of Manak."

The high priest paled visibly. "Alert the soldiers. They should clear the streets, and be ready to kill it if it should appear. We shall show these Demons that they cannot enter our towns without suffering the consequences." He continued out of the temple.

"What are you going to do?" his acolyte asked, following him.

"I shall inform my fellow priests of the situation. We must beg the gods' help," he replied. Seeing the rioting townsfolk in the street ahead, the high priest turned and made his way through the back streets to the temple of Somri-Galin. He arrived quickly, and was escorted straight through to the highest-ranking priest's room.

"How can I help you today, high priest?" he asked, in his rasping voice. "Do you need more assistance in dealing with the heretics?"

"In a way, yes." The high priest pulled himself up to his fullest height. "It may have escaped your attention, but there are rioting mobs of peasants in the streets. They seem to have the idea that we have been lying to them about the Lightning Demons, and are demanding the truth. I require your assistance in dispelling the crowd, and silencing the ones who are spreading this blasphemy."

The priest of suffering stared at him for a moment, a wicked grin slowly creeping onto his face. "I cannot help. My god has forbidden me from intervening; it seems the People are doing his work for him, and he has no desire to stop them. Perhaps you should commune with your god," he suggested cruelly. "Unless, of course, the almighty Creator is still refusing to answer you."

The high priest spluttered indignantly. "I… you cannot… you…" Composing himself, he continued. "Very well. I shall seek help elsewhere; and do not believe I will forget this insolence." He turned on his heel and stormed out, leaving Somri-Galin's priest grinning to himself.

Making his way through the deserted back streets to the temple of Fakro-Umdar, he wondered who had begun this fresh wave of lies. True, there had been a sudden rise in heresy over the last few months; scholars teaching things that went against the word of the gods, people speaking about the Demons without fear. He had even heard one blasphemer saying that the Demons were not truly Demons, but beings of energy with their own ways and customs. He had, of course, had the man arrested and staked out within the day.

The temple of death loomed into view at the end of the street; a dark shadow hanging over it that lent an ominous feeling to the place. When he reached the large wooden doors a silent acolyte escorted him to a private room to wait. The death priest entered soon after.

"What is it?" he asked lazily. "You want help with all these mobs?"

"Precisely. I intend to quash this heresy, cut out its source, and save as many souls as I can. Will you and your acolytes assist me?"

Fakro-Umdar's priest shook his head slowly. "No. All things must end, including eras. When a period of stability in time dies, we have a choice. We can either change with it, thus gaining a new lease on our own lives, or we can die with it. It seems that the times are changing, and I will be changing with them. What choice will you make, high priest?"

"How can you be so accepting of this? You know as well as I do that the Demons are evil," the high priest began.

"I know what we have been telling the People for decades," the death priest interrupted. "I know that we have been keeping them in ignorance because we have been too afraid to learn more. Perhaps it is time to shed our fears. It is no-one's fault but your own that you have become fanatically narrow-minded, believing blindly in your own dogma."

Frustrated and angry, the high priest stalked out without saying another word. He went straight back to his own temple, wondering what he could do without the others' help. After a few moments' thought, he decided to organise his own acolytes and priests, along with any shamans he could find, to wait outside and within the Creator's temple. The heretics would likely be making their way there, to attempt to spread their irreverence further and corrupt those in the temples. He sped up, wanting to reach his temple before the mobs did.

Jindar stood framed in his window, staring out over the town. He watched the orange glow of torches competing with the greenish light of the setting sun, wondering how things had gotten so bad. *Surely,* he thought, *I cannot have been so blind for so long.* He was roused from his thoughts by a faint sound behind him, and turned to see what it was. His new son in law had appeared.

"Chief Jindar, I have been asked to take you to your daughter. From all reports, things are getting a little fraught here and she wishes you to be safely out of harms way." He extended a hand, which Jindar took, and then transported them both directly into Jindara's rooms.

Jindara had been waiting for them. "Thank you, husband. Now my father is safe, you can go help the others," she said. Braklarn inclined his head and vanished again. She turned to her father. "I am glad to see you well, if a little paler from staying indoors so long," she said with a small smile.

"I am glad to see you healthy also, daughter. You must tell me of your wedding; it must have been grand," Jindar said, taking a seat next to her.

"Perhaps later, father. There is something I wish to discuss with you first, namely your apology made last winter." Jindara met her father's eyes, the pain of two decades clear on her face.

Jindar looked back at his eldest child. "I meant what I said. I am truly, deeply sorry for causing you and your siblings so much pain. My wife –your mother relied on me for support in her final days, and I let her down. I let all of you down; I should have listened to you when you told me to get a healer to see her. My own blind faith convinced me that prayer alone would heal her, that she had no need for medicine if our belief was strong enough," he said, as long distant memories came flooding to the surface of his mind. "Can you forgive me for my errors?"

"I can, father. Mother would have wanted us to make up a lot sooner, I think. It's a shame we both share the family trait of stubbornness, else we would have let it go long before now," Jindara said, hugging her father for the first time in twenty years.

Jindar hugged her back, not wanting to let go. "So, what exactly have you been up to this past year? I only know what your sorcerer husband has told me, and I suspect he left a lot out."

The Vice-Chief sighed, about to begin a long, complicated explanation. "Well, from what I understand it began with the punishment of a young girl from Manak, by the name of Kandrina..." She talked for over an hour, and by the time she finished the sun had completely sunk below the horizon and the lanterns had been lit outside. She lit her own lamp, throwing light across her father's shocked face.

"Daughter, if what you say is all true," the Chief began awkwardly, "and I have no reason to doubt that any longer, then the priests' deceptions run far deeper than anyone suspected. I hope your friends are doing alright." He gazed out of her window at the stars, noticing a faint orange glow on the horizon to the north.

As the sun reached the top of the hills, just touching the crest of the highest hill like a shining crystal on a pedestal, Remlik fought his way through the charging crowds of townspeople. Some of the people had got hold of torches, and were holding them high above their heads like beacons. The gods only knew what they were planning to do with them. He finally reached the Sitting Horse, checked his sister and the young scholar were still with him, and pushed the door open. The inn was almost deserted, with all of its patrons out marching in the streets. Kandrina and the others waited at a table in a corner, and he walked over to them.

"I think that's the majority of the town out there now," he said, pulling over a chair. "With any luck it will be enough to get the priests to listen to us. Anyone know what they're planning to do with those flaming torches?"

"Burn things," replied Dranjari. "What else does one do with a flaming torch? Anyway, we have a more pressing issue here. The high priest has ordered the soldiers to clear the streets and restore order, so someone's going to lead a group over to the barracks to distract them, so that we can get to the temple without any trouble. Remlik, you should do that. We waited here until the street outside cleared a bit then made our way over to the temple."

Mikrald spoke up. "I'll go with him. They might need an extra hand," he said.

Remlik nodded. "Fine. We should go now, there are a lot of people just outside we can take."

"Sounds good to me. We'll see you ladies later," said the young lad as they rose to leave. Outside, several people were hurrying up and down the street, waving their torches and shouting. "How are we going to get this lot over to the barracks?" he asked Remlik.

"Like this. Hey, listen up!" Remlik shouted, getting a few people's attention. "I just heard that the high priest has got the soldiers out to stop us. Let's go and meet them before they can get too far," he cried. The mob roared in agreement, and started running towards the barracks. Remlik and Mikrald ran after them.

They arrived outside the army barracks a few minutes later to find two regiments remained outside, receiving orders from their sergeants. The rest of the army had apparently already left. Braklarn suddenly appeared next to Remlik.

"Have I missed anything?" he asked, looking around.

Remlik shook his head. "Not much. The action's about to start," he said, seeing the regiments on the other side of the yard marching towards them. "A few protective spells would be greatly appreciated about now," he said before rushing forwards with the mob.

Braklarn nodded and cast a hasty spell to turn the soldiers' swords into wood, making the two sides a little more evenly matched. The two groups clashed, the soldiers immediately gaining the upper hand through their well-organised tactics and greater numbers.

"You lot in the centre, pull back!" someone shouted. "If you just surge forward, you're practically handing yourselves over to them!"

Remlik glanced over everyone's heads to see Mikrald attempting to organise the mob a little better. The people in the centre followed his directions and stepped back, leaving the soldiers who faced them to follow.

"Now left and right close in!" The mob closed into a circle, with a group of soldiers trapped in the centre. They were quickly clubbed unconscious and carried out, evening out the sides. "Use your damned torches, they can't fight if they're on fire!"

Within seconds, several soldiers were aflame, and they retreated to extinguish themselves and regroup. Remlik took advantage of the lull to speak to Mikrald quickly. "Where did you learn that tactic? I've never come across it in anything I've read," he asked.

"Setting them on fire? It seemed obvious. They already had the torches, it only made sense to use them," Mikrald replied.

"No, the first bit, getting the mob to encircle the soldiers. Have you done this before?"

Mikrald looked around. "Of course not. I read about it, that's all," he replied evasively. "Looks like they're coming back for round two. Right you lot, follow my lead," he shouted, rushing forwards at the head of the mob and leaving Remlik to wonder who exactly he was.

The soldiers were eventually sent back into the barracks, and a slightly depleted mob marched back down the street triumphantly, heading for the nearest tavern to have a few drinks. Remlik hung back, touching Mikrald and Braklarn on the shoulders. "Wait," he said. "Let them go. There's something I want to go and check, and it will be easier if you two come and help me."

They watched the mob go round the corner before turning and heading through some back streets. "What are you looking for?" Braklarn asked quietly.

"I want to look up something in the library, if it hasn't been burnt down," Remlik answered.

As the soldiers desperately attempted to keep order in the streets, a small band of women proceeded through the mobs with ease. A fair few buildings had been set on fire, whether accidentally or otherwise was unclear. There were still quite a few people around, but Nerlarina's presence helped to clear their way. They headed straight for the temple of Vrenid-Malchor, which was guarded by a handful of acolytes and shamans.

"We'll deal with this lot, you get inside and sort out the high priest," Yantrola said, readying her staff. "Go on, get in there." She strode over to an acolyte near the door and bonked him on the head. Crenkari began a distracting argument with a couple of shamans, which left the door clear for a moment. Kandrina led the way in, the others close behind her.

They headed straight into the main prayer hall, where the highest-ranking acolytes and the priests waited. "You?" exclaimed a surprised voice from the chair behind the altar.

Kandrina looked to see the high priest staring at her. "Yes, me. And a few friends," she said coolly. "We're here to put a stop to your fanatical nonsense. The people know the truth about the Colourless now, and it won't be so easy to change their minds back."

"I for one would like to know why you have been so intent on spreading fear and hatred of our kind," Nerlarina said, drifting forwards. "I thought that holy men were supposed to be kind and understanding. Or is that another of your kind's false truths?"

As the high priest spluttered indignantly, Dranjari simply stood behind the others and smirked.

"I'd like to know how you're sleeping," Remlika said. She stepped forwards and glared at him. "You really don't look well. How are those burning women, high priest?"

He stared at the dark skinned mage. "How did you know... You are the one who cursed me, aren't you?"

Remlika smiled at him. "You are the one who put my friend's life in danger, along with countless others over the years. A little revenge for the ones who weren't as lucky as Kandrina."

"This is all your doing!" The high priest shouted, staring at Kandrina. "You caused the fuss in Tewen, you brought the Lightning Demons to this town, you are the one behind all of this!"

"Actually, I had a lot to do with it as well," Dranjari said, raising a hand like a schoolchild. "You see... oh wait, we've met before, haven't we? I think you thought you were dreaming though. Anyway, I'm Dranjari. And yes, that does mean what you're all thinking," she called to the other priests, who had begun muttering between themselves when she said her name.

The high priest sprang to his feet, furious at the presumptuous women who had invaded his temple. "Enough of this preposterousness! You two are heretics of the foulest kind, to bring this demonic abomination into a holy temple," he cried, pointing at Kandrina and Remlika, who stood either side of the Colourless woman. "You shall both be sentenced to a slow, painful death in the temple of suffering, while a mage loyal to the temples will deal with the Demon. And you, who claim to be a holy aspect, will suffer along with them. I intend to follow the wishes of the gods throughout this outpouring of blasphemy, and all who continue to stand against the temples will be punished." Yantrola and Crenkari crept in unnoticed as he finished speaking.

"You are not following the wishes of the gods, priest. We are not pleased with your actions," Dranjari told the high priest firmly. "Your sermons are less than holy, as you twist the gods' words. You persecute any who dare question you, on the pretence of punishing heretics. You hound those who run, to the point where they are afraid to leave their own houses, and you threaten their families. You are nothing but a cruel oppressor with delusions of holiness, and now the people see you as such. Repent now, you may be spared the full wrath of the gods."

"Lies! I am the highest authority within this temple, I hear the words of Vrenid-Malchor, and you have no say in how I conduct my business! I refuse to take orders from a blaspheming woman!" the high priest shouted. "Now leave, before I have my acolytes throw you into the cells!"

The aspect of the Goddess of Time inclined her head. "I knew you would not listen to me. But you will listen to your own god, will you not?" she clasped her hands and called a single, unearthly syllable. The priests and acolytes began to shout objections, and then –

A deep, resonant voice rang throughout the temple, silencing everyone in the vicinity and causing the high priest to fall to his knees, cowering. "You have displeased me, mortal. You and your kin have spread falsehoods and terror to suit your own desires. The young woman Kandrina is innocent. You will answer to me for your discretions," the voice boomed.

There was a flash of blinding white light, and the high priest vanished. All that was left of him was an echoing scream. Dranjari turned to face Kandrina with a radiant smile upon her face. "That's the end of that. Your story is only just beginning, though. I know what you're going to do, and it's going to be fantastic." She began to walk away, fading as she did so, and by the time she reached the temple door she had vanished into the sunlight.

Yantrola cackled at the bemused expression on Kandrina's face. "The gods can be very cryptic at times, and Dranj-Aria is the worst of them all. But I suppose, 'knowing all that is now, has been, and ever will be'," she quoted, "would make even a goddess wary of revealing any details before they should. Ah well. I'd better be getting back to my temple in Tewen. I'd wish you luck, but somehow I don't think you'll need it. You appear to have the blessing of the gods, Kandrina."

"I hope we'll be seeing you very soon, Kandrina," Crenkari said. "You can teach us a lot about the Colourless, and probably about ourselves too." She trailed out after Yantrola, leaving Kandrina, Remlika and Nerlarina alone amongst the remaining acolytes and priests of Vrenid-Malchor. They all seemed unsure what to do with themselves, as though the first to speak would also be struck down by a vengeful Creator. It was all Kandrina could do not to giggle at their expressions.

"Let's get out of here," Remlika suggested. "Leave this lot to sort out their temple." She turned and headed out of the doors, clearly trying not to crack up herself.

Once they were outside, self control failed and both women laughed themselves silly. Nerlarina gave them both a quizzical look. "Why are you laughing?" she asked.

Remlika was the first to regain some sensibility. "I'm not entirely sure. Probably something to do with priests being afraid of the gods. You'd think they would be comfortable in the presence of the gods they pledged their lives to serve."

"Or maybe it's just satisfying to see them getting the comeuppance they deserve," Kandrina said, her giggles finally subsiding. "Either way, it's nice to be able to laugh after all this."

"Yes. I'll go tell my brother that everything is dealt with here," Remlika said, and walked off to find her twin.

Kandrina watched her go. "That should be the end of the matter. Now the high priest is gone, the others should calm down. With any luck, Chief Jindar will keep a closer eye on the next high priest," she said. "So, are we going to stay here or go back to Tewen? I'm sure there are several questions the temples would like to ask you."

Nerlarina made a very human expression of exasperation. "I'm a little tired of questions for now. Can we go back to the dwarven villages? I think Enkarini would be glad to see you again."

"I don't see why not. I wonder how Father is coping out there?" Kandrina said. "Shall I find us a cart?"

Before they could move, however, Remlik came running around the corner, clutching a thick book and accompanied by his sister. "Kandi, I found something!" he called, skidding to a halt in front of her. "You remember the lizard men, and Dranjari said we'd find out more for ourselves when the time was right? Well I took an opportunity to visit the library while the mobs were busy rioting, and I found something about them in here. It looks like they are very skilled in the magical arts, and according to this they have no inclination to live peacefully with each other, let alone any other races."

"Do you mean the Li Buqu?" Nerlarina asked them. The others turned to stare at her. "They live far to the north, beyond the Serpent Hills. We have encountered them before, in our distant past. They killed many of us before we fled to these lands, and established our hidden city."

"So you know of them?" Kandrina exclaimed. "I knew I should have asked you before. What can you tell us?"

"Not a great deal, myself," the Colourless woman replied. "If you wish to know about them, I could retrieve the information from the whole. It may take a few days; the information is buried deep."

Remlik nodded vigorously. "That would be greatly appreciated, Nerlarina. There isn't much in here, most of it is about other races or mythical creatures like dragons and forest spirits," he said.

Nerlarina promptly vanished, and the other three looked at each other. "It looks like visiting Enkarini will have to wait," Kandrina said. "I have a feeling we're going to head north."

Epilogue

Kandrina sat quietly in her chair before the fire, watching the dancing flames slowly consume the logs beneath. She had returned to Tewen with Remlik and his sister, to wait for Nerlarina's reappearance. She had spoken to her father and sister, explained everything that had happened and told them she would visit on her way north. Enkarini, in typical nine-year-old fashion, had thought it was all a great adventure and had even asked if she could come home and join them on their journey. Harndak had been the concerned parent and at first told her not to go, that if there was truly any danger from these lizard things then the Chief and the army should handle it, but had relented when she said that she was going with Remlik and a few others.

"Kandi, Nerlarina's back," Remlik called through, pulling her out of her reverie. He led Nerlarina into the front room and sat down opposite Kandrina. "What have you found out?"

Nerlarina, in her usual cloudy form, drifted to the centre of the room. "The Li Buqu are a strange people. They have no chiefs, or governing body, rather a matriarch and patriarch. They have very little control, however they do decide who is protected and who can be attacked. If you can convince them you are no threat, you ought to be safe. Their culture revolves strongly around the use of magic; they almost revere their sorcerers. If you are indeed planning to venture north and explore their lands, I will be unable to accompany you. Magic is an integral part of their lives; we have long thought they are unable to live without it.

"They are not mindlessly violent, but they do spend much of their lives duelling one another in competition for supremacy. Superior strength, whether physical, arcane or mental, is everything to them. You would do well to have Remlika with you; I understand she is a very powerful mage. They share an ancestry with the predatory creatures you call nayrim, and can manipulate them easily. Also, be warned they hold a deep mistrust of any race that is dissimilar to themselves. That is all I could find, and I hope it is of use to you," she said, her voice crackling as it always had.

The room was silent for a moment as Remlik and Kandrina took in what she had told them. "Thank you, I'm sure we'll find that very useful," Kandrina said, breaking the silence.

"We were planning to go with my sister, and possibly Dekarem if he can make it," said Remlik. "From what you've just told us, I think we might need them both when we go up there. Kandi wants to go and see her sister in the dwarven village first though; would you like to accompany us there?"

"Perhaps. It would be good to see the dwarves again," Nerlarina replied. "I will be around Manak for a while; I have agreed to stay here and teach Crenkari and the other scholars about us. Contact me at the library when you leave, I will go with you."

Remlik nodded, and rose. "We shall. Thank you for the information, and good luck with your lessons," he said, taking her back to the door. When he returned, Kandrina was once again staring vacantly into the fire. "You still want to do this?" he asked gently.

She lifted her head and looked into his eyes. The firelight caught her hair and made it shine mesmerisingly. "Of course. They took my brother from me; I owe it to him to make them pay. If we leave this week we can be in the dwarf village by the end of summer; a few weeks there and we can head to the Farm Valley. We should avoid the worst of the snows once we get there, I've heard the hills protect the valley from much of the winter."

"Alright. I'll get Dekarem to come with us, I have a feeling we'll be needing more than one mage when we leave our lands."